DRAGON'S GROUND

SHANNON MAYER

HiJinks

ISBN-13: 978-1984035547

Cover art by Raven

Created with Vellum

Acknowledgments

Thank you to my family for an endless supply of angst, emotions, and contrary personalities. Without you, I would never have truly understood that truth was stranger than fiction, and I'm not sure my stories would have the depth they currently do without my crazy background.

Also, I would be remiss if I didn't thank Maria Potter for her help in this series! (I forgot in the first book damn it!) She helped me start the process of Zamira, Lila and Maks's personalities and names. 🖤 SO, thank you, they would not be what they are without you!

I lay on my back in my bed inside the place I called home and thought of all the ways I could kill my ex-husband and get away with it.

Poison in his food.

Smother him with a pillow.

Trampled by giants.

Trampled by anything big enough to trample him.

Knife him right in his stupid face with a dull blade. Or maybe a spoon.

The list was long, and sure, you might say those sorts of morbid thoughts are a common fantasy for an ex-wife when her husband turned out to be a cheating, lying, manipulating asshole of the kind the world sees only once in a generation, but for me it was a bit more.

I was actually plotting how to make it happen.

Because my ex-husband was not only *all* of those things, but he had threatened my life and the life of my brother.

The scene still reverberated through my skull and it made me boil with rage, homicidal thoughts rolling through me all over again.

Steve grabbed my arm as we left Ish's chamber, right after we'd returned to our home in the Stockyards. As our mentor and leader, Ish had given Steve the position of alpha of our pride. Sure, the decision was based on lies, but I couldn't prove it. I glared at him, slowly looking to where his hand gripped my arm.

"If you value your fingers, you'll take them off me now, you camel-fucking asshole." I snarled the words but didn't jerk away. He would either drop his hand or I would go for his throat right there and not feel an ounce of sorrow over it.

"You are not in charge, Zam." He peeled his fingers from my arm, slower than I wanted but at least he let go. "Be glad your brother isn't here to see this."

I narrowed my eyes farther. "Don't you dare *even think it, Steve."*

He smiled, his canines showing clearly in the light of the flickering candles. "He's a blight, a weak link in our pride. He should have been put out of his misery years ago."

There was no thought process for me at all as I launched myself at him.

Darcy caught me around the waist in midair and held me back —but barely. "Stop, Zam, stop! This won't do anyone any good, least of all your brother!"

She was right, but in that moment, I wanted nothing more than to grab Steve's stupid, sneering face and shove it into a deep water bucket until he stopped thrashing.

He snorted and shook his head and spoke as if he'd read my mind. "You should have been drowned as a cub, Zam. Useless and weak. That's you and your brother."

I sat up, and my bed springs creaked as I swung my long legs over the side. My emotions rolled from anger to worry, to hatred and fear, leaving me unable to sit still.

Above and behind me, my horse, Balder, stuck his head in through the window that connected his stall to my bedroom. His lips flapped as he wiggled them against my head, messing up my long dark hair before he let out a big snort that sent horse boogers all over my scalp.

"Nice, thanks," I grumbled and pushed him away gently. He was as antsy as I was, being cooped up for three days. Three days of finding ways to avoid Steve, because the truth was, I wasn't sure I wouldn't attack him.

He'd threatened me before, lightly, subtly. But never my brother.

That I wouldn't stand for.

I blew out a long breath and scrubbed my hands through my hair. "Fuck, we need to get moving, Balder."

He bobbed his head in agreement, but of course, there was nothing he nor I could do about our current situation.

Three days ago, we'd returned to our home in the Stockyards.

Two weeks before that, I'd pulled Steve, his current girl, Kiara, and my best friend, Darcy, out of the dungeons of the Ice Witch of Pojhola. The Witch's Reign had nearly killed me on multiple occasions and I'd thought that our mentor and leader, Ish, would have been happy to see us all home and alive.

Yeah, that hadn't been the case, not in the least. She

wanted the Ice Witch's jewel—a sapphire that would give her additional power over the weather. She'd been furious that we'd not returned with it. Or at least that was what I let her believe.

I reached under my shirt and touched the sapphire that hung on the chain around my neck next to my father's ring. A part of me knew I had made things worse by not giving it to Ish. If I'd done that, I could have proven I had been the one to save the day against the Ice Witch. Could've shown clearly that I should be the one to lead our lion pride despite my size and gender.

I should have given it to her. I really should have.

But I didn't, and that other part of me knew I'd been right to hold it back. Something was off with Ish, something dangerous and dark that I'd never seen in her in all the years I'd known her.

That took my thoughts down a path I didn't like, one that left me unable to trust even the woman I'd thought of as a mother. I frowned and let go of the sapphire. At least, for now, it was safe with me. I was no mage, so there was no call on me to use its power.

The caw of a raven startled me and I spun around.

"Balder, am I hearing things?" I asked as I climbed onto the bed and peered out the connecting window.

He snorted and flicked his head up and down as if agreeing with me. I smiled and reached out for him. He was such a good boy, steady and . . . a second caw cut through the air and a flash of white whipped across the courtyard I could see through Balder's stall.

I grabbed my kukri blades and leapt through the

window, then over the half-open Dutch door in a single bound. I landed in a crouch, the two blades held out to either side of me. I kept very still while my mind raced with all the possibilities. I'd faced the large, magical White Raven in the land of the Witch's Reign. I'd traded for my life by giving her the flail of Marsum, a weapon that was powerful and deadly.

I'd considered it an excellent trade, seeing as the weapon had tried to kill me more than once.

I shifted in my crouch, leaning to the side so I could check out the overhang above me. No bird sat there. Probably I was just on edge because I'd been—

A caw shattered the air and my heart clattered into overdrive. I wanted to leap up and fight, but the caw of the raven came from all around me.

"We made a deal!" I shouted.

"We did . . . that is true," she called out, her words bouncing around me like the ping pong balls in the game room.

I pushed my back against the wall of the building and slid to my right, one quiet step at a time. "What do you want?"

"I bring you a gift." The Raven's words were suddenly soft on the wind. "My mistress regrets . . . things."

I couldn't help but laugh at her choice of words. "Regrets . . . things? You mean like trying to kill us, or worse, handing us over to the Jinn?"

"Yes, those things, amongst others." There was a sound of talons on metal and my head snapped up. Above me to the right was the curve of the tip of one talon as she gripped the metal roofing. I continued to move her way.

"Okay, fine, let's act like that wasn't a fucking shit show. Why would she send me a gift?"

"Maggi went to the Oracle . . . who told her that you need your weapon back." The talon lifted from the metal roof, disappeared, and then came back into view with . . .

"Oh, fuck no." I stood and stepped out from under the overhang, staring hard up at the huge white bird. "Are you serious?" I pointed at the flail in her claw. It looked small in her grasp. But it was a fucking monstrous weapon that not only killed with glee, but drew the energy and life off anyone who used it for killing.

So, you'd kill your enemies, but you still died. What a deal.

The raven tipped her head to one side as her eyes narrowed. "The Oracle knows better than all of us. You will need it. Do not let it out of your sight again." She let go, and the flail dropped to the ground, a clatter of metal against the scattered paving stones.

"Wait!" I held up both hands as she crouched, her muscles bunching to launch her into the air. "Just . . . is Maggi really Ish's sister?"

That probably wasn't the best question, but it was the one that burned in me. Because of all the implications it led to. That Ish had held information back. That Maggi had thought Ish cared enough for us to save us from her. And Ish had done nothing of the sort.

The raven crouched, bringing her deadly beak

within inches of my face. "They are sisters. You were lucky to survive Maggi, I believe, and you gained her respect for the allegiance you showed to your pride. She holds loyalty as a quality above all others."

I swallowed once and then gave the raven my secret. "I didn't give Ish the sapphire."

I didn't think birds could smile; I was wrong. The corners of her beak turned up and her black eyes glittered with humor. "Then I believe Maggi was right in returning the flail to you. Be strong, little cat. You're going to need every ounce of your inner power before this is done."

A shout came from across the courtyard. The raven pushed off the roof and launched into the air. I stumbled back with the downdraft of her thickly feathered wings, going to one knee to stop my backward slide.

More shouts.

I had to move fast. I shot forward and scooped up the flail. It warmed instantly against my hand, and if I didn't know better, I'd swear it . . . purred against my skin.

"Knock that shit off. You aren't happy to see me. You're a fucking weapon," I snapped, irritated and upset with what had just happened. The purring sensation stopped, but the warmth didn't. I grimaced, wanting nothing more than to throw my hands over my head and rail to the sky.

What the hell? The Ice Witch was now my, hell, I didn't even know what to call her. Mentor? Patron? Cheerleader?

"Fuck me," I grumbled as I strode back to Balder's

stall. The shouting behind me was still heavy in the air, but it was just the other residents of the Stockyards—a mixture of humans and lesser supes. They would run and tell Ish what they saw, and I'd tell her I'd made the raven go away. But I was a shitty damn liar so this could go south rapidly.

I climbed back into my room and laid the flail on the bed. Yes, the weapon was powerful, but the truth was, I couldn't use it unless I was willing to die.

I shivered, thinking of the drain on my body when I'd slammed it against the White Wolf. Yes, I'd survived his claws and teeth, but the flail had laid me out as it drained my life in payment for its help. Or some shit like that.

I'd barely been able to save myself and couldn't guarantee I'd be able to do it again. I just stared at it. "Seriously, what the hell am I to do with you?"

A knock came on the door and Darcy poked her head in. "Am I interrupting something?"

With long blond hair, bright gold eyes, and a smile that normally lit up a room, she was the epitome of a Bright Lion. Unlike my dark hair and green eyes that could not have made me stand out more. Today, though, her sunny disposition was missing, and that made me nervous.

I snorted. "No, just talking to myself again."

Her face was sober and my joke didn't so much as lift her lips into a half smile. "Steve wants to leave today. I think Ish will allow you and me to go as well. I'm assuming you do want to go."

"Does he?" I had to fight to keep the sarcasm from

dripping off even those two words. None of this current situation was Darcy's fault. Well, maybe a little of it was —in my mind, anyway. She could have stood up for me against Steve at any point.

We could have taken him down together, but when I'd suggested it, she looked at me like I'd lost my mind.

"That's not how things are done in a pride; you know that," she'd said.

"Well, maybe things need to change then" had been my reply, and she'd turned her back on me and walked away, stiff-legged and angry.

More and more, I doubted our friendship, and that cut deeply. I'd risked everything to save her from the Ice Witch. But after having Lila at my side for just a week, the little dragon had shown me there were better friendships out there, even if they weren't between the same species. I just didn't want to let Darcy go. She was my kind—a lion shifter. We had been friends since we were children . . . but things had changed somewhere along the journey to this moment, and I had been ignoring that truth for a long time.

Darcy sighed and stepped into my room, shutting the door behind her. "Listen. We *must* let him lead. We don't have a choice here, and you know it, so don't even think about asking me to jump him again. Ish put him in charge of recovering the Dragon's gemstone. I trust Ish, and she wouldn't do this if he wasn't the best choice."

Oh, that fucking stung. Steve was not the best choice, not by a long shot. I held those thoughts back. "And what about Bryce? Did she say anything about him? Did she say we could send someone to look for him?" I felt like I was living in a fucking loop I couldn't escape. Only a month before, Steve had been sent into the Ice Witch's Reign to recover the sapphire for Ish while Darcy was being held captive by the same power.

Ish claimed Darcy was lost, and not worth trying to bring home even though Steve was going to the *very* castle where she was being held. Ish said all our efforts should be for the jewel and the jewel alone.

Which just meant I'd gone after Darcy with only a supposed human at my side for help. Thoughts of Maks —said supposed human—stirred up a ragged set of emotions I didn't have the energy to deal with on top of the worry for Bryce, so I pushed them aside.

"Bryce, what about Bryce?" I asked once more seeing as she didn't answer the first time. "He's out there, on his own, and he is going to need help. You know that. He loves you, Darcy. Does that mean nothing?"

Because here we were again. In the balance was a loved one and a jewel held by those who were physically and magically stronger than us. What was more important to Ish? I didn't really have to ask, but I wanted her to say that Bryce was worth saving. I needed Ish to show me that she still cared, at least a little. Or . . . hell, I didn't even know the answer to that.

Darcy lowered her eyes, and with that, my heart dropped. "She . . . she said he is lost to us. Those were her exact words. He made his choice to leave when he is not physically strong enough to take care of himself."

And there it was again: Ish had made her stance clear.

The jewel she desired was more important than Bryce.

I realized that Ish had solidified that stance by making us wait three days before we were even *allowed* to start out. She'd kept us pinned down to make a point.

Steve might be the new alpha, but Ish was truly running the show. And she wouldn't have any of us defying her—or more clearly, she wouldn't have me defying her to go after Bryce when she wanted my energy to go into bringing the jewel to her.

I would have snuck off on my own, but Ish knew me too well and put a lockdown on the Stockyards.

I don't know what the spell was, but it was a bitch, and I was still hurting from it.

Yes, I'd tried to sneak me and Balder out on the second night we'd been back.

I rubbed the palms of my hands, the burns from the magical, and fucking invisible, fence line still healing. Whatever spell she'd laid, it had sunk in deeply, and it seemed to only affect me, as I'd seen servants and others from the Stockyards going in and out, no problem.

"Will you at least talk to Ish before we go?" Darcy asked softly. "She—"

I held up both hands, stopping her. "She doesn't give a shit about Bryce any more than she gave a shit about you. And I'm not going to let him die out there any more than I let you go without a fight. That's not how a pride works. You know that. We stand together, we fall together."

Something churned in my guts, and while deep in me I knew what it was, I didn't want to give voice to it. Not yet. Truth had a way of forcing itself to the surface whether we wanted or not, and this particular truth was hard for me to let out. Soon, I wouldn't be able to stop it. But *soon* wasn't now, so for the moment, I'd stuff it down. Like everything else that made me uncomfortable and introspective. I snorted to myself. I didn't have issues at all. Nope, not a one.

Darcy sighed and her shoulders slumped. "Well, let's get ready. Knowing Steve, he'll try to catch us off guard to make us look stupid in front of Ish."

I gave her a nod, frustrated that she could see him for what he was and still back him. But she was deep in the throes of being part of a pride . . . and I was not. Goddess, I was not.

She turned to go, then paused at the door. "You really think Ish doesn't care about us?"

I made myself lock eyes with her as I nodded because I didn't dare speak. Her question was too close to the truth that bubbled to the surface of my mouth.

I closed my eyes for all of two heartbeats, and when I opened them, she was gone, and I was alone in my room. My saddlebags and bedroll were already packed, of course. Ready to go at the drop of a hat. I grabbed them from beside my bed and set them on top.

I ran my hands over them, lightly touching the most important pieces of my gear. My weapons—two kukri blades that I wore strapped to my outer thighs, a shotgun with limited ammo and a grenade launcher under the barrel, multiple smaller blades, and the big bad of them all, the flail. I reached out, drawn to the flail more than I wanted to admit.

"You're a right fucker, aren't you?" I muttered.

Magical, it was made by the Jinn, but even more than that, it had been forged by Marsum, the Jinn who'd killed my father. He'd made the flail to be a killing machine of epic proportions.

Two long chains hung from the shaft's end. At the bottom of each chain, a spiked ball clanked against the other as I picked up the weapon. Light in my hand, it felt as though it weighed nothing at all—another of its perks as a traditional flail was heavy, usually forty or fifty pounds. This flail, though light as a feather, hit with the power of hundreds of pounds, and drank up the blood of my enemies as payment.

Nice, right? In theory, it was a grand weapon. One that any smart person would want to have on their side rather than in the hands of their enemies.

Except there was a downside as mentioned. That whole drawing on my life force when I used it to kill. Or maybe it was just geared to take the life of anyone who used it that was not its master, or not a Jinn. That could be it too.

"Maybe I should leave you behind," I said. Sweet baby goddess, I was talking to the thing now. But . . . I could take it and use it only if I had no other recourse. A last resort, and until that last resort happened, the weapon would stay strapped to my back. Satisfied with my decision, I let my fingers trace the weapon.

It made me think of the Jinn which led me to

thinking of a Jinn I didn't hate as much as I would have liked to.

Maks. I tightened my hand on the weapon as I thought of the blue eyes of the man who'd claimed to be human, but was in truth a Jinn masquerading as a weak creature to get close to us. He'd told me he'd been sent to kill Steve and Bryce. He never tried to hurt me, and I'd put myself in a vulnerable position with him more than once.

Zam is mine. His whispered, sleep-laden words still sent shivers down my spine that I couldn't deny made my skin hot and my heart pick up its usually steady pace.

I put the flail down with a sigh and pulled on my long deep-hooded cloak over my riding pants and simple short-sleeved cotton top. The hood hid my face from anyone trying to get a good look at me and blocked the worst of the weather. I reached up, thinking I could almost feel Lila there, curled up against the cold and wind, huddling close to me.

Lila, the little dragon who'd wormed her way into my heart in record time. Lila who'd helped me get to Darcy. Lila who was now on the run from her own kind because she believed they would come for her, and if she stayed with me, I would be killed too. She was the friend of my heart, and even though Darcy would say it was stupid to trust someone not in our pride, Lila was different. She got me, and I got her.

If I believed in past lives, I would have said she and I had been sisters in another life, another world.

I rubbed a hand over my face. So many people . . .

so many lives on the line, and so many lives destroyed, all for a fucking jewel.

If it were up to me, we'd stop hunting for them completely. How many of us had been lost looking for them already? Previously, I'd thought the cost was worth it.

But now, I wasn't sure at all.

Ish had told us the jewels were tied to her life force and that she couldn't survive long without them. But from what I could see, that wasn't entirely true—if I were being honest, and that was something I was doing my best to be, at least with myself. If anything, the jewels seemed to hurt her more than help her. Or they were changing her. Yes, that was a better assessment.

I shook it all off. We were leaving soon, and that made me . . . well, happy wasn't the right word. Determined, maybe, eager to go. As soon as we were out of the Stockyards, I'd track Bryce and split off from Darcy and Steve.

That would make Steve happy.

I frowned and rolled my neck, shocked at my own thoughts. I assumed Darcy wouldn't come with me to save Bryce, an assumption I hated even while I felt it in my gut to be true. She would follow our new alpha as much a slave to our old ways as any other female in our pride.

"Well, fuck that misogynistic shit," I muttered.

I grabbed my gear and shooed Balder back from the window so I could crawl through and end up inside his stall. I'd avoided Ish for the last three days. I wasn't about to face her now as we left. The last thing I wanted was for her to try to make me stay behind, or worse, have the truth of my thoughts spill out my mouth.

Horror flickered through me and I froze, crouched on the sill of the window. She wouldn't dare stop me from leaving, would she? Even as I considered it, I realized it was a distinct possibility. She knew me well. She knew I would leave Steve and Darcy to go after Bryce. Unless I made a convincing act. I snorted and shook my head. I was no actress. I couldn't so much as keep my thoughts off my face for a second.

I dropped into Balder's stall and put my gear on the straw-covered floor. I ran a hand over his steel gray hide, scratching him here and there where he liked it most. "You ready to go, my friend?"

He snorted and bobbed his head, butting it against my chest, shoving me a little. I had him brushed clean of the loose straw and saddled up in a matter of minutes, my gear attached to the back of the saddle along with my bedroll and additional bags. I slid his bridle on and did up the throat latch and chin strap, then took him by the reins and led him out the stall door into the central courtyard. Steve was there on . . . Batman? I couldn't help the gasp.

"How is that possible?" I couldn't believe what I was seeing, and I knew my jaw was gaping in absolute shock. Batman had been with Maks. The horse had chosen the Jinn over me. So, what the hell was he doing here? I hurried to the horse and put my hand out. He nuzzled my palm, looking for a mint, so I fished one out of my pocket.

His muzzle felt different, more prickly and whisker-covered. I stared harder. No, it wasn't Batman after all. But a big boy who was almost identical in color and body shape. The only thing different was this horse's left hind leg had a snippet of white on it. Otherwise, the two horses could have been twins. A strange sense of relief flowed through me. If Batman really had shown up, then Maks . . . he would have been in trouble.

And I didn't like the fear that induced in me. Obviously, I was not the only one who noticed my strong reaction.

Steve smirked. "Missing your human? Maybe you shouldn't have let him die then, Zamira."

I spat at him, yes, literally, hitting him right in the face with a great gob of saliva. He roared and flailed backward with his arms windmilling as though I'd punched him in the nose. For that kind of reaction, I wished I had.

"Enough." Ish's voice rang through the courtyard, power curling through her words and freezing me in place. A tremor shook through me, not fear, but the magic that Ish was spreading across us. The flail on my back heated, dispersing the cold touch Ish had given me.

I flicked my eyes to see her approach me and Steve. Darcy stepped out from the other side of Steve. Her horse, Pig, gave a soft nicker when she saw Balder.

Ish was tall, slender, and elegant as always as she swept toward us, and I was reminded of the Ice Witch. The Ice Witch who'd implied that Ish was her sister. The Ice Witch who'd said she'd thought we were of value to Ish, that Ish would have come to save us. And when she hadn't, the Ice Witch had fucked off because . . . well, because we were not the trap for Ish that her sister had thought.

That said all sorts of things about our value to our mentor. You didn't rescue tools that could be replaced.

The Raven had said they *were* sisters, and that it was good I hadn't given the sapphire to Ish. Fuck, would Ish ask about the big white bird? How the hell was I going to explain having a chat with her sister's pet as it brought me a gift? Sweat trickled along my spine.

The time to be a good liar was right now, but I wasn't sure I could pull it off.

I made myself turn and face Ish, feeling the shards of my life and the truths of my world cracking under the strain of learning more than I'd ever wanted to. Why now? Why did this have to be happening now when Bryce needed me more than he ever had?

"Steven," Ish said. "You are charged with leading the way to Dragon's Ground, to the hill that the jewel lies under. You are charged with returning to me the gemstone of flame that was given to the dragons by the Emperor himself."

Steve put a fist to his chest. "I take the charge on willingly, my lady."

"I was not done," she said. He went red in the face and I grinned. Her eyes swept to me, but she spoke to Steve. "Do you believe that Zam will be able to follow you in this task, or will she be preoccupied by the loss of her brother's life?"

My heart plummeted to the cobblestones beneath my feet. She spoke as though Bryce were already dead. Something we didn't know, something we couldn't possibly know. He'd left, headed for Dragon's Ground in search of a healer.

There had been no news to the contrary, and I refused to believe him dead until I saw his body with my own eyes.

Steve shook his head, a glimmer of malice in his eyes. "I do not believe she will listen to orders. But that is nothing new, Ish. You know that as well as I do."

I stared at Ish, the mother of my heart, the person I no longer was sure I could trust, the center of my internal conflict. "Do not tell me I can't go, Ish. This is what I do. This is all I know."

"Or what?" She lifted herself, straightening her body. "What would you do if I required that you stay here to protect me, Zamira?"

If I thought my heart had plummeted before, it was nowhere near to the depth it dropped with her question.

How the fuck was I going to answer this?

Chapter 2

I shot a look to Darcy next to Steve, both mounted and ready to leave the Stockyards, to see how she was reacting to Ish's question. Because I wasn't sure how I should respond. *Of course*, I wanted to go to Dragon's Ground, but not for the reason Ish wanted us to go. And she knew it. We all knew it.

Bryce was there, but how did Ish know I didn't give a shit about the gemstone? How did she know when I'd said nothing regarding Bryce after that first night back? I'd kept to myself and made sure to keep a low profile. So, who the hell had told her how little I cared about the gemstones now?

Darcy looked away from me, lowering her eyes to the courtyard's dusty ground.

"Fuck it all, seriously, Darcy?" I whispered the words, even while I understood why she'd told Ish. I felt the sting of her betrayal though that wasn't the worst part. She was not the friend I'd thought her to be. I'd once believed that Darcy would have come for me had I been the one trapped in the Ice Witch's castle, but seeing her now and the betrayal . . . I knew in my heart that was false.

Darcy lived the laws of our lion shifter pride about as fully as one could. Which was part of the reason why she'd given in to Steve's attentions when he'd pursued her when he and I had still been married. Back in the day, there was only one male in a pride, just like natural lions. And he got to fuck all the ladies as much as he liked. My father had changed that, and the Bright Lion Pride had been healthier, happier for that. One mate to one mate.

Steve wanted things the way they once were where he benefited from all the ladies. And there was no physically strong male lion to gainsay him.

I drew a breath as I worked the words out in my mind. "I would do as you asked of me, Ish. You know that." I lied right through my teeth with only minimal effort. I had to make her believe I could behave. If only long enough to let me get the hell out of here.

Once, I would have thought Ish trusted me to make my own choices, but I could see that was no longer the case. I wasn't sure that Ish would know I was lying, but I did know I was a terrible liar. This was not a game I had any skill at.

Her eyes left me and went back to Steve. "You are ready to go then?"

A breath escaped me. Thank the desert gods, she believed me.

"We are, but are you sure about Zam?" The crease

in his brows deepened. I wanted to flip him off with both hands since I was behind Ish's back but I didn't dare move.

"I am quite sure about Zamira. This is excellent." Ish clasped her hands in front of her, resting them against her long blue skirt. "Zamira will stay with me. Darcy, you will go with Steven."

Except for the tightening of my hands on the leather reins and the freezing of the air in my lungs, I did not move while Steve and Darcy filed past me. Steve with a smirk, Darcy with tears in her eyes. She mouthed something to me but I looked away from her. She would always be my friend, but I knew now not to trust her. Nor did any of this mean I could just take this camel shit lying down.

And people wondered why I had trust issues. I'd trust Lila and Maks over the pride I'd been raised in at this point.

That idea rippled through me like a little shock wave, because it was truer than I'd thought possible for the two of them, two friends who'd lied to me at different times for different reasons. One of whom was my natural enemy. But their lies had been backed by truths that were tangled and complicated. And in the end, they'd both come through and had my back.

I turned and tugged on Balder, leading him into the stall, keeping my temper in check but barely. I un-tacked him and put all my gear away, tossing it into my room through the connecting window. Ish might think she had me trapped, but I would find a way out. No matter how long it took.

I felt the air pressure change more than I heard Ish behind me. I stopped what I was doing and bowed my chin to my chest, adopting a look of submission. "What is it you need of me . . . Mistress?"

She sucked in a sharp breath. "Why would you call me that?"

I turned slowly to face her, the truth inside me bubbling up slowly, like lava curling toward the surface of the earth right before it went on a killing swath a mile wide.

I could hold the heat back no longer. "You are my master, are you not? You command me and I must go where I am sent because of what you wish from me, correct? My own desires are not considered. Other people's lives are not taken into account. I am not free to go where I want. I am held captive here, which makes you my mistress. You own me, Ish. I am a slave to your whims." I was proud of myself; I delivered the words calmly, almost in monotone. No anger took hold of me.

"You are a child yet then, if you believe I do not know what is best," she said, and any other time I would have said her eyes were sad, but I saw the flash of anger. Now that I knew it was there and growing, I saw it more and more.

I forced myself to stare her down even though she was taller than me, even though the cat in me wanted to curl away in submission. My jaw ticked. "You would have left Darcy to die. Someone you claimed to care about, a woman who I heard you once call daughter. What if I were out there? Would you have given a shit? No, I don't think you would have." I didn't feel an ounce of fear while I faced her. I was not afraid, but I should have been.

She waved a hand at me, dismissing my words as if they were nothing more than a bad smell. "I was willing to send Maks to find you when Steven came back from the giants without you, or have you forgotten so quickly?" She paused, and again there was that strange flash in her eyes. "I will always want to keep you safe, Zam. And it has always been with great reluctance that I send you out into the world on my behalf. You are too small, too weak, to be able to truly protect yourself. I let you go only because I knew you would chafe being held here. But no more. You must stay out of danger. I will not allow you to be hurt, or worse, killed."

I felt my face getting hot, and I wasn't sure if I was more embarrassed or angry. Her desire to protect me should have made me feel loved, but it only left me feeling owned. "You are avoiding the question. You don't give a shit about the others then? Just me?"

Her eyes narrowed, and she spun on her heel, throwing her command over her shoulder as if she didn't even need to look me in the eyes to make me obey her. "You will not leave the Stockyards, Zamira Reckless Wilson. Not *one* foot will leave its safety."

I watched her leave, anger and frustration vying for the surface of my emotions until I finally exploded.

"Bryce will die if he's left out there alone!" I screamed the words at her retreating back, and she finally stopped, turned, and faced me.

"He was dead the moment I pulled you two from the Oasis. It's only that neither of you realized it."

Just like that, I was there again in the past, standing in front of the Oasis, the water lapping at my feet.

I'd run back to the Oasis after trying to warn the rest of the pride. The Jinn hadn't stopped with our pride though, but had swept the area, killing as many of the Bright Lions as they could.

My father was dead; that was a truth I felt to the center of my bones. That he was no longer in this world. But Bryce . . . he'd been alive when I'd left him to warn the other prides. I'd been too late to save them.

Perhaps I could save my brother, though. Maybe his injuries weren't as bad as I'd thought. Though I knew in my heart if he wasn't injured badly, he would have kept fighting.

I raced across the sand in my cat form, leaping and bounding faster than I'd ever gone before. The sand was hot on the pads of my paws, but I didn't slow. My eyes watered with tears and from the grit of the blowing wind sweeping across the dunes. Over the rise that preceded the Oasis, and then I was sliding down the slope toward the bodies strewn around. Bright gold fur stained with brighter red blood was everywhere I looked and the world swayed. I used a trick my father had taught me. On the field of battle, keep your eyes on your goal, nothing else.

I narrowed my eyes, staring only at my brother, and the spear that still rose out of his lower back.

I slowed as I approached him, fear taking me down more than a few notches. He wasn't moving, and I wasn't even sure he was breathing still. My ears flicked back and forth, but I didn't dare scent the air too much for fear of all the death I would inhale.

"Bryce?" I whispered. He couldn't be gone. I couldn't have lost him too. I shifted and wobbled on two legs, grief making me weak in the knees. Carefully I knelt next to him and put my shaking fingers to his neck.

For a moment, I felt nothing, and then there it was, a heartbeat that, while it wasn't strong, it was at least there. He wasn't dead.

Breathing hard, hope giving me a burst of energy, I twisted around to look at the spear. There would be no way he would heal with the weapon still in his spine. As a shifter, he should be able to heal once the spear was out.

I stood and stepped over his back, straddling his wide hindquarters so I would have better balance. A clean jerk, that was what Father had always said about removing a weapon from a body. Clean, and as much at the same angle as the weapon went in. I let the spear rest in my hands, feeling the direction it needed to go. Toward me, toward Bryce's head, which would be good for a clean pull. I could do this.

I bit my lower lip and put my hands on the haft of the spear. The haft rested against my palms. "Hang on, Bryce. This will hurt but then it will be done." I tightened my hold on the spear and then pulled it as hard and as cleanly as my thirteen-year-old self could.

Bryce grunted, and for a moment, I thought he was going to get right back up. I tossed the spear to the side and knelt at his side again. "Bryce, come on, you have to get up." I shook his shoulders. He didn't move, and I wasn't sure what was going on, but all the sound in the world singled down to just the breath in his chest moving in and out. "Bryce, get up!" Even my words echoed weirdly.

"He can't, child." A woman's voice cut through the strange white noise buzzing in my ears. I gazed up at the stately woman with the raven-dark hair and the crystalline-clear eyes. Sorrow was etched into her features as deep as my own. "You should not have pulled the spear out, Zamira. You have broken him. He will never heal now."

I put my hands to my mouth, the horror of her words bringing bile up the length of my throat. "No," I managed and nothing else before I vomited to the side, unable to keep it back. I'd damned my brother.

"You have lost so much, little lion. Will you come with me? Let me protect you and your brother from the Jinn." Her hands were on my back, soothing me as I retched, as I sobbed for what I'd done to Bryce. He would hate me forever and I would never fault him for that.

The offer from the woman was sincere. I believed her every word and the guilt that I'd hurt my brother rather than helped him overwhelmed any other sense I might have had in that moment.

"Yes. Please, I don't want him to die. I . . . was only trying to help him." I looked up at her through the tears.

"My name is Ish." She held a hand out to me. "And your brother will not die, though there may be times he would wish he had."

She bent and smoothed her hands over his head. I watched in fascination as deep purple lines spilled out around his hair, matching the throb of purple that emanated from a dangling bracelet. Magic, she was using magic.

"Are you a Jinn?" I'd never heard of a female Jinn, but there was a first time for everything.

"I am not a Jinn, child. There is no such thing as a female Jinn, you know that." She spoke gently with only the mildest of rebukes. I would do whatever she wanted if only she could heal Bryce. She could scold me all she wanted.

"You can heal him, right?" I whispered. "You can fix him?"

She turned to me then. "If you help me, Zamira, I can fix him. But you must be strong enough. You must listen to me and do my will."

I stared up at her. "I am yours."

I swallowed hard though I could not seem to push the lump down my throat. Yet again I'd failed Bryce. The only blood relation I had left, I'd failed him because that seemed to be my lot in life. My chin touched my chest as the pain of the past curled around me, tightening its hold on my heart.

I'd never told Bryce I'd been the one to pull the spear, and as far as I knew, neither had Ish. How could I? He already hated me for being able to walk when he couldn't, for being a thief for Ish and ruining our family's honor as he saw it. But how could I not when she was the only hope he had of being healed? And now . . . he'd run off to Dragon's Ground to find a cure on his own because it had taken too long.

What a clusterfuck this was.

I stood there, breathing hard, fighting the guilt and the sorrow doing its damnedest to choke the shit out of me. Finally, I lifted my head. Ish was gone, and I was alone in Balder's stall, the past finally fading behind me.

For all that it was, I could do nothing about it now. I had to move forward. There was no choice for me now but to find Bryce and . . . tell him the truth. Then maybe we could find a way to heal him together. I drew a big breath, filling my lungs fully before slowly letting the air out, and then nodded to myself.

"I should have told him years ago, Balder. But I was too afraid to lose what family I had left," I said softly. Which meant that now, I had to find a way out. I stared out into the desert, past the territory that was the Stockyards.

Whatever barrier Ish had put up around the Stock-yards to keep me in was powerful magic; she was growing stronger with each gemstone we brought back to her.

Basically, I needed some powerful magic of my own to break through it. Because if she thought for one fucking second I would leave Bryce out there on his own, she had another think coming.

The real question was where the hell did I find magic that would offset whatever spell she had going on?

A cold spot centered on my chest and my hand shot to the sapphire dangling from my neck. The Ice Witch's stone *could* have that kind of power, but I didn't know how to use it. And if I did manage to use it, I would tip my hand to Ish, showing her I had the stone she so desperately wanted. That she wanted more than she wanted those in her charge to survive.

A stone that would give her greater power yet.

"You ain't getting it," I growled under my breath, my hand dropping from the stone hidden under my shirt. No, I couldn't use it unless I could think of nothing else. In part because I wouldn't know what to do with it. Throw it at the barrier and hope it did something was about all I had in mind.

But what else was there? I paced the courtyard, wracking my brain. There was someone else who had power like Ish. But. . . he was less than reliable. He had, however, offered to help me out.

"I feel stupid," I muttered to myself. I took a breath. "Merlin, this would be a perfect time for you to show back up and help, you know," I said out loud. I perked my ears, listening for a response. "Merlin? You said I could call on you. So. . . I'm calling you, you fickle bastard."

Nothing but the wind blowing across the winter desert. I crinkled up my nose and resumed my pacing. Not that I'd really expected him to show. He had said he'd wanted to help me get through the Witch's Reign, nothing more. Damn it.

As I strode past Balder's stall, he stuck his head out and butted his nose against my back.

Right against the flail.

A flail made by a Jinn, a flail that soaked up blood. A magical weapon if ever there was one. And Maggi had delivered it back to me on the day I needed it. I did not think that was a coincidence now.

I slowed my pacing, turned and looked at him. "My friend, you are surely not just a horse inside that head of yours, for you are far too smart."

I would only get one shot at this, that much I knew. I slipped into Balder's stall and tacked him up faster than I'd ever done before, apologizing all the way, but he never flinched. Ish would not expect me to try to run this soon after being told I had to stay. At least, that was what I was banking on. The cover of night would be the smart time to try this, so obviously, I was going right now.

I had Balder's gear on in well under a minute, checked his girth, and then slid on his bridle.

"Where are you going?"

I cringed at the familiar voice. Fucking desert sand up my ass crack, this was not what I needed at all.

Chapter 3

S tanding in Balder's stall, I fought with the desire to swing around and punch Kiara in the face, but that was a no-no for a lot of reasons, least of all that I didn't really blame her for what had happened. She'd been a pawn of Steve's, and now she was likely checking on me for Ish. If I didn't think fast, I had no doubt she would tattle on me. She could easily run to Ish now that I was all geared up and ready to get the fuck away from the Stockyards and whatever weirdness was taking hold of Ish.

I slowly turned to face her. "Nowhere. I'm going nowhere but a ride around the Stockyards so Balder can stretch his legs. We've been cooped up for days, if you recall."

Her golden eyes fluttered closed to half-mast, making her look demure and even younger than her eighteen years. "I know you hate me."

"Yup." No point in denying that shit. I might not blame her, but she'd betrayed me as much as Steve had.

"And I know you hate Steve."

"Well, to be fair, I hate him more than I hate you," I said. "You're just. . . young. And dumb to the ways of a fucking manipulator like him. You can't see what he's done to all of us." I didn't take my eyes from her. "So maybe I don't hate you. I hate what you've become, what you let him turn you into."

"I love him," she said softly. "And he loves me. He's not manipulating me."

I glared at her. "Yeah, well I loved him at one point too. Hell, I loved you too. But he doesn't love either of us. He wants a fucking harem of women so he can have a new body under him every night because he's a manwhore."

She cringed. "He told me that he loved me best. Out of all the women he's been with."

I rolled my eyes, somehow not surprised that she was aware and okay with the fact that Steve was still sleeping around on her. "Okay, great, fine, he loves you best. I'll give you that. Why are we having this conversation again?"

She drew a big breath and it was only then that I saw she was dressed for travel and that Lacey, one of the other horses, was tied to a stall a few doors down. A speckled black and white paint horse that wouldn't hide well on the wide plains, but in the snow, would be hard to spot. Too bad we were going through the plains.

"I want to go with you. Something is wrong with Ish and. . . I'm afraid for my baby, Zam. And I know you might not care for me, but surely you would help me keep a cub safe?" she asked softly.

My lips curled up with distaste, not so much for Kiara but for the words she spoke. Because there was a feel of truth to them I didn't like. The same truth I'd been struggling with myself—that something was very wrong with our mentor. "Did Ish threaten you?"

Kiara's heart-shaped face fell, her eyes filling with tears, making her look like the little girl I'd rescued so long ago. "She said that if Steve didn't come back with the jewel, that. . . something bad would happen. That she'd seen it in a dream that I'd lose the baby, that I'd die, that our pride would die with me."

A threat cloaked within a dream. I'd seen Ish pull that stunt once before, but it had been with an interloper who had been trying to worm his way into the Stock-yards. A wolf shifter with no pack, and a disease we could smell on the wind.

But that was then, this was now. Seriously, what the fuck was going on with Ish? In all the years I'd known her, she'd *never* been cruel. I frowned, thinking about when it had all started. When had she stopped being the woman I looked to for comfort, the mother of my heart? The steps had been slow in this new direction, but there had been a leap toward the cruel. . . with the stone that we'd brought from the giants. Icy fingers clenched my heart. They were just gemstones we were bringing back, gemstones to magnify her strength, weren't they? Suddenly the sapphire against the skin of my chest seemed to cool, reminding me that it held power too. A hell of a lot of power.

What if they were a power unto themselves? That would mean we weren't just saving Ish's life as she'd said we were, but we were giving her more power.

I tapped my finger against the stall door, thinking fast, trying to outmaneuver whatever was happening here. Because suddenly the problems I faced weren't just my missing brother, Kiara being threatened, or the dragons' gemstone falling into the hands of Ish. The problem was Ish herself was a powerful mage who I didn't want to cross for more reasons than I could count.

That left us only one recourse. One I didn't like all that much.

"Something is wrong with Ish, that much I'd agree to." I nodded, keeping my thoughts to myself for the moment. "But I can't slow down for you, Kiara. And I can't take you with me."

"As soon as we get to Steve, you won't have to worry about me at all," she said, her eyes full of hope. "And. . . I'm sorry I lied to Ish about what happened at the Ice Witch's castle. I. . . just want Steve to see that I support him in every way. So that he would know how much he means to me."

"Even if he's a camel's pizzle?" I arched an eyebrow.

Her lips wobbled. "Yes. He needs to know I stand with him. Even if he's wrong, he's our alpha and we need to support him."

Goddess of the Desert, that was bloody fucking messed up. A leader should be held more accountable than anyone else, not given a free pass just because he got handed the job. A mate was the same in my mind. But I wasn't about to give her relationship advice to improve her partnership with my ex-husband so that he would see her as more than just a warm body at night.

I sighed. "I don't know if what I'm going to try will work. Did Ish tell you that you couldn't leave the Stockyards too?"

She nodded. "I think she knew I wanted to go with Steve."

Of course, she did. Kiara was no better at subterfuge than me in that regard. Which was how I'd caught her and Steve together.

I rubbed a hand over my face. "Fine, you will keep watch while I try to break the. . . whatever it is keeping us both in here."

"You have magic?" Her eyes widened.

My hand went to the flail's handle. "Not mine, the Jinn's. But it should be strong enough to cut through the spell Ish has laid on the Stockyards." That last bit was just speculation at this point. Ish had always avoided the Jinn, and I'd always thought it was because of us—the only lion shifters in the world were here.

But maybe there were more reasons than that.

Kiara's mouth dropped open, and she stumbled back a few steps. We'd all been at the mercy of the Jinn's magic more than once, so I wasn't exactly surprised by her reaction. We'd all lost loved ones to their strength and their spells. And maybe I relished the reaction she had a little more than I should have. But come on, I'm not perfect.

I smiled as I opened the stall door and handed her Balder's reins. "You hang onto the horses and get ready to blast through when I say."

"Okay. What happens if you can't break it?"

My hand went to the sapphire, but I stopped myself from touching it, lifted my hand higher and rubbed the base of my neck. No need to tip my hand to her, just in case she was lying about wanting to get away. In case she was still somehow working for Ish. "I have a backup plan. I don't want to use it if we don't have to."

She nodded, trusting me, which was nuttier than a peanut bush in my eyes, and then she fell into step just behind me. Submissive to me. I was older, that was likely it more than anything else. That and I'd just told her that I had something of the Jinn's magic.

Though she was Steve's mate, and he was playing the alpha right now, she was still so young and really, she was no alpha to begin with. Hell, she wasn't even out of her teens. I drew a slow breath, knowing that no matter how old she got, she would never be an alpha. She just didn't have the spine or the heart for it.

Some were born alphas. Some weren't. She was most certainly in the second category.

"I remember when you found me," she said softly as we walked. "You fought off the gorcs trying to kill me near that muddy watering hole."

I nodded but said nothing. Thirteen years ago, it was hard to believe it had been that long, that she'd ever been that little and that. . . I had cared so much for her. Back then, not now.

No, I would not go there.

"I never forgot that," she said. "You were always my hero. I wanted to be you."

I snorted but kept sweeping the area with my eyes as

I spoke. "I'm a fucking house cat, Kiara. You don't want to be me."

"But it never stopped you. Even Steve says that. You never let anything get in your way. If you saw something you wanted to do, nothing could be done to convince you otherwise. It's why. . . he. . . "

"Wanted someone who would behave?" I offered her. The Stockyards were quiet for the moment, which was good, but again I kept looking. Watching for a servant or another shifter who might notice us headed toward the boundary.

"Something like that, I think," she said, and I heard the frown in her voice. I wondered if she understood that he liked her because she was weak-willed, a damn doormat if ever there was one. Not a fun realization no matter your age.

"Enough talking. We've got to get out of here," I said. We approached the eastern side of the Stockyards. Ish would expect me to try to escape out the north or the west side, putting me closer to the path I'd need to be on in order to head toward Dragon's Ground at the fastest speed. I sucked in my cheeks and clamped them between my teeth. This was a piss-poor idea at best, and my nerves suddenly bit at me. If I was wrong, I wasn't sure I'd get another chance, even with the sapphire hanging on my neck.

And I remembered all too well the feeling of the flail as it sucked the life out of me, how close I'd come to dying because I'd used it. I cleared my throat.

"There's a chance that there could be some kickback for what I'm going to do," I said. "If I fall over and the barrier breaks, toss me onto Balder and hiss at him, okay? He'll follow you and Lacey."

"Hiss?" She blinked those big golden eyes at me as if she didn't understand the word. "Why would I do that? And I can't throw you onto Balder, I'm in a delicate—"

"Just do it, Kiara. We don't have time for explanations. And you are strong as an ox even pregnant. Don't act like suddenly you can't bench press your own weight two times over." We were close enough to the edge of Ish's magic that I felt it humming against my skin, raising the flesh and hair alike. My fingers tingled where I'd burned them the first day of enforced captivity. Yeah, Ish had supercharged the fence she'd put up. A cage, she'd caged me.

She had to know I would try to fight my way out, even knowing the chances for success were slim. The hair on the back of my neck stood, and I looked around again. Nothing, we were still unnoticed.

I made a quick check that all my gear was tied down, that the shotgun was lashed in tightly. I was stalling. I could admit that much to myself. I was afraid of what could happen here.

I really did not want to go head to head with Ish, and that was basically what I was doing by breaking her barrier. I was throwing down a gauntlet, putting myself on one side of a line in the sand and Ish on the other.

Stupid, this was stupid, but I was doing it anyway. Like the dumb-ass I was because my brother needed me, and now, so did Kiara. She might not have been born with alpha tendencies, but I was. And I couldn't help but want to protect her.

"Ready?" I asked with a quick glance at her.

Kiara nodded and her hands clenched around the reins of the two horses. "Yes, ready. But why do you think this won't work?"

I gritted my teeth a moment before answering. "The barrier is keyed to you and me. We can't see it, but we can feel it. I think if I go forward with the flail, the barrier will think it's a part of me and try to stop it."

"And the Jinn's magic should break it just because?"

"Fuck, enough questions, Kiara," I snapped in part because I didn't want her poking holes in my theory. Either this would work or it wouldn't and hesitating would not help us one damn bit.

I pulled the flail from my back and the wooden handle immediately warmed becoming almost tacky against my skin. Like it wanted to be held, and held a *lot*. "No doubt a man made you," I muttered. "Always wanting his stick held."

Kiara snorted. "Are you talking to the weapon now?"

"No, that's fucking stupid." I flicked my wrist and began to spin the unearthly lightweight flail in an ever-increasing loop until I had it going as fast as I could. Smashing the shit out of the magical barrier was now or never.

With a grunt, I drove it directly into the barrier that held us back. There was a resounding crack, like bone snapping in half, and I grinned. Damn straight, my theory was sound! The air around us shimmered, spider web breaks scattering out around us, thin and barely seen but there. The barrier we couldn't previously see came into view, fuzzy like one of Bryce's TVs he worked on with the screen out of focus.

"Again!" Kiara said. "You have to hit it again!"

I didn't like agreeing with her, but she was right. I spun the flail again and smashed it into the distorted screen. It dug into the barrier this time, sticking to it. There was a pulse of black mist that curled around the twin spiked balls and I realized the flail was doing the same thing as when I fought with it.

"Holy. . . hell fire on the sand dunes," I whispered.

The flail soaked in Ish's magic like it soaked in the blood of my enemies. Horror flickered through me. This was Jinn's magic, and I didn't know what the hell I was doing. Being an idiot, that's what I was doing.

I yanked it out with a hard pull, and with a growl of frustration, spun it and slammed it into the barrier again. There was a shout behind us. One of the servants had noticed what we were up to. Seconds, we had seconds before Ish would be on us.

"Mount up!" I yelled at Kiara as something caught the corner of my vision as it sailed our way, twisting through the air like a snaking cord.

She scrambled onto her horse just as a net slithered our way. A catch net. The woven threads were black and green and moved as though they were alive, curling and crawling toward me and Balder. He danced sideways, tugging Kiara and her horse Lacey with him. He knew better even if Kiara didn't. I spun and slammed the flail down into the catch net.

The magical threads burst apart, dying where they were.

"The barrier, Zam, it's still there!" Kiara cried out.

"Not for long," I snarled. I had to believe this would work, we were too close to fail now.

I spun my entire body, throwing my weight into what would be the final blow either way. We'd be caught, or we'd escape. The time was now. A yell escaped me as the flail buried deeply into the barrier and the spiderweb of cracks spun out farther than before, cracking even as the flail pulsed and tugged on my hand. I yanked the flail out and jammed it onto the holster on my back. For the moment, it wasn't pulling on my life force and even if I didn't understand why, I would take it as a win. I jumped onto Balder's back and booted him forward, toward the still-shattering barrier.

"Are you crazy?" Kiara screamed.

I grinned over my shoulder. "Fucking bananas, girl."

Balder and I hit the barrier and there was a moment of resistance, a stretching sensation that made me hold my breath and pray to the gods of the desert, before it gave way in a sparkling, shimmering explosion that sent dancing purple dust out into the surrounding air around us. I ducked my head and closed my eyes, feeling Ish's magic slide over my skin as she fought to hold me back. To keep me from going into the world and saving my brother, to keep Kiara where she could control her life too.

I gave Balder the sign to go, dropping the reins so my hands were free to fight if I needed to, and he bolted forward. Three days of pent-up energy unleashed in a single bound. I reached for the shotgun and pulled it up, but it wasn't needed. There was no one giving chase.

Kiara's horse kept up, and we raced east. My plan was to come around in a big loop to the north, to throw Ish off our trail in case she did send someone our way.

Behind us there was a scream that was nothing but pure fury, a screech that made the hair on my neck stand because it sounded so like the Ice Witch I'd faced not that long ago. I looked over my shoulder. Ish watched us as we raced away from the Stockyards, already out of her grasp. Watching us boot it the fuck out of there. Her long hair snapped in the breeze and for just a moment I thought I saw her raise her hand, and I tensed, waiting for a spell to come sailing our way. But it happened so fast, the motion was there and gone before I could be sure.

When I could no longer see her and the shimmering haze of the Stockyards faded, I let Balder slow, though he still wanted to run. He pranced underneath me as I brought him down to an animated trot. Kiara and Lacey caught up to us. She looked across at me.

"Ish was never like this before. She was never mean."

I nodded my agreement but kept my thoughts on Ish to myself. "We'll loop north after another mile or so. It'll take us longer but if we get too close to the Stockyards again, I think she'll try to bring us in."

"She doesn't leave the Stockyards. Not ever. And the servants are no match for us. We'll be fine, we can cut close and save time," Kiara said. She straightened her back and lifted her nose. Like she was going to run the show now.

If I kept rolling my eyes like this, they were going to fall out of my head.

"And from what we know, she's never been cruel before either," I pointed out. "Things are changing. I don't want to take the chance that we could get taken back by someone we think might try to kill you and your cub. Do you?"

She bit her lower lip, her eyes lowered and her posture softened. A moment or two passed before she spoke again. "The jewel. . . I mean, the Dragon's gemstone. You don't mean to bring it to her, do you?"

I'd give Kiara at least that much, she wasn't stupid even if she was dumb as a bag of brightly colored rocks when it came to Steve. "No, I don't. Whatever is going on, I don't think we can trust her with more power, and I think the gemstones are giving her that. It's not just about her life, it's about strength. Steve is trying to get it for her regardless of that fact. He can't see past his own desire for power to realize Ish is becoming dangerous to us all."

Kiara said nothing, and we rode in silence while we continued our road east. I didn't think she agreed with me, but she didn't argue on Steve's behalf, which was a nice change.

I could only take so much of "how great Steve is" before I wanted to start killing things.

"How do you know where to turn north?" Kiara asked.

I glanced at her, reminding myself she didn't leave the Stockyards often. "There's a stone that's been cut in half. It's the marker to let people know that any further east and they are headed out into the wilds."

She shivered, and I kept my eyes forward, watching for the stone.

Whatever waited for us out there, no matter how bad, was better than sitting in the Stockyards waiting for word of my brother's death. No one would fight for him like I would.

Just like I believed he would fight for me. Like I believed Darcy would have fought for me. I frowned, not liking the comparison my brain made between the two people who I thought were the most important in my life.

Oh, if only the desert gods were not so cruel, that would have been true about Bryce fighting for me. But the truth was far uglier than even I knew.

A truth I would learn soon enough.

Chapter 4

M erlin leaned back in his seat before the orb, watching Zamira break free of Ish's magic. His eyebrows shot up and he had to blink a few times to see if he was in fact seeing what was really happening. "I did not expect that."

Flora snorted and smacked the back of his head. "You did it, didn't you? You softened the barrier for her to get out. She's better off there. As crazy as Ish is becoming, Zam needs to stay safe."

He rubbed at his head where she'd messed his hair up. "Actually, I didn't." And that was what concerned him. The magic of the flail was a creation of the Jinn. That it hadn't taken retribution on Zamira when she'd used it against the barrier was at the very least alarming. The flail was designed to kill any who held it who were not a Jinn. But he knew that as a weapon of magic, it would want to be used. . . it might be growing attached to Zamira, and that could be as dangerous to her as if she were being attacked by it.

"Excuse me?" Flora leaned so she was right in his face. "Did you just say that the weapon is meant to kill any who aren't Jinn?"

Merlin cleared his throat and then smiled. "Said that out loud, did I?"

"Guessing you didn't mean to?" She arched a brow.

He sighed. "No, I didn't. The weapon is important, Flora. The Oracle said so."

"No, she didn't, Merlin. Unless you have something more to tell me?" Flora didn't move an inch. The woman had the stare of a hawk when she wanted to with those sharp green eyes of hers, and Merlin began to squirm. Flora, in her days as a priestess of Zeus, had been formidable. As she'd aged, her temper had mellowed and her true strengths had shown—wisdom, cunning, and the ability to see to the core of people. Now it seemed that since her youth had been given back to her, she'd managed to blend both that fierce spirit and the wisdom she'd gained.

Her gaze narrowed farther. "Unless you mean you asked the Oracle questions before or after I was there? Hmm?"

"Before," he muttered. Damn it, he had a hard time lying to this woman. Probably part of the reason he liked her so much. He didn't like weak women. Though Flora was almost too strong, too stubborn even for him. As a priestess of Zeus, she was used to taking control of situations and the people in them. Including himself. He found a smile had worked its way onto his face.

"Gods, you are. . . impossible! Why did I think you and I could work together? I was a fool to marry into your family." She pushed away from him, her curvy figure swaying as she walked.

"Marrying into my family saved your family line, if I may remind you." He pointed a finger at her. He only wished he had convinced her to marry him instead of his brother.

She waved a hand at him. "Do not distract me. What else did the Oracle say?"

Hard to sidetrack that one. He grinned again, and then the smile slipped. "The weapon she has, the flail, is important. As are the last four gemstones Ishtar is collecting. We need her to collect them, but. . . " He didn't know how to say the last part. Because he'd kept it from Flora for this reason. Part of him had hoped that Steve would be the one to face down the guardians of the wall. That he would be the Wall Breaker they needed. Mostly because he didn't think much of the Bright Lion that had cheated on Zamira, and in general been a self-serving ass. So if he died in the process, there would have been no real loss.

He'd hoped that he could spare the young woman he was coming to admire that same loss.

"How bad is it?" Flora asked softly, those green eyes of hers sucking him in with the sincerity in the depths. From hard to understanding in a flash, she was like lightning in a bottle.

"It is very bad, Flora. The Emperor is waking. We have maybe a week at best before he is fully aware of the world once more." He rubbed a hand over his face.

The Emperor was the strongest mage the world had ever seen, stronger even than Merlin. And he'd gone batshit crazy with that power.

Flora slumped to the floor, her legs buckling. "I could call on Zeus and the pantheon. Alena would come; I know she would."

"No." Merlin shook his head. "Do not bring them into this unless there is no other choice. And only if Zamira fails the tasks in front of her. They. . . are not stronger than the Emperor."

Flora approached him slowly, taking his hands in hers. "You put the Emperor to sleep once. You can do it again. I know you could."

He closed his eyes and tightened his hands on hers. "The humans believe I put the barriers up to keep them safe, and I did. But not from the supes, Flora. From him. I did it to keep them safe from him. And I tricked him. That's how I got him to drink the draft that knocked him out. He won't fall for it again." He grimaced. There was more to putting the Emperor to sleep than even that, but he could not say that to Flora. The steps taken had been many, and he knew in his heart there would be no duplicating them. Much as he hated it, they needed Ishtar to regain her power.

He opened his eyes, expecting to see anger flashing in those green jewels of Flora's.

Compassion was written clearly in her eyes and the lines of her face, taking him back to the woman he'd known the longest, the older, wiser Flora. "We'll find a way, Merlin. While Zamira lives, there is hope."

He looked at her, wishing and hoping she was

right but knowing the truth of it already. "That's just it, Flora. In creating the wall as I did, I am bound by my own spell, and it forces my hand. I am bound so that I *cannot* fight my father if he breaks free. It is the balance of creating a wall like this one and holding him back for so long. It is the price I had to pay."

Her fingers slid from his. "What are you saying?"

He drew a breath, opened his mouth, paused, and then finally spoke. This was not going to be an easy sell. "Either Zamira finds a way to break the wall and stop the Emperor, or the world—human and supes—will become his slaves, and you and I will be among the first to be killed."

Flora raised her eyebrows. "Oh, is that all? Good thing you picked the strongest of all the supes here to save us then, right?"

Merlin turned to face the spinning orb, and it zoomed in on Zamira's face. On the sharp lines of her cheeks, and the determined turn of her mouth, but more than that was the fire in her eyes that reflected the strength in her soul.

He nodded, feeling the certainty flow through him. "She may not be the strongest in body, but she is the one, Flora. She has the strength of a hundred lions flowing through her veins and driving her heart. She only has to find it."

Flora cleared her throat. "If she hasn't found her strength now, after all she's been through, she's not going to, Merlin. She's faced the death of her family, the loss of her marriage, injury, betrayal, and hardships that most will not face in their whole life, never mind within the short span she has seen it all."

While he didn't want to agree with Flora, her words struck a sharp slice of fear through his heart and the hope that had been building there.

The fear that the things she said were exactly what would happen.

That Zamira was too hardened by what she'd faced already, and instead of strengthening her, had cut her off from her own power.

"Then we must help her, Flora. We have to help her break through those barriers and find the reasons to fight for this world. To fight for us all."

Chapter 5

Riding through the desert plains alongside my ex's pregnant—what was she? fiancée, mate, girlfriend? I wasn't sure what to call her—I tightened my jaw to keep my mouth from running away with me, and kept my eyes forward, sweeping the path in front of us. This was not how I'd planned to leave the Stockyards. And because she was pregnant, I was taking it slower than I would have on my own even though I said I wouldn't. That and her horse, Lacey, was slower and out of shape compared to Balder.

That first bolt of speed had knocked the piss out of the black and white mare. We'd turned north about three miles back at the stone marker and were now making the long, slow route around the Stockyards. Out of sight, out of mind, was what I was hoping.

To our left was an expanse of hard-packed desert plain dotted with a few buildings here and there left over from the human civilization. The humans had stayed as long as they could but eventually most of them died or migrated to the east, away from the hotbed of action this western wall had going for it.

To our right were the foothills covered in broken rocks and boulders leading up to the mountains. The issue was all those boulders and dips gave lots of places for an ambush to be set up.

Kiara shivered, and I knew why without asking. About twenty miles north of our position was where the gorc territory officially started and where we'd found her stuck in the mud so many years before. She was from a lion pride that had left the southern desert and had wandered out on their own months before the Jinn attacked us. What we didn't know—those of us who'd survived the attack on the Oasis—was that the Jinn had made a coordinated attack on Bright Lions everywhere. They'd killed not only our pride, but every pride of Bright Lions they could find from the south end of the wall all the way through the north.

The Jinn had split up and roamed the lands looking for every lion they could in a blow that would have wiped us all out completely if not for the few survivors that had dodged the death squads. Kiara had been young, a brand-new cub, and her mother had run with her when the attack had come. They'd survived for a few years on their own before the gorcs caught them.

There had been too many for her mother—lame and weak from years of living hand to mouth—to fight off. And Kiara would have died too if we'd not heard her screaming on a routine sweep of the area.

I'd found Kiara in a mud bog, just like she'd said. To

be fair, Steve, Darcy, Richard, and Leo were with me too, but I'd been the first to Kiara, scooping her out of the sticky mud and running my blade down the gullet of the gorc who'd had her in his sights. I'd been a teenager full of rage at the unfairness of the world, and certain I could conquer anything.

I glanced at her again, watching her react to the cool gusts of wind. "You aren't a cub anymore, and now you have your own to protect. Don't show the gorcs weakness. Don't give them that power over you."

Her back stiffened. "I do not need you telling me how to feel."

"You look like you're about to fall out of the saddle from fear, so yeah, I think I do need to say something," I said.

She flashed a snarl at me and I laughed at her. "That ain't going to work, not on me. You are no alpha, Kiara. So don't try to put me in my place with a curl of your lips."

"That's right, you respect no one," she snapped, her words thick with the fear that had to be humming through her veins.

I shrugged, but she was wrong. Maks had bested me in a fight, the first time since I'd been a child wrestling with my brother that a man had actually taken me down. I might not be the strongest supe out there, not by a long shot, but I had a mean streak about a mile wide down the middle of my spine, and I depended on it for my survival. That and I was fast, faster than the bigger lions that I often trained with.

Such was the nature of being the smallest in a

group. You learned to bite hard and fast before anyone took a shot at you.

"I respect those who deserve it. Not a child who's not yet figured out how to be brave." I didn't look at her, but kept my eyes roving the rolling hills around us. My skin prickled here and there, as if eyes had come to rest on us, and I didn't like it. Gorcs were. . . difficult to kill in large numbers. One or two, even three, I could handle without too much effort. Many more than that, and we'd have to outrun them. I patted Balder on the neck and he tossed his head, his mane flipping this way and that, tangling with the breeze that cut through the rolling hills, whistling between the boulders. I tried to scent the wind, but there was nothing out of place, no smell of gorc that I could pick up.

Balder blew out a long snort and slowed his walk, surprising me. A whisper of wood smoke reached my nose along with the sudden stench of gorc. Fuck that shit.

I gave Balder the lightest tap with my heels. "Come on, get moving."

He planted his feet. What the hell was this ridiculousness now? I frowned and slid out of the saddle.

"What are you doing?" Kiara's words were a half-strangled whisper. She'd picked up on the smell too.

I frowned and shook my head. What was going on with Balder?

"I'm checking his legs and feet." I quickly ran my hands down Balder's legs, picking up each hoof and checking them. Shoes were all on tight, no sign of bruising or heat in his joints or tendons. There was no reason for him to stop.

A rattle of rocks down the hill closest to us snapped me around. I leapt straight up onto Balder's back, spinning him so I faced the noise. Kiara let out a whimper that was most unbecoming of a lion.

The noise came again and then. . . the distinct and horrifying sound of a goat being throttled.

Kiara gasped. "What is that?"

"Not what, but who." I grimaced, shook my head once and then urged Balder forward as I spoke over my shoulder at Kiara. "Stay here."

"By myself?" The words were strangled syllables.

I shrugged. "Gorcs are on the other side of the hill probably torturing a satyr."

Her face paled, and I looked away from her. What she chose to do was up to her. I was not forcing her hand one way or another. But I wouldn't let someone I knew be killed by a band of gorcs. Typically speaking, they didn't rove in numbers bigger than four, so I was banking on speed and surprise.

Balder climbed the hill, leaning into it, and I leaned forward in part to keep my head down, in part to help him by at least not throwing my weight around. As we crested the hill, I found myself behind a pair of fifteen-foot-high boulders. I sat straight up and moved Balder with my heels, quietly getting us around the curve of the boulders so we could look down into the small depression between hills. I found myself looking at a curious scene. One that didn't seem to fit with what my brain had been telling me I'd find.

There was a fire pit at least five feet across with four gorcs in various stages of reclining around it, and with them was a satyr—Marcel to be exact. He seemed to be telling them a story by the way his hands were going, but I did note rope hanging from his left wrist that went to a metal bar hammered into a large boulder.

More than that was the body of something over the pit. Long legs, a torso, and human features that had been burned to a char. Nubs on the head. Shit, they were eating a satyr. The gorc closest to me leaned out with a knife and cut a chunk of flesh off the torso, bringing it to his mouth.

I narrowed my eyes, seeing the sweat run down Marcel's face, seeing the fear in his eyes. Four gorcs were no small thing, but if I caught them off guard, I might be able to pull this off.

I slid from Balder's back and ground tied him just as Kiara rode up beside me. I put a finger to my lips and motioned for her to get off.

She slid from the saddle, and I saw the way her knees shook. We couldn't speak, not this close to the gorcs. As a beast, they were large, over seven feet tall, and a cross between ogres, goblins, and something else. They were a creature created by the Jinn to harass the legitimate supes that lived on this side of the wall. Ugly, tooth-filled, claw-tipped hands, and powerful, they were not something I liked crossing. The worst was that they were not stupid. Or at least not as dumb as I would have liked.

The more gorcs we killed, the better. As far as I knew, there were no females, only males; which meant that the more we killed, the more the Jinn had to make, and that should sap the Jinn of their energy.

At least that was the running theory at the Stockyards. We didn't really know much about them other than the fact they worked exclusively for the Jinn. I wished Maks was with me. He would've had at least some info on the gorcs.

I put a hand on Kiara and mimed for her to take her clothes off. That would allow her to shift without ruining a perfectly good set of threads. I, on the other hand, could shift and take my clothes and weapons with me in the form of a collar around my neck. A very small perk for the rather large fact that my form was about as un-lion-like as one could get.

I turned my back on her, letting the shift take me. For me, it was like walking through a door, stepping between two legs and four. The change was swift, and painless, and in only a few seconds I was on four legs, standing between Balder's front hooves. He dropped his nose and breathed softly across my thick black fur, ruffling it. I reached up and batted his nose gently, pushing him away.

I glanced behind me and saw with some surprise that Kiara was naked and making her way to shift. Honestly, I'd have expected her to tell me to fuck off. I also couldn't help noticing the tiny bulge of her stomach, the telltale sign of a child on its way. The first Bright Lion born in more years than I wanted to think about. Much as it was hers and Steve's, it was still a good omen. Even I could admit that.

She shifted and gave a shiver, her golden coat shimmering in the dull winter light. I motioned for her to draw closer with a flick of my left ear. Kiara crept forward on her belly, her golden eyes wide with anxiety and fear as her tongue hung out, panting.

I put my mouth into the rounded cup of her ear closest to me. "Let me go in first. I will call for you if I need help. This will be good for you, to face them, and put them on the end of your claws."

Her ear flicked once and I took a step back and turned to face the slope down. Dropping to my belly, I crept forward, one step at a time with my eyes locked on the scene that was playing out. Marcel was telling the gorcs a story that was a little too familiar.

"I'm serious, this woman gallops along the canyon of the giants, the entire rush of them right on her very pert, very lovely ass, and she comes to a dead end. But that doesn't stop her, no. Her horse is injured, and like any lovely, thoughtful creature, she sends him up the treacherous slope first." He drew a breath and his eyes scanned the area, landing on me for the briefest of seconds before darting away. Of course, he didn't know that I had a second form. Or that I would be of any help. All he saw was a simple black house cat.

But I wasn't so sure that him telling my story of fooling the giants would keep the gorcs entertained. Not when they were most of the way through the first body. Even in the time it had taken me to shift and tell Kiara the plan, most of the flesh had been stripped off the first satyr.

Marcel cleared his throat. "Anyway, she climbs up,

the queen is behind her, and this tiny, beautiful woman starts cussing out her ex-husband."

"Why she do that?" the gorc closest to him asked. "No good in sack?"

"Well," Marcel gave a nervous grin, "according to her, he was a no-good, cheating, tiny-dick man who couldn't satisfy her."

The gorcs laughed together and I used their laughter to cover me as I shot forward, tiny pebbles rolling down around with me. I slid to a stop, some scrub brush working for a bit of cover. Not really a cover, but then I was a six-pound house cat. Not exactly hard to hide if no one was looking for me.

I let out a slow breath as Marcel went on with the story. His words washed over me as I focused on the closest gorc. If I could launch myself onto his upper back, I was pretty sure I could slash his throat. While I might not be able to break bones with my bite, my claws and teeth gained strength from the weapons I carried, as strange as that might seem. And currently the flail of Marsum was a part of that strength.

Booyah for me.

The best part was, in my house cat form, the power drain that happened if I used the weapon on two feet didn't happen on four feet. I didn't know why, and I wasn't going to question it.

I pushed my way through the scrub grass, the spines brushing through my thick fur.

"You tell another story before we eat you." The gorc closest to me thumped his big flat foot into the hard-packed earth and the concussion of it crept up through the pads of my paws. "I like your stories. You keep talking, we no eat today."

Marcel gave that braying goat cry that set my skin to crawling as if it would run right off my body. That was nervous satyr laughter if I ever heard it.

I drew my breaths carefully, keeping the sound of my breathing as quiet as I could while I waited for the right moment to pounce. I was only going to get one shot at this.

A gorc who sat across the fire leaned forward, his eyes narrowing as they landed on me. "What is that? A pussy cat?"

Well, fuck. So much for surprise.

I launched up and onto the back of the gorc in front of me, landing on his shoulders and neck. I dug my claws into his thick hide and they cut through his skin like a razor blade through silk and with about the same tearing sound.

He shot to his feet, his hands reaching back for me while his companions laughed and slapped their hands on their legs. Because let's be honest, it probably was funny as a camel in a three-legged race with a rhino. The gorc howled, and I kept slashing at his neck, light pink blood splattering all over the place. If I didn't have to bite him, I was going to avoid it at all costs.

Gorcs tasted like rotting flesh.

I swiped my claw across the veins in his neck, finally getting deep enough to hit them. The resounding spurt shot across the fire, hitting one of his buddies in the face. The gorc went from trying to grab me, to grabbing at his neck.

"Get the cat!" he screeched, but I was already off him and racing across to the next gorc. That wound would kill him soon enough. The next gorc was still laughing, not grasping what had just happened to his buddy. There was no time. I wouldn't be able to reach the second one's neck. But there were veins in the inner thigh that would work just as well, much as I didn't want my face that close to his dirty, unwashed junk.

The gorcs wore a light brown uniform that helped them hide in the desert and the surrounding hills, but it wasn't made to protect them, and it wasn't much of a barrier to me. I cut through it in a single slash, the strength of both the flail and the two kukri blades I carried giving my claws and teeth the edge I needed.

This time, though, it would be my teeth doing the damage. No matter that I didn't want to use them on the foul-tasting shithead. I grimaced as I shot upward in a single bound and landed on the gorc's thigh, sinking my front and back claws in to hold myself steady. I looked up at him and batted my eyelashes as he stared down at me in utter shock.

"You're going to die, big boy," I said.

He swiped at me with a big meaty hand and I dodged it, then bit him hard, sending him onto his ass as I chewed my way through layers of meat and muscle, gagging on the taste of his blood. The pulsing vein was there. I knew it was, and I went for it with every ounce of energy I had.

"Watch out!" Marcel's warning was all I needed.

I let go and bounded off the gorc as one of his buddies brought a spiked club down on his leg, right where I'd been. The snap of bone and the explosion of blood and roars of pain set the scene on fire. Two down and out of commission, two to go. This was Kiara's chance to face her demons.

"Kiara, now!" I screamed for my backup.

I shot forward, heading for the fourth gorc who was closest to Marcel. As I drew close, I walked through the doorway in my mind and went from four to two feet in the space of a single breath, faster than I'd ever shifted before, and it stole the wind from me.

The gorc's eyes widened and then narrowed. "Zamira."

"Ah, good, you know me. Can't say I know your name." I yanked my kukri blades out, still moving forward, and slashed toward him with a yell, the scream of one seriously pissed off woman.

He met me with a blade of his own, big and bulky, slow. But if I let him hit me, it would only take one blow to snap me in half.

The dance of blades between us clattered through the air, but more than that, I listened for the sound of a lion roaring into battle. A sound that never came.

Well, fuck.

Chapter 6

T he gorcs behind me around their campfire were starting to gather themselves, and that was not good since I was apparently on my own in this. I could take them, or at least I thought I could.

Marcel had pinned himself as far away from the action as he could, and it was then I saw the chain around his one fetlock tying him to a large ring near the fire. As if the rope on his wrist weren't enough.

"Marcel, nice to see you," I said as I parried the gorc's blade, flinging it back at him with a grunt.

"Well, probably not as nice as it is for me to see you. You are getting a free flouncing for this, Zam. Two. Three. However many flouncings you want, just get me out of here," he yelped as we drew close to him.

I couldn't help but laugh. "Flouncing is the last thing on my mind right now. How about we settle for killing the gorcs?"

"Sure, I guess." Even in that moment, he sounded disappointed. Like I'd turned him down again and his ego just couldn't take it. I grinned, and the gorc glared at me.

"The Jinn. . . are they still looking for me?" I spun into a kick that I managed to land on the gorc's kneecap, snapping it sideways with a satisfying crack. He went down, but that didn't mean he slowed. He punched me in the gut, sending me stumbling backward, gagging as I fought to draw a breath. I tripped over the logs near the fire and ended up on the ground. I took a quick glance at the other gorcs.

Two were down, the third was coming my way.

"They are always looking for the females of the pride, you know that," the first gorc growled. "They want you as they want them all."

"Why is that again?" Might as well get info while I was here. Assuming I made it out alive, this could be seriously good intel that, for all we knew, would pinpoint just what in the sands of hell the Jinn were up to.

"Don't matter to a dead kitty cat," the gorc behind me said.

My skin prickled, and I ducked and rolled to the side as the spiked club sailed through where my head had been only a moment before. I didn't bother to yell for Kiara, not again.

She knew I needed help, and she was going to just sit up there and watch me fight it out on my own.

"Marcel, the chain!" I yelled. "Use it!"

I needed whatever help I could get.

Even if it was from a sexually amped satyr.

I dropped to the ground and spun with a leg extended, knocking the second gorc to the ground. I didn't wait to see if he was knocked out. Without thought, my right hand reached for the handle of the flail, and I grabbed it before I could stop myself. Almost as if someone else was controlling me, or maybe as if the weapon was calling me.

"Shit," I growled as I yanked it from my back and began to spin it, the twin balls clanking almost like metallic bells. The gorc on the ground scrambled backward, crying, both hands out. "No, no! Not that!"

I stared in shock as he pushed to his feet. . . and *ran away*. I turned to face the last gorc standing. My breath came hard and pain filled. I could feel a crack in at least one rib from the punch, but it was the fear on the last gorc's face that had me captivated.

"You cannot be using that. It's impossible." He held both hands out in front of his body, pointing a single finger at me with each. "Not possible!"

"You don't know me well enough to say what I am and am *not* capable of." I took a step toward him, picking up speed on the flail. He took a step back and then another, and another, before he spun and ran from fear of me. But that wasn't the truth, and I knew it.

They recognized the flail. They knew it had been made by Marsum, their master, and they knew the flail's power. But they acted like it was more than a weapon. The handle warmed under my fingers, making itself tacky and hard to pry them off. But pry them off I did.

"Off, you fuck," I muttered at it. No, I would not start talking to the weapon.

I turned around. The second gorc who'd had his leg smashed was flat on his back, a pool of blood around him. Between my slashing and the break from his friend, he was unconscious. I walked over to him, pulled a kukri and thrust it through one of his eyes, hurrying his end.

I checked the first gorc I'd attacked, and he was dead, bled out.

Two dead gorcs and a chained-up satyr were all that were left. I went back to Marcel and pulled the flail, swinging it hard against the chain on the ground. The metal shattered like glass and Marcel brayed with excitement. I gave him a stink-eye. "Seriously, shut your goaty little guts the fuck up. We don't need to draw anyone to us."

He made a zipping motion across his mouth, even while he grinned like the fool he was. Another time I would have grinned back. But not in the midst of this mess. I grabbed a kukri blade and sliced through the attached rope.

"Thanks." He rubbed at his wrist.

With some effort, I put the flail back in its sheath across my spine, wondering why I'd pulled it in the first place. While the fight hadn't been going great, it also hadn't been so close to being a full-out rout on the gorcs' part that I'd need to pull the powerhouse weapon that liked to suck my energy away.

That spoke volumes about the attachments the magical weapon could have, which should have made me nervous. But it didn't.

"Marcel, let's get the fuck out of here before they bring their friends back." I turned from him, checking the gorcs' bodies quickly to see if they had anything worth taking. The only thing of interest I found was a sheaf of papers in a leather satchel. I flipped through them. They were blank. I took it anyway. Good for lighting fires at the very least.

Marcel followed me with a small length of chain dangling behind him. "How did you know I was there? You must really like me, to save me from the gorcs. I didn't think you really liked me, seeing as you turned down my offer to flounce."

"Or I really don't like gorcs because they are creatures that belong to the Jinn, and I'm not an asshole to leave anyone with them, maybe?" I offered.

"No, I think you really like me. Ten flouncings for you. The question is, all at once or spread out over one glorious night?" He made a reach for me, and I stepped out of the way.

I couldn't help the laugh. I really tried not to, but he was so dumb, he was funny. "Marcel, seriously. I do not want a flounce of any kind from you."

We climbed the loose scree slope to where I'd left Kiara and the horses. Though I was irritated with her, I wasn't really pissed. At least not until I stepped around the boulder to find only Balder left standing where I'd given him the command.

Kiara and her horse were gone.

I sighed, anger and frustration coursing through me. She was a fucking child having a baby and obviously couldn't be trusted. I was babysitting her. Fuck me sideways. I looked at the satyr.

"Can you keep up on foot?" I asked Marcel.

"Of course." He sounded indignant. "I can outrun any horse."

I lifted an eyebrow, doubting he could outrun Balder, but kept that to myself. "Then why didn't you outrun the gorcs?"

He frowned, and a wave of sadness rolled off him. "I was caught with my friend. We were. . . busy."

His friend. The one on the spit that had his bones picked clean by the gorcs. I reached out and put a hand on Marcel's shoulder. "I'm sorry for your loss. Truly."

"We've been friends since we were boys, I never thought. . . " He closed his eyes and big fat tears rolled down his cheeks into his sparse beard.

I turned away from him, his grief making me feel more than I wanted to. "Well, unless we want to end up the same way, we need to move. Where there is one gorc, there are more. And two ran off to tell their buddies we are here." Not to mention they knew my name. That couldn't be good in any scheme of things.

He bobbed his head, and I mounted up on Balder. I turned him, and we started down the slope toward the flatter plain at a jog. As soon as we hit flat ground, I urged Balder into a gallop. Kiara and her horse couldn't be that far.

I had to give Marcel credit, he kept up even with that uncomfortable length of chain dangling. Two miles away, I slowed Balder and Marcel followed suit. "We need to get that chain off or it's going to rub you raw."

"We need to get farther away, I think." Marcel turned and squinted into the distance.

I froze. "You see something?"

"No, not yet."

"We can move faster if you are free of it." I slid out of the saddle and searched for my lock-picking kit in the pack.

Jewel thieving 101. Never leave home without all your tools.

I dropped to the ground and slid the pick into the iron lock, working it for only a few seconds before it popped off.

The fetlock was raw, fur gone, flesh torn. I put my picks away and grabbed my hacka paste. Without a word, I rubbed it over the wound and Marcel let out a low sigh. "You're not like the other supes, you know that, right?"

"Yeah," I muttered. "I know." Did he really have to point out that I was a house cat now? Like right after I saved his hairy goat-bellowing ass?

"No, I don't mean your cat shape, though I do find that interesting." He crouched, and I had to look up fast so I wasn't staring right at his crotch, a definite invitation to a satyr. "I mean you look out for others. That's not normal here. It hasn't been normal for a long time. Not since the massacre."

A chill swept down my spine. "What do you know of the massacre?"

He shrugged and stood. I followed his lead and chose to walk Balder for a bit.

Marcel sighed. "We all knew that the lions took the brunt of the Jinn's anger. We knew it and we let them because we were afraid and they were the strongest of us. As long as the Jinn were occupied, they let the rest of us live our lives. Once they massacred your kind. . . we no longer had the safety we once falsely believed we had. We all should have stood together."

I frowned, unsure how to take that. As a compliment maybe, but also a confirmation that other supes didn't look out for one another any longer. It was one thing to know that, of course, but to hear it so blatantly put was a little hard.

He was quiet a moment. "Where are you going?"

"Dragon's Ground," I answered without much thought, simply because it was no secret. And I doubted Marcel was going to run off and tell the dragons I was on my way. I grinned at the thought of him asking one of the dragons for a quick flouncing.

"Funny, I've been hearing a whisper of a rumor about a dragon that was an outcast." He tipped his head to one side, as I slowly turned to him.

"What did you say?"

He paled, and I realized that perhaps my intensity level had gone a little high.

I reached out for him and grabbed the tip of one of his nubs. "What rumors?"

He tilted his head to one side, then pushed my hand away so he could scratch at the nubs on top of his head. "Well, Rev, that's my friend I was meeting, he came from the western slopes. He said there was a dragon sighted there, but. . . "

"It was very small?" I couldn't help the hope in my voice. Lila, it had to be her!

"Yes, how did you know?"

"Could you find where Rev was? Where he heard about the little dragon?"

"Well, yes. I know where he lives, but his wife hates me. I really don't want to go there."

I put a hand on his shoulder and tightened my fingers until I knew he was feeling the pinch. "You owe me, Marcel. And besides, you should probably tell his wife that he's gone, don't you think?"

Horror flickered over his features. "Tell her that Rev is *dead*? Good goddess of the mountains, you want me to be killed, don't you?"

I fought the irritation that wanted to climb up and out of my mouth. "I doubt very much she's that bad. She cannot be worse than the gorcs who wanted to roast you on a spit and eat your liver for breakfast."

"Says you," he muttered under his breath, causing my lips to twitch. I'd never met a more spineless creature and yet he made me laugh.

"Come on. Maybe we can catch up with the cowardly lioness." I hopped into the saddle once more and Balder broke into a fast trot, picking up on my energy. There was only one dragon that was too small to be believed, and I wasn't about to let her go this time.

Though she be but little, she was fierce, and she was my friend, damn it.

Chapter 7

Two more miles and we caught up to Kiara and her horse. I wanted to roll my eyes when she first caught a glimpse of us, and booted her poor horse in the sides. He just didn't have the energy to give her more than a half-hearted gallop.

I let Balder take the reins, as it were, and we took them over in a matter of minutes. "Kiara."

She stared at me as if I were a ghost come to haunt her. "You're alive. I didn't know it was you, I just saw something chasing me and I thought. . ."

"No thanks to your sorry hide." I threw the words at her. "I know you were scared, but we could have taken them together. Now they know we're here. I couldn't stop them all!"

She slowed her horse and Marcel jogged up beside me. "Is she available?"

I waved a hand at him. "She's pregnant."

"Oh, perfect," he cooed. I spun in the saddle to look at him.

"What? How can that be perfect?"

He grinned, and I knew it would be in his mind as perfect satyr logic. "Well, I can't knock her up, and I know she likes to flounce a bounce. How could that not be?"

Yeah, satyr logic.

Kiara frowned. "Who is that?"

"The satyr I pulled out from the gorcs."

Marcel waved at her, winked, and blew her a kiss. She blushed and looked away, and I remembered all too clearly the curl of magic Marcel had at his disposal. Sex magic was a real thing and if you weren't aware of it, you'd end up flouncing a satyr before you thought better of it. I sighed and smacked the top of his head. "Leave her alone, Marcel."

"Okay, but only for you, pussy cat," he said.

I whipped around and glared at him until he squirmed. "I mean, Zam."

I nodded. That was better. "We're making a pit stop."

"No." Kiara shook her head. "We're not."

I stared at her a moment and then laughed. Because she was out of her mind if she thought she was in charge.

"What's so funny?" She glared at me. "You ran into danger without any thought of me or my baby. Just like Steve always says you do to him."

I rolled my eyes. I couldn't help it. "*Please*, Steve is an idiot."

"WAIT!" Marcel roared the word as he skipped and hopped so that he was in front of us, trotting backward. "Do not tell me this girl is the one that your ex flounced around with?"

His eyes were wide with a mixture of shock and hope.

Kiara huffed. "It wasn't like that."

He held up his hands. "Right, I'm sure Steve loves you the best."

If I hadn't been sitting in the saddle, I would have fallen to the ground laughing. As it was, I bent over the saddle horn and struggled to breathe for a good solid minute. "Oh, my gods! Marcel, you are my fucking favorite satyr of all time."

"Well, no doubt, you did save me," he said.

Kiara was not amused.

I was in my fucking glory.

"That was good, right?" Marcel danced around us. "I mean, it took only a little putting of the puzzle pieces together, but damn. Too funny."

He gave a hop and a kick with both feet, flicking his tail as he did.

I grinned. "Yeah, that was good work."

The wind swirled around us, bringing the smell of rain right before a roll of thunder cut through the air.

I hunched my back. I was no different from most other felines. I did not like getting wet if I could avoid it.

"Marcel, how far to your friend's home?"

He cocked his head. "If we're going full speed, maybe half a day's ride?"

I bobbed my head. "Then we go now, as fast as we can."

Outrunning a thunderstorm was one thing, but there were still gorcs behind us. I wasn't going to assume we'd lost them. In fact, we were going to ride like they were hot on our asses. I couldn't throw the feeling that they would come after us.

They know your name. Of course, they are coming after you.

"My horse is tired," Kiara whined.

"Then shift and run on your own feet," I said without another look. "We need speed and you need to give it up."

"I'm pregnant. I don't want to shift again. It hurt."

She was clinging to an old wives' tale that shifting too much while pregnant could harm the child.

But I couldn't force her to do it.

What if something did happen to the baby that had nothing to do with the shifting? She'd blame me. I'd blame me. I hunched my back further. "Fine. We go as fast as you and your horse can go."

As fast as they could go turned out to be a quick walk. Fuuuuuk. I wanted to tip my head back and howl like a wolf shifter.

I finally got off and walked beside Balder. I might as well give him a break where I could. And the blood flow would help when the cold came—

The rain slammed into us without any warning. There was no gentle patter that led up to it, just an opening of the heavens that left us soaked in a matter of seconds.

Marcel was as bedraggled as I was, and I could see

him shivering, his upper body naked except for the dusting of fur that protected him. I went to Kiara's pack; she yelled as I yanked her blanket out and handed it to Marcel. He bobbed his head and wrapped the blanket over his shoulders.

"That's mine!"

"Well, then, you should have thought about that before you condemned us to all get soaked, you selfish twit!" I snarled back at her. She cowered from my anger and I didn't feel a stitch of sorrow for it.

We stopped after a few hours to eat and feed the horses to keep their energy up. The rain hadn't eased off a single drop. If anything, as the day began to wane, the rain came down harder, pushing across us in sheets and waves. The only thing keeping us from full-on hypothermia was the fact that we were all walking, moving, and keeping the blood flowing.

As we stood in a tight circle to eat, a rumble slid through the ground and up the soles of my feet. I blinked away the raindrops hanging from my eyelashes and looked back the way we'd come.

A dark mass of bodies rumbled our way, their large flat feet slamming into the ground, which was the only warning we were getting. The gorcs had found their friends. A hell of a lot of them.

"Mount up, time to run." I spun toward Balder and pulled myself onto his back, the weight of my sodden clothes hampering my movements.

"What is it?" Kiara asked.

"Gorcs, lots of them." I put my heels to Balder and he took off, Kiara and her mount right behind us.

Marcel dropped the blanket and kept up surprisingly well.

This was very bad. I couldn't fight off that many gorcs on my own, not even if I pulled the flail. That seething mass had to hold at least eighty, maybe more of the Jinn's creations.

Eighty.

I'd not seen a horde like that in years, not since my father had still been alive.

"Water, find water. They don't like it and aren't strong swimmers," Marcel yelled through the weather at me.

Normally I would have laughed in his face. This was, after all, a desert, but with the rain coming down like this, water was a distinct possibility.

My mind raced as I tried to piece together the terrain in front of us. This close to the Stockyards, I knew it better than others, but I was turned around with the weather. A bolt of lightning lit up the sky as we galloped across the terrain that was turning from hard-packed footing to sloppy mud bath.

"Kiara, where is Hangman's Gorge?"

She shot a look at me. "Are you insane? It will be flooded and running too fast!"

"The horses can swim it. I'm sure." I was sure of no such thing. But I knew if we didn't survive the gorcs, there would be no one to go after Bryce, no one to tell Lila that she was important and still a part of my family. Kiara wouldn't survive, nor her child.

"Where is it?" I repeated louder with a growl to the words.

Her jaw tightened, and she tipped her head for me to follow. I tucked Balder in tightly to her horse's rump, and as we ran, I tied them together.

Kiara's eyes widened. "We can't. We'll all die!"

"You want to get eaten by a gorc? That's a sure thing. This is a chance to make it."

I wasn't sure she heard me over the pounding rain and the boom of thunder that was coming faster and harder, but she gave a single shake of her head. Yeah, I didn't think so either.

"What about me?" Marcel yelled.

I yanked a rope from my saddlebags and threw him an end, then tied the middle to me, then handed the end to Kiara. "Together or not at all. That's how this works!"

The horses stopped, and we stared down the long loose slope that led to Hangman's Gorge. The valley was normally empty, dry, and barren except for the occasional hawk hunting for a rodent.

Now the water raged, frothing and mud-filled, as it seemed to jump over itself in an effort to gather speed. Clumps of bush and sticks washed through the water, and I knew the debris could be as dangerous as the water itself. The river was at least a hundred feet across. More in places.

I looked back and in a flash of lightning saw the gorc horde. They were not even a mile back now and they saw me.

"Hang tight to your horse, Kiara. We all swim hard, we all swim together, and we can make it across."

"You aren't really sure, are you?" she asked.

I grabbed her by the arm and shook her. "I would not do this if I did not think we could survive. So, get your spine and straighten it the fuck out."

She blinked away the rain, or maybe it was tears, I didn't know and at that moment didn't care. But she did give me a nod. I stepped back behind Balder and took hold of his tail. "Here we go."

I gave him a soft kissing noise, and he started down the slope, his back feet sliding deeply into the loose and muddy soil all the way up to the top of his hocks. The angle was steep enough that the best we could do was a careful slide that sent rocks and sand rushing down the slope. A gallop in the dark in this footing would leave us with broken legs and necks.

I kept up a running set of instructions because I knew Kiara was scared, and I had no doubt Marcel wasn't happy either. Satyrs were not known for their ability to swim.

"When we get to the bottom, let Balder lead. He'll swim first and pull Lacey behind him. You and me will hang on to their tails. It's easier for them. Marcel, you do what you can. Keep your head above water and try not to get snagged on anything."

"Got it," Marcel said. "But you're earning yourself pretty much anything you want after this. I might even offer to marry you."

"Ha!" I barked a laugh. "Been there, done that, got the ex to prove it."

Kiara said something that was rather unladylike that might have been along the lines of "fucking witch." Marcel made a fake gasp. I grinned at him like an idiot as the rain hammered around us. The thing was, with certain death behind us, and possible death ahead of us, letting off a bit of stupid steam was not a bad thing.

We were near the bottom of the slope when the first arrow slammed into the ground, the tip of the feathers blazing with a blue flame to mark where we were.

"Time to run," I said and then hissed at Balder. He bolted forward, taking Kiara's horse with him. I wrapped his tail around my wrist a split second before Balder plunged into the frothing waters. My horse trusted me above anyone else, and even though most horses would have hesitated at the deadly rush, he dove in, swimming hard as the current caught hold of us.

"Good boy!" I yelled at him as blue flaming arrows shot through the air around us, sizzling as they hit the water. I didn't dare look back to see where Marcel was, I could feel his weight on the end of the rope. Worse, I could feel him drag me down, the rope tightening around my middle and making it difficult to breathe.

I fought to stay afloat, fought to keep enough air in my lungs as the water pounded around us. A stick swung at my face, the end of it catching me in the side of the head. For a split second, I saw stars and I thought that was it, I would die in the water, the gorcs would feast on my bones and that would be the end of my story.

A cat dying in the water seemed such an ironic way to end my life after everything I'd faced.

But as suddenly as we were in the river, struggling through it, there was solid ground under my feet and I realized that Balder and Lacey were literally dragging us down the bank of the river, away from the gorcs. At top speed, our bodies hitting hard.

I bounced along, smashing into rocks and dips in the ground and feeling the inevitable bruises bloom, unable to get my feet under me any more than Kiara or Marcel could. Or I assumed, anyway. With my free hand, I grabbed a kukri blade and cut the rope between me and Marcel first, then between Kiara and me.

"Balder, ease up," I hollered, and he began to slow, dropping from a full-out gallop to a slow trot and then a walk. Even there, my legs didn't want to cooperate. They wanted to buckle and leave me kneeling on the loose soil. I brushed water from my eyes and looked around. We'd taken a few corners in the valley and put distance between us and the gorcs. More than that, the river was wider where we stood now, which had to help. Thank the desert gods that gorcs weren't the brightest stars in the sky. It would take them days to realize they could go around the gorge.

Kiara lay on her side. I stared at her. "Think shifting to lion form is tough on your body now?"

"I hate you," she whispered.

I shrugged. "You wanted to come along for the fun. Remember that you could have stayed with Ish and trusted Steve to get the job done, but you didn't. Deep down, you know he's a fucking loser or you would have let your life ride on his abilities."

She sat up, and for a second, I thought she'd launch herself at me. That would get ugly fast and my heart didn't want to go there. Because a part of me still loved that little girl I'd saved from the gorcs all those years ago.

"You didn't have to save that satyr. You could have left him and the gorcs would have never found us!" she screamed at me while the weather crashed around us. I stared at her.

"You're a selfish, self-centered, little girl. Someone was in trouble. It's our job to help them if we can," I said, knowing she would hear me over the pounding rain. "My father was right to run your pride off."

Her eyes widened. "What?"

I shook my head, cursing myself for saying that. For letting it slip. "Get up, we need to move."

"What did you say?" She grabbed my arm and twisted me around, the most aggression I'd ever seen from her. I sighed.

"Your pride was a blight. They were weak. They cared nothing for anyone besides themselves. My father ran them off before you were born."

She stumbled back from me. "No."

"You don't have to be like them, Kiara. You can be better." I turned my back on her. "I want you to be better."

Marcel let out a low groan from the water's edge. "We're headed north east from here."

Good enough for me. I didn't wait for either of them. They would follow me, or they wouldn't. Either way, I was done babying them. I was trying to get to Lila and then Bryce. These two fools had chosen to come along for the ride.

Three, I supposed, if I counted Kiara's child. I gritted my teeth and stumbled along in front of Balder. My horse was in no better shape than me. How long had we been in the river? I couldn't have said. It felt like hours and over in a split second at the same time.

Balder and I stumbled, leaning on one another down the valley until it widened enough that there was another path heading up and out. Again, I held onto his tail, letting him pull me up the steep slope. By the sounds of the hooves behind us, Kiara and Marcel were still following.

As we crested the top of the slope, I leaned against Balder, staring at the figure in front of us. A satyr, yes, but she was twice the size of Marcel with breasts that somehow fought gravity and won even though they were easily the size of watermelons. I stared at her through the rain, putting the pieces together.

"You must be Rev's wife," I said.

She drew close to me, and her face twisted with a fit of rage I'd not counted on. With the cold wet soaking through my muscles, I couldn't dodge the large wooden weapon that came crashing down on my skull.

Chapter 8

Merlin let out a groan. "That's putting her right in the path of the Jinn. Damn it, you said that thunderstorm would push them the other direction."

Flora stomped a foot and brushed past him to look deep into the orb. "Well, if the girl had any sense, she would have let the river block their path and push them back the other direction."

"You forgot about the gorcs."

"Nasty beasts," she muttered. "There is nothing for it. She will just have to avoid the Jinn."

Merlin nodded slowly. "Unless we can do something about it. The Jinn are not far from us, Flora. They do not know you or me. We can perhaps give them something to chase?"

"You are kidding me, right?" But she was already following him as he led his way out of the small domicile they shared, at least temporarily. He got the two horses ready and Flora mounted without another question, despite her obvious reservations. Now that she was working with him to help Zamira do what she had to do, Flora would not hold back. He knew that much about her. Once she committed, it was with her whole heart.

They rode out in silence through the middle of the night. There was a time to talk to Flora about his plans, and a time to surprise her. This was one of the latter moments.

She wouldn't agree with what he had planned, so best to throw her into the deep end with no warning.

Ahead of them, the rain had eased off, but not in a natural manner. No, the Jinn were holding the weather off themselves. Well, except for their prisoner.

As they drew close, Merlin could see something—a body perhaps?—staked out, hands and feet spread wide, face-down in the mud as the rainstorm hammered his body. Other than that body, there were four Jinn, all lower than Maks in power but together they could hold him. Interesting. If that figure in the mud was Maks, it said a great deal about his placement in the Jinn hierarchy.

"Hello, there," Merlin called out with a hand over his head. "Could we share your fire for a bit? There are some nasty-looking gorcs out hunting tonight. Perhaps stronger numbers could keep us all safe."

Flora snorted at his words, but he knew the Jinn perhaps better than anyone else. That being said, they reported directly to the emperor. He would have to tread carefully.

Very, very carefully.

"Go away," the smallest of the Jinn said. "We don't share our fire with other supes."

Flora dismounted and sashayed into the middle of the clearing, her soaking wet clothes clinging to her lovely, dangerous curves. "I just want to warm my hands a minute if you boys don't mind then."

All four Jinn perked up. Powerful supes they might be, but they were still male, and Flora was most *definitely* a beautiful woman. Merlin had to hold back a smile of appreciation for how quickly she took control of the situation.

Men should be warned not to trifle with a priestess of Zeus.

He stood on the outskirts and let her do the magic that only a woman could. His ears picked up a noise that sounded like a groan and he turned his head ever so slightly. Outside the circle where the rain was being kept clear, there was indeed a figure pinned face-down. The dirty blond hair and wide shoulders confirmed his suspicion. . . Maks was on the shit side of the Jinns.

"Those gorcs, they were running south hard." Flora gave an over-the-top shudder. "You think they could be headed for something big, maybe? A fight?" Flora flicked those eyelashes of hers a few times, and the Jinn closest to her leaned her way. While they were occupied, Merlin slowly made his way toward their prisoner. The Jinn normally didn't take their own kind prisoner. In fact, he had never heard of a case where one Jinn had turned on another. Ever. So just what was going on with Maks and his fellows here?

Why would they pin him down like this? Had he. . . fought them? Considering who his father was, Merlin struggled to see how this situation could have come to be.

Standing just inside the barrier that kept the rain from falling, he glanced down at Maks. "What exactly are you doing out here?"

"Fuck," Maks muttered into the mud, which made Merlin inexplicably happy. He didn't like the Jinn any better than Zamira did, but for different reasons. They belonged to the Emperor and the Emperor was his enemy.

"Really, flouncing the mud?" he asked softly.

Maks pulled against his bonds, but there was a trickle of magic running through them, telling Merlin that Maks was not going home to any sort of glory or honor. He was being taken back to the desert against his will. Likely to be killed.

"Is Zam okay?" Maks asked.

Merlin just stared down at the young Jinn as the shock settled around him. The Jinn were not known for caring about anyone, most certainly not their sworn enemies. "What does it matter to you?"

Maks tried to turn his face, but the magical bonds held tightly. "Is she okay? Did she make it back to Ish with the jewel?"

Merlin tapped the bottom of Maks's boot with his own, his thoughts circling around this Jinn and Zamira. "Zam is of no concern for you. You should know that. This is not Romeo and Juliet, Jinn. You cannot have her in your life. It will end up killing her, but not before it shatters her heart."

Maks's back muscles bunched under his shirt. "I just. . . can you make sure she's safe. Can you handle that much, mage?"

Merlin frowned. This was not the behavior of a Jinn, not by a long shot. The whole situation was screwball. "What are you really, boy? You aren't a Jinn, are you?"

Maks pulled at the ropes again and Merlin took a step back. He couldn't help Maks and get away with it even if he wanted to, and he really wasn't all that interested.

But Zamira needed to find her strength, and she was drawn to this one. . . much as Merlin might hate it. Besides, if Maks wasn't a Jinn in truth, that changed things.

Merlin walked over to where the horses were tied, finding the one that belonged in the Stockyards. "Batman, is it?" he muttered softly. He didn't dare place a spell on the beast to be able to find Zamira, but he was betting she was close enough that the horse would find her on his own. He cut the hobbles from around Batman's fetlocks and then made a shooing motion with his hands.

As soon as Batman backed up, Merlin turned and strode toward the fire. Flora had kept the Jinn watching her with the attentiveness a starving man gave a buffet. He grabbed her arm and kept walking. "Time to go. I just remembered I left a pot on the stove."

"What?" she squawked, and he tugged her arm a little harder.

"Wave goodbye to the nice men. Thank you for allowing us to warm up a bit."

She waved but frowned at him as he all but shoved her onto the back of her horse.

He climbed aboard his own mount and gave it a hard boot, sending it out into the weather.

Flora kept up and he ignored her questions as they galloped away from the Jinn's encampment. To the left of him in a flash of lightning, he saw Batman race northward.

Toward where he knew Zamira lay unconscious.

Flora finally got in front of him with her horse, forcing him to stop. "Are you insane? What is going on?"

He opened his mouth but didn't dare tell her what he'd done. That he'd acted on a whim, on a belief that maybe love had a place in this world after all. That maybe love was what Zamira needed, not more challenges. Because he knew what Flora would say. That he was a sentimental old fool who had no idea what he'd just done.

"I think that's enough time. I was worried they would pick up on our abilities."

She frowned. "Why do I get the feeling you aren't telling me all the truth? What did that boy Maks say?"

Damn, so she noticed him talking to Maks.

"Nothing of importance. Protesting his innocence. The usual words of a condemned man."

As soon as he said condemned, he knew it was true even though Maks had said no such thing. Marsum would not allow a traitor to live, and if they'd staked the young Jinn out like that, then that was what Maks was. A traitor.

The question Merlin had now, though, was far more complex.

Just what the hell was Maks if he wasn't a Jinn?

Chapter 9

Noises all around me made me think perhaps I was having a psychedelic dream, but I was *fairly* certain I'd not eaten anything that would create what my ears were picking up. A pair of goats being strangled, the roar of a lion, hooves everywhere, and was that one of old Will's insults. . .

"You cream-faced loon!" she screeched. Lila's voice was the best thing I'd heard all day.

I turned my face into the rain as it poured over me, so happy, I couldn't hold the grin off my stupid face. "Macbeth and it's *thou*, not *you*."

Blue and silver scales, and seemingly giant violet eyes came into view, then a familiar weight settled on my chest. Lila grabbed at my face with her tiny claws, squishing my cheeks. "You're alive! Look, she's alive!"

I groaned and tried to sit up. But between Lila's weight, as little as it was, and the spinning inside my skull, the attempt ended with me puking to one side.

The sounds of strangled goats continued, and I made myself look at the chaos around me.

Kiara had shifted and stood between me and the two satyrs who were arguing violently. Shit, who knew that female satyrs were so damn big? She was easily eight feet tall and three hundred pounds of pissed off half-goat woman.

I lifted a hand to my skull and my fingers came away sticky with blood. "What did she hit me with? A spiked club?"

"Wooden spoon," Lila said.

A wooden spoon. Who the hell used a wooden spoon as a weapon? I groaned and pushed to my knees. Lila swept into the air, giving me room. I wobbled and leaned against Balder who'd not left my side. I clung to the saddle, the shouting between the two satyrs and the roaring of Kiara making me want to pull my own head off.

"ENOUGH!" I shouted the word and instantly regretted it, swaying with the force of my gorge as it climbed my throat. I clutched at the side of my head, but blessedly there was silence after that. I looked up to see all three of the noise makers staring at me. "Kiara, shift back. I need your help."

The words would have been difficult to say another time, but not then. My head hurt too much to let my pride get in the way of help. Kiara shifted, and I pinned a look at Marcel. "I've saved your ass twice now; get your friend to help us."

"You, I will not help you!" Rev's wife screeched, and she came at me with the wooden spoon. Before I could do anything, Lila shot between us and let out a miniature roar.

"Damn it, Stella, these are my friends and I will pour my guts out on you if you don't let them come in out of the rain." Lila held her ground even while Stella held her wooden spoon high. Rain, was it still raining? I barely felt it through the throb of my head and the horrid taste of bile on my tongue.

This was where Lila had been hiding? With the female satyr?

This was quite the standoff if I ever saw one. Something like a laugh slid out of me and then Kiara was there, helping me stand, and we were being hustled out of the rain and through a door big enough for Stella to stand upright to pass with plenty of clearance.

"Horses, someone take care of the horses." I handed the reins to Marcel and then I was out in the black night of unconsciousness again. I knew I'd heal, that wasn't the concern. The concern was how fast I'd manage to heal. Because there were gorcs behind, and dragons ahead. And Bryce needed me to find him somewhere in between.

If Steve got to him first, the dragons would be the least of my brother's worries. I didn't doubt what Steve had said before I left—that he thought my brother and I should have been left to die.

And with Bryce on his own, I had no doubt Steve would take advantage of that fact.

Speaking of dragons. . . Lila curled up in the crook of my neck as I came to. I was on the floor, and my clothes had been stripped off me, but at least I was dry and warm.

"I'm sorry," she whispered. I turned my head slowly, her words confusing me.

"What for? You got us out of the rain. You kept Stella from smashing me with a wooden spoon again. What a psycho that one is." I reached up and laid a hand on her back.

"I'm sorry for leaving, for betraying you at the very end. There was no other choice for me, you must know that. I was still not in control of myself."

Right, there was that. Maybe I was finally gaining some wisdom in my later years, but I understood her better than she probably realized. I patted her back. "You thought you were doing the right thing. I get it. I really do. Besides, it's turned out. . . " I wanted to say it had turned out okay, but I wasn't so sure about that. At the moment, things were looking pretty ugly, but that had little enough to do with Lila leaving my side.

She buried her face under my hair, tiny sobs wracking her body. "They cut me off, Zam. They cut me off. I'm no longer a dragon. I can't feel them. I'm no longer bound to them at all. They cast me out like I'm worthless."

I kept my face as neutral as I could as I tried to absorb this new information. She went on, the words bubbling out of her. "I was coming to find you when the rainstorm hit, and I was blown off course. I saw the Jinn, and I think. . . I think they have Maks."

Of course, she didn't know the truth about that bastard. I put a hand to the back of my head, feeling the lump there, wincing as my fingers slid over it. "He's one of them, Lila. Maks is a Jinn."

She flicked her tail violently from side to side, thrashing the air. "No, they had him staked out, face-down in the mud. You don't do that to your own unless you hate them." She lifted her head so we were nose to nose. "I know you care for him. I know he cares for you. Maybe we could go get him. We could be like before, just the three of us."

Just the three of us against the world. It would have been simpler if Maks had really been a human.

I knew she was in part trying to keep me from asking too much about being cut off from the other dragons. But her words forced me to consider what she was saying. "Even so, he doesn't want us in his life. He left, Lila. He's trying to escape the wall."

Those big eyes of hers blinked a few times. "Maybe he's got a good reason for trying to get away, Zam. I left because I was trying to protect you; what if he was doing the same? We need to save him. We need to give him that chance."

I sat up, holding the blanket to me. There was no wave of nausea, so score one for me. "We do not need to save him, Lila. He chose to leave."

"So did I," she whispered. I looked at her, sitting beside me.

"You also chose to come back," I pointed out.

It was at that moment Marcel decided to chime in. "He can't come back if he's tied down in the mud."

I rolled my eyes, but Kiara's voice made me cringe. "Maks is a *Jinn*?"

Well, shit, that wouldn't go well once we were back at the Stockyards. Everyone thought Maks was a human, and he'd let it slip that he'd been sent to the Stockyards to kill Steve and Bryce. But in the six months he'd lived with us, he'd been nothing but a model servant and human. There hadn't been a single "accident" in all that time that would've left me suspicious of his behavior. Had he been telling the truth or just lying once more.

"Kiara, hand me my clothes." I pointed at my drying garments by the gigantic fire.

"Not until you tell me the truth. Were we living with a Jinn?" The horror and fear that laced her words was not surprising. The fatigue it gave me, though, was.

"Yes. As far as I know," I said. "I think he was on the run from his own kind."

She sucked in a sharp breath as she made her way to the clothing stretched out to dry, picking up my pants and shirt. She tossed them to me and I caught them in midair, pulling my shirt on with only a low wolf whistle from Marcel.

"Nice rack."

"Shut up," I growled.

"I thought shifters liked being nude." Marcel grinned at me from across the way.

Kiara nodded. "We do, but she's not really a shifter. Not like the rest of us."

She might as well have slapped me across the face. Even Marcel's eyebrows shot up. "Miss Preggars a friend of yours?"

I shrugged. "A child whose mouth runs away with her."

Kiara blushed, and I pushed to my feet, yanking my pants on. They were mostly dry, which meant I'd been out a few hours. The house we were in was made of mud and straw, and through the shuttered window, I heard the rain still pounding down.

I frowned. Pounding. . . the rain didn't fall like that, like the sounds of galloping hooves.

"Fuck, the horses are loose." Something had to be chasing them to send them into a gallop in the rainstorm that still thundered around us. I ran out of the house barefoot. No one followed.

Idiots, did Kiara really want to be on foot the rest of the way?

It was hard not to grab them and shake them until their teeth rattled. I stared through the rain to see a horse galloping straight for me. "Easy, easy, buddy. . . " I trailed off as he slid to a stop, his dark coat slicked with sweat, steam rolling off him while the rain sluiced across his body and all around us.

"Batman?" I whispered his name as I slid a hand up slowly. He breathed into my palm and bunted me. When I reached for his dangling reins, he pulled back a step and flicked his head.

"I am not following you out in this," I said. "You're insane."

He snorted and bobbed his head again. The mud squelched between my toes, turning my feet into ice blocks. I had to make a decision.

Did I care enough about Maks to make sure he was

at least okay? Even if that meant walking right into a Jinn's encampment? The very thought took my breath away.

Maks as a Jinn didn't frighten me, as foolish as that was. Maybe because I knew him. I knew his laugh and knew even if he was inherently a bad Jinn, he'd not even tried to kill me. And I'd given him plenty of opportunities where he could have, and no one would have been the wiser. And I'd known him before as he'd masqueraded as a human. I couldn't seem to not see him as that man no matter how hard I tried.

The taste of his mouth, the feel of his skin on mine, the safety in his arms, those sensations caught me off guard. I turned away from Batman, my heart pounding with the memory of Maks and me in his lap. Of his body warming me after my fall into the river.

Of him calling me back from the brink of death.

"I need my boots first," I said. Batman snorted as if he understood.

I walked through the door and went directly to the fire and wiped my feet off on some of Kiara's clothes while she spluttered and tried to snatch them away from me. Without a word, I pulled on the rest of my clothes, boots, cloak, and weapons. I was out of my mind. There was no other reason for me to do something like this—to attempt a rescue of one Jinn from his Jinn buddies. But that wasn't stopping me.

"Lila, you with me?" I turned to her as I settled the flail on my back.

"Where are you going?" She flew up to my eye level, the wind from her wings blowing my hair back.

"There's someone stuck in the mud."

She grinned and nodded. "The course of true love never did run smooth. I'm with you." She flew to my shoulder and settled, and I shifted my balance to accommodate her as if I'd been doing it my whole life.

"Midsummer Night's Dream," I said. "And it's not love."

I turned, and Kiara stood in my path. "No, you are not going after Maks, and you have the sapphire," she said with her hands on her hips.

Well, fuck a duck, I had half-forgotten about the jewel.

"You are not in charge here, Kiara. And if he's really being held against his will, he's their enemy, the same as us, so he needs our help. I'm going to check it out. I won't bring him back if he's with them. And the sapphire is no different from the dragon's gemstone. It will only make Ish meaner and give her more strength. We don't need that right now."

She put an arm out as if to block me and a crackle of tension rolled between us, thick like the air before a lightning strike.

I pushed into her arm. "This is not complicated," I said softly. "I am the stronger shifter here. *Not* you."

She let out a long growl, and I locked eyes with her, knowing that to even look away for a split second would be considered a sign of submission. Instead, I pushed my body into hers until our noses touched. I might not have the low growl she did, but nobody outstared me.

The seconds ticked, and I leaned into her farther. "I

do not want to hurt you, but if you make me, I will put you in your place."

Her eyelashes fluttered, and her growl softened until it was nothing. She looked away and dropped her arm. "I had to try."

"Actually, no, you didn't." I pushed her gently out of my way. "I'll be back as quickly as I can."

That's what I said, but already I knew I wasn't coming back for her or Marcel. They were dead weight and I needed to move fast. The gorcs would come for me. They were hunting my name, not Kiara's. I stepped into the rain and made my way to where the horses had been tied. With all their gear on, and only water to drink.

Anger snapped through me and I softly apologized to both Balder and Lacey, giving them each a couple of the camel fat balls of oats. It was the best I could do. I untied Balder and jumped onto the saddle.

Lila clung to me. "You aren't coming back for them, are you?"

I shook my head. "No, I'm not."

Dead weight. . . those words would come back to haunt me. I just didn't know it in that moment.

Chapter 10

I held tightly to Batman's reins so I didn't lose him in the rain as we galloped through the splattering mud and wet. We were running out of night, and that did not work in our favor.

Because if Maks did need a rescue, then we needed the cover of darkness to do it. I broke out in a cold sweat just thinking about facing Jinn.

"What made you change your mind about the toad?" Lila asked, and I grinned. Toad, that was what she'd taken to calling him at one point after one of her favorite Shakespearean insults.

"If he really is against them, we could use a Jinn on our side. Besides, the gorcs are on my ass, and my brother went into Dragon's Ground to look for a healer."

"Oh." Just that, nothing else. Because she knew better than I did just how fucking stupid and dangerous it was for anyone to trespass into the Dragon's Ground.

Even to find a legendary healer, there was no acceptable reason the dragons allowed for anyone to come into their territory.

It seemed, though, that luck was not on our side, and the sun began to rise before Batman took us all the way to wherever he'd gotten loose. Assuming he was taking us back to Maks.

Assuming Maks really was in trouble.

The sky wasn't bright exactly, but the jet-black of the night faded a little. I wished the rain would've faded with it.

Lila hopped off my shoulder and made her way to the pommel of the saddle where she perched. "You mean to go into the Dragon's Ground then, don't you?"

"If that's where my brother is." I nodded. "I'm hoping he hasn't gotten that far." But if he hadn't, it could mean Steve had found him first. I clamped down on the growl that wanted to roll up my throat. Steve had better not have put his hands on Bryce.

Lila's jaw worked side to side and a deep frown creased her brows. "You want the dragon's jewel too, don't you?"

I sighed and looked down at her. "Yes and no. Steve and Darcy are going in after it as we speak. I don't want Ish to have it, Lila. She's. . . not stable. I think that some-thing within the giant's stone that we brought back has made her mean. Like the giants are mean. I don't understand why, but it is the only thing that makes sense to me." I realized as I spoke that my thoughts had been circling around this conclusion for days.

Lila's eyelids fluttered. "Then the stone from the

dragons will not help that. It will make her more suspicious, meaner, quicker to anger and she will turn into a true hoarder. Like the dragons."

I just stared. "You know all this? How?"

"I always knew. I just couldn't really tell you before. But I'm free of my bindings now so I can explain a bit more. Or at least explain what I know. The stones and jewels that the emperor's son handed out before the emperor was put to sleep, they carry some of the traits of the creatures who've owned them for so long. A weak heart could never carry a stone without feeling the effects." She reached up and tapped the sapphire through my shirt. "You wear this with no effect that I've seen. You've got the true heart of a lion, Zam. Not that I'm surprised."

I would have blushed if I hadn't been so fucking cold. "Thanks, Lila."

She shrugged. "It's the truth. And I think the stones are partly what make the dragons such bastards, to be honest." Her violet eyes caught the light from the sun and seemed to be jewels of their own. "Dragons weren't always this bad, Zam. We were heroes once too. There are stories about the dragons of old. Of their great deeds and battles to save others."

I believed her. There were stories of dragons helping, healing other supes. But those stories were old, almost more like legends and fairy tales than truth.

But they had been enough to draw Bryce in hopes he could gain his legs back.

The sun rose at my back, but the rain didn't slow a single drop from what I could tell. I grimaced. I was nearly soaked through, yet again, but at least my head had stopped hurting and my cracked ribs were healed.

Batman tugged on the reins, nearly pulling them out of my stiff fingers. I clamped my hand closed at the last second and he instead jerked me halfway out of the saddle. I yelped and pushed Balder closer to the big horse.

"Close, are we?" I asked softly.

Batman blew out a big breath and pawed at the ground. He really loved Maks, that much had been obvious almost from the beginning. Something that didn't fit with the Jinn.

Animals hated them.

I frowned, wondering why I hadn't thought of that before.

"I think there is something ahead." Lila was above me, using her height advantage to get a lay of the land. "Maybe your eyes are better than mine, though. I could be seeing things."

I nodded and tied Batman's reins to my saddle before I took my feet out of the stirrups. The cold had seeped into my bones and made me stiff, like a two-hundred-year-old woman, and I grimaced while I worked to get the blood flowing again. With a groan, I pushed my feet up onto the saddle, then carefully stood, balancing on Balder's back.

That bit of extra height made the difference. Ahead of us on the flat plain, I could see a small group of figures moving about. Maybe three miles away. I dropped to the saddle and turned the horses north.

"We need to keep a low profile until tonight," I said.

"There's no way we can go in the light of day to check on him."

"They'll move today, and if they go, we'll never be able to keep up," Lila said.

"Maybe. Maybe not. Jinn like the heat and the sun. They're probably hunkering down against the weather," I said. Though I was not altogether sure, it seemed a high probability.

I swallowed hard because a sudden swell of nausea flowed up and through me. Jinn. . . I did not want them knowing I was alive, or that any of my pride had survived. We'd lasted this long because they hadn't known. I frowned. Then again, Maks had said he'd been sent to kill Steve and Bryce. Someone had to have blabbed about where we were.

I sighed. Another mystery for another day. "There's a stand of boulders over there. We'll duck behind them for the day." Because while Jinn could be lazy, they were not stupid.

They'd notice us if we just stood there out in the open of the plain watching them.

We hurried to get to the boulders, which also stood out in the middle of the plain in a circle, but they were more cover than we had on our own. I should have thought about just what they were, and why they were there, but I didn't. I only thought about getting out of sight of the Jinn.

The horses picked up a quick trot, and though Batman stared back toward Maks and the Jinn encampment, he kept up with only a slight limp. I'd have to look at his legs and feet and see what ailed him. I hoped it would only be fatigue.

"We'll get you back to him, one way or another," I said as we rounded the first tall standing stone. I stared up at the gigantic black boulder, the grooves drawn into it anything but natural.

"Lila," I said. "This might have been a bad idea."

"Why?" She was just ahead of me, her wings cutting through the air.

"These are standing stones." I expected her to understand, to get exactly what I was saying. Standing stones were known to appear on this side of the wall and they were usually connected to a supernatural of great power.

As in the Emperor himself.

But they had not been seen in my lifetime, though my father had taught me about them.

I swallowed hard, halted the horses and asked them to back up. Lila swept out from between the stones and the sense of foreboding that crawled over my skin eased off.

"The Emperor is. . . he must be waking." I breathed the words and a low rumble of thunder seemed to laugh at me and my fear.

Lila squeaked and shot to my shoulder, burying herself inside my cloak. "Sweet goddess, we were right in there. Why didn't he steal our lives?"

Apparently, she had heard the legends and rumors too. The stones were a place of sacrifice for the Emperor's acolytes. They'd used the stones to hand over the lives of their enemies. At least, that was how the story went.

I turned the horses so we rode around the outside edge of the stones until we were behind them. They still blocked us from the Jinn's sight, but they would give us no shelter from the cutting rain. Which was fine. We'd all survived worse.

To be fair, though, that was probably one of the most horrendous days of my life in terms of sheer discomfort and length of each minute. The rain slashed through every layer I had. I might as well have been naked. There were moments I considered shifting and standing under Balder as Lila was so smartly doing, but I needed to hold myself ready for a shift later.

The hours passed slowly, and the horses huddled together, but even they didn't get too close to the black standing stones behind us. I kept turning around to make sure they were still there. Or more accurately that they hadn't drawn any closer. There were stories about the stones appearing, but like with dragons healing those in need, I'd thought they were just stories with no basis.

"Lila," I needed to break the silence, "you know about the stones?"

"You mean how the emperor uses them to gain his strength back so he can rule us all again?"

I nodded. "Something like that."

"You mean like how they suck the life and soul right out of you?"

"That too." I breathed the words and peered down at Lila who was peering up at me from under Balder's belly.

"What are you thinking?" She flicked her wings several times, flinging water droplets every which way.

"That the stones are waiting for something powerful to come along, and neither you nor I are that." I smiled, though I knew there was a sour twist to it. "Score one for the weaklings."

Lila laughed, but there was a bitterness to it that I did not miss. "Yeah, score one for us."

After that, we fell into silence again for hours more, and finally the sun began to drop. I slid from Balder's saddle and ground tied him. "I'm going to shift, Lila. Can you climb high enough that they won't notice you, but you can still see in the dark what is going on below?"

She bobbed her head. "Yes, I think so. What are you going to do?"

"I'm going to see if Maks needs rescuing," I said. "If he does, I'll do what I can. If he doesn't, then we book it out of here as fast as we can."

She gave a single flick of her tail and shot into the sky, startling the horses after so many hours of inactivity. For just a moment, I wished I was with Marcel and Kiara in that mud hut with the roaring fire. But then, I'd be back with Marcel and Kiara and the mud hut, and have no way of slipping away from them.

I sighed and let my body slide from two feet to four, barely blinking, and it was done. Faster and faster, I was getting better at the shift after so many years of ignoring that side of me. I should have been using the gifts I had instead of ignoring them all these years. I startled, my tail twitching. That was the first time I'd ever considered the shifting ability I did have to be a gift.

I jogged around the standing stones, giving them a wide berth. Just in case the Emperor changed his mind and decided any power was worth a grab.

A shudder slid through me.

The sun was ahead of me and I watched as it dipped below the horizon; the clouds blocking the light worked in our favor. And miracle of miracles, the rain eased off to a light mist that was damn near heavenly after the pounding rain we'd sat through for the day. But it could mean that the Jinn might be ready to leave.

I ran toward where I'd last seen the encampment. When I was a mile away, I heard them, their voices carrying across the flat ground.

The laughter, the raucous talk, the clink of plates and such. I slowed, dropping my body so I was less noticeable. The whoosh of leathery wings high above me made my ears twitch. Lila had my back, there was that, and it gave me a boost of courage.

Still, if I'd been in my human form, I'd have been sweating. As it was, my tongue hung out and I couldn't help myself. I was panting like crazy as the fear cut through me. Jinn were not to be trifled with, they were not to be engaged, they were to be feared.

They killed lions, cutting them down with no thought.

A hundred feet away, I crouched beside a series of crappy little scrub brushes. The darkness was my friend, especially with my black fur. Even if the Jinn were looking my way, they would not see me.

I crept forward, flat on my belly now, my eyes narrowed so their gleam didn't catch in the firelight.

The camp was not new by the looks of the shit every-where. I mean that in a most literal sense. There was horse shit everywhere.

It looked like the Jinn had set up camp before the rain had come and just hunkered down. I swiveled my ears toward them. Their conversation froze me.

"How much longer, Orlow?"

"Tomorrow, we move tomorrow. We'll see if we can pick up one of the lion shifters Maks told us about. Didn't he say there was a female?"

Laughter followed, and my blood seemed to freeze. Maks had given us up after all. I turned to leave, and actually took a few steps before their words stopped me.

"Not much of him left. Why don't we just kill him? Tell Marsum that he fought us too hard and we had to. Bastard did put up a good fight, and we have the scars to prove it."

If I thought my blood had run cold before, the ice now in my veins made the previous chill feel like a blis-teringly hot summer's day. I made myself creep closer again, my eyes searching the ground around the camp. Lila had said Maks was pinned to the ground, face in the mud.

But there was no movement, not even the exhalation of breath that should have given a body away. I tipped my head sideways to give my nose better access to the scents. The Jinn came through loud and clear, the smell of desert and death. A faint whiff of a man I knew, of the smell of someone I cared for, was there too.

Barely.

Maks was on the far side, of course. I worked my

way slowly around the camp, moving only when I thought the Jinn were preoccupied with each other. Their conversation flowed over me as they discussed killing Maks.

"He was never really one of us, so what loss is it?"

"Marsum wants to make an example of him. Show what happens to traitors. Besides, he'll power the Emperor."

"Hmm. Marsum will be pissed if we don't come back with a lion too. The female, the one that's pregnant. We need her. That will soften the blow of losing Maks. A two for one deal." Laughter followed that last bit.

Oh, fuck, they were talking about Kiara now. Gods and goddess of the desert, none of this was going to help me get to my brother any sooner. How the hell did they even know about her though?

Bryce would understand why I had to go back for Kiara first before going to him. Protect the children first, and Kiara carried the first child in twenty years.

The strongest lions of the Bright Pride stood between danger and the member that could not protect themselves. That was our creed, our family, and I would not fail it.

So I thought.

I got all the way around the camp and the Jinn had settled in to play cards of some sort, betting on them and throwing things into the fire as they lost. I split my attention between them and the man who was on his belly at my feet. He had his face turned to the side, but even so, the mud had climbed over everything but one nostril. The air fluttered in and out slowly against the mud as if he were peacefully sleeping.

Or out cold.

I could smell the blood on him, the injuries that weren't healing.

I wanted to rip his bonds from him but knew our survival depended on doing this right, and that meant doing it quietly with all the stealth I had. I slowed my breathing and went to his left wrist. I cut through the rope tying him down with my claws, the strength in them buoyed by my weapons. I quickly went to his other wrist and legs. One eye on the Jinn, one eye on what I was doing.

Maks didn't move an inch. I needed him to shift into his caracal form so we could run, so we could get away. I nudged his head with my nose.

A burble of air bubbled out of the mud and his face sunk under the thick sticky mass. I grabbed his hair with my mouth and yanked his head up. It was then I realized he was bound by the neck too.

You're lucky I don't hate you, toad, I thought as I stuck my face under the mud, my mouth searching for the rope that held him down.

The mud was foul, tasting like horse piss and vomit making me gag, but I worked my way through it until I found the rope on his neck. A single bite and I was through it.

But none of that mattered as a hand settled onto the scruff of my neck and yanked me upward.

I was spun around to face the one thing I feared above all others.

A Jinn.

He held me tightly by the scruff of my neck, immobilizing me. I stared at him and a hiss slid out of me. He frowned. "What the fuck is this, a cat?"

I hissed again because I realized he didn't know me. He didn't know what I was, and that was about the only thing that was saving my furry ass. I stopped myself from shifting and just twisted around, hissing and spitting as any normal, ordinary run-of-the-mill house cat would.

Goddess save me. I was in deep shit.

"Put it down, Bart," one of the others said. "They are all hair, not worth eating at all, and that one is fucking scrawny. Couldn't be more than five pounds!"

The Jinn threw me down and I scrambled backward, out of the firelight while my heart pounded out of control. Part of me said I should have fought, should have tried to kill him while I was so close, but the truth of it was, I wasn't strong enough. I couldn't have killed him. Jinn made the Ice Witch's pets look like stuffed animals.

I scuttled to the edges of the flickering firelight but. . . Maks was still face down in the mud. Fuuuuuk. I let out a tiny snarl of frustration that made the Jinn laugh, but then they all turned their backs on me.

I scooted forward the second time and grabbed at Maks's hair with my teeth, yanking his head up.

He wasn't breathing.

There was no more choice, I had to shift. I didn't let myself think about it, but instead let the shift take me. I lay on my belly, breathing hard as I grabbed

Maks by the shoulders and yanked him partway out of the mud.

I didn't look at him but kept my eyes on the Jinn. They were totally ignoring this side of the camp. I pulled Maks a little farther, the wet ground making little sound under his sliding body.

When we were ten feet away, I twisted around, flipped him onto his back and turned his head sideways, sliding my fingers into his mouth and clearing it of mud. I tried not to think about anything but getting him breathing.

I put my mouth to his and blew into him. Filling his chest with my air. I paused and listened to his heart.

Nothing. Again, I pushed air into him, again I listened. I used my elbow and drove it once into his chest, then breathed into his mouth again. Not exactly what I'd call expert CPR, but it was the best I could do. If he didn't start breathing soon, I would have to leave him here.

Panic like I'd never known caught hold of me with that thought. Of Maks dying.

Breathe, damn you, breathe! Inside my head I screamed at him, demanded that he take a breath. I chose not to notice how wet my face was. It had to be raining again.

I put my ear to his chest just as he took a slow, labored breath. I spun around so my face was by his and my body in line with his so I could watch the camp.

"Do not move," I whispered as quietly as I could into his ear. "Breathe, catch your wind. Then we shift and run."

I had my cheek pressed to his, and he lifted a hand

to touch my face but said nothing. His breathing came stronger with each lift of his chest. At least he was going to bounce back fast.

That was the only good thing about him being a Jinn: they healed like a speed demon.

The seconds ticked by as I lay on my belly in the mud with Maks with his hand on my face and my cheek pressed to his. A weird sense of calm flowed over my body and through my limbs.

This was what he did to me. Good or bad, my heart had decided that Maks was good for me. Fucking traitorous chest drum.

The calm fled as the Jinn began to move around, restless. As if they knew something was up but couldn't quite pin it down. They didn't look toward where Maks had been pinned. Likely they wouldn't have cared if he'd died in the mud right there.

How the fuck was I getting us out of this mess? Maks's hand pressed a little harder, then slid through my hair, trailing a tingle of energy everywhere he touched until he left off and reached for the flail's handle.

I put my hand over his, stopping him. That was not a good idea. If he started a fight we couldn't win, we'd both die. I couldn't fight one Jinn, never mind four, even with Maks at my side. They were not gorcs, and I knew my limits.

Apparently Maks did not know his.

I leaned closer to see those blue eyes of his were open and snapping with an anger I'd never seen in him. Rage was a good, dangerous look on him that sent my blood pounding into overdrive.

Don't judge me. I have a thing for men who can take charge, and Maks was that with a soft heart that gave me the best of both worlds.

But did I trust him enough to take the flail? The weapon was beyond destructive, and though he'd used it once before, something in me told me not to let him take it. I pushed his hand away and the anger etched deeper onto his face.

So be it. He could be angry with me all he wanted, but we needed to get out of here as fast as we could. I shifted into my cat form, which did two things. It hid me from the Jinn, and it hid the flail from Maks.

He rolled to his belly and shifted to his other form of a desert caracal. Sandy brown with black tips on his ears and points, he wasn't that much bigger than me, really.

We just needed to creep away.

Except we were too late.

"Maks, you fucking shit, get back here!" The Jinn, Bart, I think, screamed his name.

We bolted, but Maks was slow and I couldn't leave him behind. Well, this was going to hell in a handbasket in a fucking hurry.

The Jinn raced after us, screaming a war cry that set my hair standing on end. A war cry I heard in my nightmares reliving the Oasis.

I pushed Maks ahead of me, guarding our rear. Which was something of a laugh, considering. We needed speed because Jinn were faster than a horse when they wanted to be.

"Lila, get him out of here!" I yelled. There was a snap of wings and then a whoosh to my side right before

Lila scooped Maks in his caracal form right off the ground.

The Jinn screamed and shot bolts of magic that looked like flaming spears at them as they climbed out of reach, high above our heads.

I spun, digging my back feet into the dirt and launched myself at the closest Jinn, knowing what I was doing was near suicide. But it would get Maks and Lila away.

Part of me knew I was being a fool for someone I shouldn't have been risking my life for.

The other part of me said fuck it, I cared for Maks, and he was becoming part of my life in ways I couldn't define. Even if that weren't true, the Jinn were my enemies and they needed to die.

The screech that left me echoed through the air as I landed on the Jinn closest to me. I hit him in the belly and slashed at him with everything I had. A wildness overtook me as I fought to find my way through his guts to his spine. I would tear it from him. I would destroy him. I would take him to the ground and snap his bones.

I knew this madness. I'd felt it before and knew it made me as dangerous as I could be, but it also put me well inside the realm of death's reach. The wild madness, though, didn't allow me to really accept that I could die. Dangerous, deadly, in those moments I was a lion, through and through.

Warm, salty blood splashed around me, coating my mouth and nose. Someone screamed, a long drawn-out wail that pitched all over the place, and then we were on the ground and I was being pulled from him while the other Jinn laughed.

"You don't think this is that idiot Dirk's kid, do you?"

Dirk, my father, the man they killed, my hero. And he was not an idiot.

A sudden white-hot fury lit up my reflexes that I couldn't have held back even if I'd wanted to.

I shifted right then and there, and in a single fluid motion, grabbed my kukri blades and swept them up through the Jinn's middle, following it with a double slice across his neck, cutting through his spine. The look of surprise stayed with him as his head rolled from his shoulders.

"Yeah," I said, "I fucking well am."

Chapter 11

With a dead Jinn at my feet and kukri blades in my hands, the three remaining Jinn stared at me, shock written all over them. Of course, they didn't think to find any lion shifters in the middle of the desert plains, certainly not one of Dirk's children. Dirk, the thorn in their side for the entire time he'd lived in the desert. Dirk, the man who'd had two children, both of whom escaped the slaughter of the Oasis.

And now they faced one of those children. I would have laughed at their expressions if I didn't think I was going to die right then and there.

The flail called to me, a pulse against my back. . . I reached for it, yanking it from the sheath and turning it, sending it into a fast spin before I could think better of it. Before I died, I would take as many of them with me as I could.

I didn't wait for any of them to move. I slammed the

two balls into the Jinn closest to me. He screamed and went flying through the air, slammed into the other two and they tumbled to the ground. Again, if not for the severity of the situation, I would have laughed. They looked like a messed-up version of the Three Stooges, a play my father had reenacted for us on dark winter nights.

Maybe I wasn't going to die. And if I wasn't dying, it was time to go. I spun, jammed the flail into its sheath and bolted into the darkness, heading toward the standing stones. Three miles wasn't that far, but it damn well felt like it in the dark with Jinn at my back. Not that I believed there would be safety there, but the horses were there, and I knew we had a better chance at outrunning the Jinn.

I shifted into my cat form partway there and turned on the speed, scooting across the black plains with twice the speed I had on two legs. But that many shifts that close together and I could feel the energy drag on me.

It was the only excuse I had for not noticing the Jinn on my right as I drew close to the horses.

"Gotcha, cat!"

He shot toward me and I veered to the left without thinking.

The path took me straight through the standing stones. I raced through the center and the Jinn followed. At least, he followed before he slammed to a stop like he'd run into one of the stones. On the other side of the circle, outside the rocks, I slid to a stop, spun and looked back.

The Jinn was floating in midair, his body stretched

out, his arms and legs flung wide and shaking as though he were being electrocuted.

Around us the rocks began to hum, singing a tune that tugged me forward. My eyelids fluttered with the warmth that pulled me forward, the call to give myself over to the stones.

"Zam, help me!" Lila screamed. I snapped out of the hold the stones had on me and bolted away and around the circle to where the horses were. To where Maks stumbled toward the circle. Already another Jinn had joined his friend. I shifted to two legs, groaning as I did, and tackled Maks to the ground. I pinned him flat on his back and he still fought with me to get up. His eyes were glazed, and his breath came in gasps. He tried to push me off and in our combined weakened states I have no doubt we looked ridiculous.

Floppy limbs, we probably appeared like rag dolls trying to fend off each other.

I straddled him, sitting on his hips as I held his arms above his head while my own arms trembled with the strain. "Stay with me, Maks."

He groaned and closed his eyes. "Let me go, Zam. The Emperor calls and I must obey him."

"No. You're here with me. With Lila. We need you."

I knew if Maks had been at full strength there would have been no contest. He'd beaten me once before, and I knew the power in his body.

He gave a sudden burst as if reading my mind and flipped me onto my back. He pushed with both hands as if to stand. I did the only thing I could. I wrapped my legs around his waist and dragged him down to me, growling through clenched teeth.

"You aren't going anywhere, Maks," I said.

Now, maybe there was something other than kissing him I could have done to distract him and break the spell the Emperor had on him. Anyone else and I would have just knocked them out, or put them into a choke hold till they passed out, but what would be the fun in that with Maks? To be fair, I couldn't think of any other way to distract him in those few seconds.

And I'd missed him. I could admit that much to myself if not to anyone else.

I grabbed his face and pressed my mouth hard against his, angling my head, inviting him in closer, opening myself to him. He paused as if he wasn't sure and then a low groan slid from him into me and he kissed me back, his body pressing down on me, the pull of the standing stones forgotten in the heat between us.

There was no hesitation, then his arms wrapped around me, curling me close to him. The heat that had been there before igniting within us on a dark, snow-filled night, seemed to have grown in the absence. The world around me faded to the points of contact where our skin touched, where our mouths touched, to the taste of him. He felt like home, like he embodied the desert and the fire deep in the sands that I loved. He fit in ways I couldn't fully grasp, in ways that no one else in my life ever had.

There was zero excuse to hide the heat between us this time, no alcohol to say it was an accident. That we didn't remember, that we hadn't meant to touch each other, to get lost in each other's kiss.

Someone cleared their throat, then a wing smacked against my forehead, startling me. I pulled back a little, breathing hard.

Lila tapped me on the shoulder, whacking me a second time. "They're gone. So if you're going to mate right here on the ground, I'm going to sit with the horses and try not to hear."

I stared up at her. I was still flat on my back, Maks on top of me, and we were pressed hard into the mud.

His blue eyes stared at me like he was seeing a ghost. "I thought I was dying back there, Zam. I thought. . . I thought you were the last thing I would see."

"Well, you were dying, to be fair." I pushed on his chest. Now was the time to act casual. Like I hadn't just kissed his face off, or he hadn't just had his hands under my shirt branding the skin of my torso with his fingers.

Yup, act casual. That was the plan.

Thank the desert gods for the black of the night that hid the growing heat in my face. Then again, maybe I was lighting the place up like a fucking torch. A giddy noise tried to escape me, and I clamped on it, turning it into a coughing snort that was anything but attractive. Maks stood and slapped me on the back.

"You okay?"

I waved him off, keeping my back to him. I needed to pull my shit together. What the hell was wrong with me? Idiot, I was being an idiot. My body was exhausted, and my emotions were spiking all over the damn place like a ping pong ball in a match with two octopi.

"What happened with the stones? What did you hear?" Lila swept around us. "You wanted to go into the stones, and I really don't recommend that after what I saw."

I turned to her. "What did you see?"

"Well, you'd know if you hadn't been so busy sucking his face off--" She grinned at me, her glimmering teeth glinting. I drew a slow breath and smiled up at her.

"I was not sucking his face off. He was under a spell, Lila. I had to *distract* him."

"Well, you *distracted* him so long that neither of you saw what happened. And the danger was long past when you finally stopped with the kissy face business." Her grin widened impossibly.

Damn it, she wasn't going to just let this go. "What happened, Lila? And I don't need anything but the facts," I asked as nicely as I could.

"They lit up from inside, their bones and muscle showing through their skin as if electrified, then they were slowly pulled apart, limb by limb, all the while unable to speak," Maks said softly, surprising me. "You did save me, Zam. I would have walked into that without question."

I knew it. There was no surprise for me there. I'd felt the pull myself, though it had been milder for sure. I'd at least been able to shake it off. "You've seen it before then?"

"Yes, and I'm going to suggest we move away from here. The call is still there under the edges of my skin. The Emperor, if he realizes I'm standing here, will try to drag me in like he did those two."

Two. Only two. I stumbled away from the stones in time to see a spark whipping across the open plain. "That's the last Jinn, and he's headed for Kiara." I knew without question.

Maks stepped up beside me but didn't touch me. Maybe that kiss had been nothing more than a passing fancy to him, like the one before. Just a mistake.

Nope, I was not following that line of thought. This was not the time to get all worried about Maks's feelings, or the lack of, that he might've had for me.

"We have to get to Kiara," I said.

Maks shook his head. "We're too late already."

"How does he even know where she is?" Lila landed on my shoulder. "Like how?"

Maks closed his eyes and slumped where he stood. I grabbed him by the arm and helped him to Batman, all but shoving him onto the big horse. Mind you, it meant I got to put my hands on his ass. A small bonus I couldn't help but notice despite the situation.

Lila snickered as I shoved Maks up. Of course, she'd taken note of just where my hands were. "Convenient," she muttered.

"Maks, how can he know?" I repeated the question as he slumped in the saddle. Whatever injuries he had were showing themselves now that the worst of the danger had passed.

"He can smell her on you, so he's following your trail right back to her," he mumbled.

I leapt onto Balder's back and spun him around the way we'd come. Lila clutched my shoulder, and I gave a long low hiss to my horse, driving into a mad gallop through the darkness.

Batman bolted after us, but I didn't look back. Maks was out of danger. But I'd put Kiara right into its path. Kiara, pregnant, the first lioness to be pregnant since the massacre.

I leaned low over Balder's neck, urging him faster than was smart for the pitch-dark night, but I trusted him and his footing. He picked up on my panic and let loose, leaving the partially lame Batman well behind us. We had to get there. I had to stop the Jinn from taking Kiara.

Otherwise. . . this was all my fault. Fuck my life. If I lost Kiara, everyone would think I'd done it on purpose, that I'd done it to get back at Steve and her for my broken heart. When the truth was. . . I would never put her in danger no matter what happened in the past. She would always be that little cub stuck in the mud with the gorc coming for her and I would always fight to protect her. It was in those heart-pounding moments as we raced along that I realized in my own way I'd tried to protect her from Steve too. That was why I'd been so angry. Because I knew he would hurt her.

And I'd been trying to stop that from happening ever since that moment I'd first rescued her.

Because she was part of my pride, and I was an alpha and protector, despite my size.

I gritted my teeth against the emotions that swelled, knowing they would do me no good.

In the distance, I saw the flames long before I saw the hut and I knew I was too late, but I didn't slow

Balder, not for a second. There was still a chance. I had to believe it was possible to save her.

We came to a sliding, mud-flinging stop twenty feet out from the hut.

Marcel and Stella were flat out on the ground, but no Kiara.

"Kiara!" I screamed her name, already knowing she would be gone, feeling her absence more than anything else. She'd been taken by the Jinn.

I jumped from the saddle and ran to Marcel, dragging him farther away from the flames, then went back for Stella. Though she was three times as heavy, I hardly noticed.

The flames around the hut burned bright gold, red, and green, the flames of a Jinn. Even if I'd had a river at my feet and buckets in hand, I'd be useless against the flames. Magic was the only way to deal with a Jinn's fire, and magic was something I didn't have in my arsenal.

I stepped backward and went to Marcel. I dropped to one knee and patted his face.

"Marcel, wake up. What happened?"

He groaned and leaned into me. "Oh, man, that was too rough. This is why we don't flounce our own women."

My eyebrows shot up. "You were flouncing Stella?"

"Giving her comfort in her grief." He slowly sat up and put a hand to his head. "Damn, I've got another nub for my efforts."

He did indeed have a third bump, but I doubted it was a horn. And I doubted it had been Stella who had clobbered him. She let out a groan. "Damn you, Marcel. You said you knew what you were doing."

I sighed. "It wasn't either of you. It was a Jinn that did this. He took Kiara." I'd been hoping they might have seen something, anything that could tell me. . . what? I couldn't catch the Jinn now, they were too damn fast, and this one was injured and on the run.

They didn't move like any other supernatural.

I narrowed my eyes and touched the sapphire on my chest. I didn't think it would help me find her. It was tied to the Ice Witch and gave her power over the weather, over the cold as far as I knew.

I crouched and tipped my head back, heartsick over what had happened. I'd rescued Maks only to lose Kiara. And I'd left her behind, thinking her safer outside my circle.

The clatter of hooves told me Batman and Maks had caught up.

"You couldn't have stopped him, Zam. Even if you'd taken her with you, he'd have grabbed her from the campsite," Lila said softly, patting a claw on top of my head. "No one can stop the Jinn."

Except I had injured him. The only reason there was one Jinn with Kiara instead of three was the standing stones. They'd saved our bacon. But not Kiara's. I rubbed a hand over my face.

Indecision flickered through me. What the fuck was I going to do?

Marcel stood and wobbled, then helped Stella to stand as well. I pushed to my feet. Bryce needed me, but now so did Kiara. This was not a time to be indecisive.

Time was not in our favor. The longer I stayed here, the more danger Bryce was in. The longer I stayed here, the more danger Kiara was in. But I knew the one I could save, and it was not Kiara.

"You two," I pointed at the satyrs who were still holding hands. "I need you to go to the Stockyards as fast as you can. Tell Ish that a Jinn took Kiara. She'll know what to do." I hoped I was right and that Ish wouldn't just be a fucking douche and say that's what Kiara got for leaving with me. Which was a distinct possibility.

"This Ish, she'll help the lioness?" Marcel frowned. "I've heard rumors that she's a right bitch. Ish, that is."

"Yeah, well, she can be, but she cares for Kiara. She'll know what to do, and if anyone can stop the Jinn from taking her, it will be Ish." I turned away because lying was not my strong point. I wasn't entirely sure Ish would help at all, even for Kiara and her unborn child. But for the moment, Ish was the only hope Kiara--and I--had.

I couldn't go after Kiara, not on my own. I glanced at Maks and he was quiet. Obviously, he wasn't going to be much help going after her either if the way he'd been staked out in the mud was any indication. He must be one of the weakest Jinn around. I sighed. Of course, he was. Just like I was the weakest shifter, and Lila the weakest dragon.

What a trio we were.

"Go," I said to Marcel. "And then I will consider your debt to me as repaid."

He gave me a sloppy salute. "The offer for a flouncing is always there, you beautiful potty mouth."

Stella snorted. "I don't think so."

Marcel opened his eyes wide and tipped his head at me. As Stella turned her back, he mouthed two words.

Save me.

"You shouldn't have flounced her," I pointed out as I mounted Balder.

Lila had been quiet the entire exchange and spoke only once Marcel and Stella were out of sight, galloping east toward the Stockyards.

"You think Ish will help?"

I wanted to say yes, but there were too many unknowns with her. "Honestly? I don't know. But I do know I can't face Jinn on my own, and he's moving too fast. He'll be back with his own kind before I ever catch up."

I turned Balder and gave him a gentle push into a fast walk. After that gallop through the dark, he needed a break. There was no stopping, though. We didn't have time to dawdle any more than I had time to wonder if I'd made the right choice.

The feeling of impending doom around us was only growing. The Jinn. The standing stones. Losing Kiara. Nearly losing Maks. Bryce in danger. Steve and Darcy looking for a stone that would make Ish more dangerous.

I shook my head as if to dislodge the feeling, but it did no good.

Something bad was coming for me, crawling across

the plains like a spell I couldn't escape. I glanced at Maks.

"You can go. I'm not going to make you come with us to the Dragon's Ground."

Lila let out a soft sigh. "We could use his help. I mean, if he really is a Jinn."

I shrugged, fatigue hitting me hard. "I'm not going to force him to come." I urged Balder forward and couldn't help but listen for the sound of Batman's hooves following. But there was no sound.

Despite everything that had just happened, despite the kiss and the fact that I'd save his life, Maks was not coming with me.

Chapter 12

F eeling Maks stay behind, not wanting to come with me, hurt my heart a hell of a lot more than I'd thought it would. Maybe it was because he said nothing. He'd not tried to argue why he should stay behind. He'd not even thanked me for saving his ass from his fellow Jinn. He'd just sat there, those blue eyes watching me, undeniably serious and lovely but giving me nothing in the way of what he might do.

The rain pounding on my head, the empty plain ahead of me. . . it had never felt more like a slap in the face.

Lila twisted around on my shoulder. "Thou art a boil! A toad! A horrible damn friend, Maks! Away, you three-inch fool! We saved you, and this is the thanks we get? Well, you aren't going to be part of Zam's pride at this rate! You don't have the heart of a lion!"

I didn't turn around though I wanted to. I wanted to rail at him too, to call him names as Lila was, to claim he was a selfish bastard, but I couldn't. The reason? I didn't really believe he was those things. He was as torn between his choices as Lila had been.

I probably would never know why he wasn't coming with us. But if he wasn't, I had to believe there was a strong reason. Maybe he thought the Jinn would come for him again. Maybe he thought we were safer without him. Both of those were possible.

But I would never know.

And I had to be okay with that lack of knowledge. I lifted my hand and touched Lila's tail. "Ease off. You had a falling-out with your people, Lila. You know the pain of that loss."

"Oh." Just that, and she crouched down. "Now I feel like a mushy little rabbit turd."

I smiled, but it was tired. "Don't. Another time and I would have been screaming right alongside you. But the truth is, he has his path, and I have mine. He's a Jinn, Lila. Nothing could have ever happened between us. Not really."

"Then why did you kiss him?"

A slow breath escaped me, turning into a deep sigh as I spoke the truth much as I hated it. "Because I wanted to. And to say goodbye, I think."

"Oh." She wrapped herself around my neck like a leathery warm scarf. "That makes me sad."

"Me too." And it did. That was the worst part. There were a lot of things about Maks that made me like him, and none of them had a thing to do with what he was or wasn't. He was a good guy. He was strong and smart, kind and thoughtful. That kind of man didn't exist in my world as far as I'd been led to believe. And a good guy like that was fucking hard to find on this side of the wall.

We rode through the night, passed by the Jinn's now-silent encampment and slowed. The ropes that had held Maks down were still there, sprawled out along with a fair amount of gear. I made myself bring Balder to a halt. The fire was still burning, and there were bags of supplies, food, and blankets along with four horses the Jinn had left behind.

"We should let them go, and then we can eat." I slid off Balder's back and went to the horses first, cutting off their halters as there were no buckles. The four of them took off, spinning northward toward the steppes. Which was good. They would be found by some herder and taken in.

I moved as if on autopilot. I couldn't help it. Everything that had happened in that short period of time had rocked me and my confidence.

I kept replaying everything through my head, trying to see if I could come up with a different outcome to the night. But no matter how I looked at things, the outcome we had was actually the best with the most people still alive.

Lila's tail stuck out of one of the Jinn's bags. "Lots of food here, Zam. What do you want?" She pulled something out and held it up for me to inspect. It was a hunk of meat of indeterminate origin. I tended to steer clear of mystery meat, no matter how hungry I was.

"What kind of meat is it?"

"Cow."

I nodded and took the heap of flesh and tossed it onto the grill over the fire. We scrounged until we found spices, and best of all, a bottle of țuică. The plum liquor made Lila giddy, and she made little grabby hands motions as she begged me to open it for her. I debated giving her any after the last time, but finally let her have a small amount. I poured a shot into the bottom of a clean plate and she lapped it up, humming happily to herself, her wingtips vibrating. I tipped the bottle back and took a sip. Rich and sweet, it slid down my throat a little too easily. I put the cork in and set it aside. "Not too much, you remember the hangover last time?"

"I remember you and Maks getting it on last time you got into it." She grinned and then the grin slid right off her face. "Sorry."

I shrugged. I didn't have the energy to be angry with Maks or to care that she was teasing me.

"We can rest here after we eat, but not too long. Dragon's Ground is still a good four days away, and. . . it's going to be a real bitch to find Bryce once we are there." I flipped the meat over, cooking both sides evenly.

Lila frowned. "The healer he seeks, she's deep into the hold. The last I knew, she kept very near to the wall itself. She doesn't like to be found, Zam. Even for another dragon to find her would be tough."

Awesome. That was just what I wanted to hear. "Are the dragons done with whelping then?"

"Close. It's actually a good time to try to sneak in. The females will be exhausted with the efforts of laying eggs, and the males will be hiding from their tempers.

That and there is a contingent at the Ice Witch's castle, spreading the numbers over a wider territory."

That all sounded a little too good to be true. I raised an eyebrow. "And what is the drawback to all that?"

She grimaced and scratched at the dirt a few times with the tip of her claw, doodling designs. "Well, that means there will be more warning spells, and traps set up because of all those things. I can help you avoid them but. . . I don't know about your brother, if he'd know what to look for. He could be already dead, Zam. You need to be ready for that."

I pulled the steak off the grill and onto a plate, cutting it in half. I put the smaller piece on Lila's plate and picked up the remaining chunk in my hands and bit into it. Warm, but bloody.

Perfect. I couldn't help the purr that rumbled through me and it caught me off guard. Lions didn't purr, and I didn't like letting that side of me out because it labeled me for what I was clearly. A lesser cat. One that couldn't roar, but I could damn well purr with the best of them. I grinned around a mouthful of meat and knew that the țuică was hitting me harder than I thought. It was the empty belly. Getting food into me would be the best cure for the țuică.

I let the purr rumble; who the hell cared? Lila hummed, I purred, and we ate our blue rare steaks contentedly side by side. Nothing better to a couple carnivores than a steak that was so rare, you could barely see the grill marks.

A horse nose bumped into my back. I growled and swatted a hand back at my horse. "Go away, Balder. You don't like steak." My hand hit something that was flat and hard. . . a man's chest, not a horse's nose.

"But I do. Is there any left?" Maks asked as he stepped into the firelight. His eyes widened and his eyebrows shot up as he stared at me. I could only imagine what I looked like. I could feel the blood running down my chin, and my mouth was full, and I don't mean a little full. I mean stuffed like a chipmunk going crazy to store nuts for the winter full, barely able to chew full.

I had to work to swallow enough meat so I could respond and still ended up talking out the side of my mouth. "You want it cooked more?"

He bobbed his head once. "Yeah, thanks."

I tossed what was left of my steak onto the grill. What the hell was happening? Was I asleep? Was this a dream? Maybe it was a drunken dream. That was a possibility. I looked at the bottle of liquor that was still half full. How potent was this stuff, anyway?

Lila tapped the țuică bottle. "He came back for this, I think." And then she giggled.

Maks leaned around, saw the bottle, and then a small smile tripped over his mouth. "I think I'll pass."

Smart. It was smart because Lila and I were laughing our asses off, already half cut from the liquor. Distantly, I knew it was partly the stress of the last twenty-four hours and the lack of food in my belly, the injury to my body, and then the alcohol just pushed me over the edge. Something had to give.

"You aren't going to ask me why I came back?"

Maks interjected as our hyena-like laughter finally subsided.

I blew out a breath, making a raspberry noise, and then shrugged. "I don't know, lonely?"

Lila bobbed her head and then shook it hard side to side so hard, I thought she would fall over. "Horny, I think," she said.

My smile slid, and I stared at her. "He did not come back here because he's horny, Lila." I turned to him, the țuică making me bold, forgetting that I should probably be as horrified as Maks by her assessment of his decision. "Did you?"

He closed his eyes, and I watched in fascination as his skin pinked up in the firelight, my grin coming back full force. "Oh, we made him blush. That's cute. You're cute when you blush, Maks."

"I came to repay my debt, Zam. You saved my life. The least I can do is help you with finding the Dragon's jewel."

Right, of course. He *would* be that guy who had the honor thing going for him. Wasn't sure I liked that reason. So, I gave him an out. "We aren't looking for the jewel, not really."

He frowned. "Then what are you doing out here?"

"Bryce went into Dragon's Ground to find a healer for his body," I said. "But. . . Steve and Darcy have gone after the jewel, and if Steve-O finds my brother first—"

"He'll kill him," Maks finished for me. I nodded and flipped the meat over. It was very nearly cooked right through. What a waste of a good steak.

Maks took it and slid it onto a plate. "I'll heal up by morning. Will you two lushes be ready to go?"

I leaned back against one of Balder's front legs and closed my eyes. "I'm always ready to ride, Maks. You should know that."

Lila screeched with laughter and I kept my eyes closed. "That's not what I meant, Lila."

A small chuckle escaped Maks. "I missed you two. I wish I could stay longer," he said. Or I thought he said it, or maybe I wanted him to say it because I missed him too, but it was all tangled up in my sleep-deprived body as I let myself drift off.

MY DREAMS WERE AS MESSED up as my waking thoughts.

I saw Kiara dragged off by the Jinn. They cut her belly open and took her cub. She screamed that it was all my fault. Maks pulled himself from the mud bog, his eyes dead as he crawled toward me, and then there was Bryce. That was the worst of the dreams. Bryce on his belly, his back punctured once more by a spear, his eyes finding mine. "This is your fault, Zamira. You did this to me, you condemned me to this life. Let me die."

I jerked awake, panting hard and startling Balder. My horse danced away from me and I fell backward, losing his support. I rolled to my knees, shaken from the dreams. Mostly because I felt like they were truths coming home to roost.

Warnings of what was coming for me. I shivered even though I wasn't that cold.

The sun managed to peek through the thick black clouds in the east, signaling what would likely be another wet day on the plains. I wasn't happy about that. And I let myself be grumpy because of the weather and not because of the dreams and how much they scared me.

I hunched my back and saddled up Balder quickly, feeding him a bunch of the oat balls I had and a bucket of grain I found in the Jinn's leftovers.

"I'm surprised you would be willing to stay here." Maks went to saddle Batman, his hands moving carefully over the horse. Damn it, why did his hands always draw my eyes? Because he was gentle and strong at the same time, and his hands were fucking magic when they slid over my skin.

I looked away.

"I'm not above taking advantage of the situation. I'd have felt worse taking over the campsite if I'd not known it was the Jinn's."

He grunted. "You aren't as afraid of them as you think you are."

I snorted. "You don't count. As of yet, you haven't tried to kill me or Bryce or Steve. Though if you want to kill Steve, have at him."

Lila groaned from near the fire and scooted closer to the dying embers. "Five more minutes."

Maks nodded. "I know you hate him, but I don't think killing one of the few remaining lion shifters would do your pride any good."

"It's not my pride. It's Steve's." I said the words out loud, much as I wanted to choke on them. Steve's pride. Ish had handed it to him, most likely because he'd knocked up Kiara.

"That's insane." Maks breathed the words, the shock coming through loud and clear.

"Yeah, well. A pride needs an alpha, and the only alpha who could truly challenge Steve would be Bryce. The other males are all naturally submissive."

"What about you?" Lila flew up and perched herself on Balder's saddle so she was at eye height. "Could you not challenge him?"

I shrugged. "I could, but the reality is he'd kill me. I know I'm outmanned there."

"I don't think you are," Maks said. "I think if you can take on a Jinn and catch him by surprise, mortally wounding him, you could take on Steve and win."

I snorted. "I did not mortally wound that Jinn. He got Kiara, remember?"

"It's why he was moving so fast. He needs to get back to the desert if he wants to survive." Maks finished tightening the girth on his saddle and patted Batman's neck. "I would know this, don't you think?"

He had a point even if I wasn't entirely sure he was right about me taking on Steve. For all the times I'd fought with Steve, I knew he'd held back. He'd not given his full strength to the fights we did have. But then again, I'd held back too. I shrugged.

"It's not the time. We need to find Bryce. That's step one."

"Actually, it's about step four if we're counting," Lila

pointed out. "Your journeys have a way of turning in on themselves if I recall."

I grunted and touched the necklace hanging on my chest holding the ring that kept my worst of the two curses at bay. The lion's head ring allowed me to live without Marsum's curse strangling the very life out of me. But the truth was, Maks had removed the ring from me once, and I'd learned to make the curse work in my favor.

That did not mean I wanted to do that again.

But the option was there if I needed it. Maybe if I had to face Steve, I could pull it off and use the curse to win.

I frowned and dropped my hand. That felt like cheating somehow. And when it came to taking the alpha position of a pride, a cheater was the last thing we needed.

I mounted onto the saddle. Balder flicked his head up and down once as if he knew we were in a hurry and he was impatient too.

Maks brought Batman into a trot beside us, though he was still favoring a leg, and we set out toward Dragon's Ground.

"Feels like déjà vu," Maks said.

I nodded but found myself at a loss for words. The last time we'd covered this path, I'd hated him because he was human. Now that I knew he was a Jinn, I should have hated him more, but it was the opposite. I sighed. Why did my emotions have to be so fucking complicated?

"Except I'm here this time," Lila said. "So, it can't

be that much the same unless you found another teeny tiny dragon to insult you prior to me."

He smiled and shook his head. "You are in a league of your own, Lila."

She flew off my shoulder and swooped around our heads, singing what sounded like a dirty limerick if the things the cobbler was doing with the sheep was any indication.

"I'm sorry—"

"How far—"

Maks and I stumbled over our words and he pointed at me. "Go first."

"I'm sorry for embarrassing you last night." I turned my face away. "That was the liquor talking again."

"Yeah, I figured. Don't worry about it." He paused. "How are we going to find your brother exactly?"

Damn it, I'd kind of hoped he was going to expand on last night. A sigh slid from me before I answered his question.

"He took the only horse that's comfortable with his weight besides Batman. Ali is a big brute, and her hoof prints will be hard to miss." I held up my hands about a foot apart to give him the idea of her hoof size, then I shrugged. "I'm hoping when we get to the marker, we'll not have to go far to find his path."

"Better we find him on this side of that marker, though," Maks said. No doubt he was recalling the mad flight we'd had along the border of Dragon's Ground to get to the Ice Witch. We hadn't even been trespassing, and we'd been attacked multiple times by the dragons guarding the border.

I grimaced. "Bryce can't fight, Maks. What the fuck was he thinking leaving the Stockyards?"

Lila bobbed along beside us. "Didn't you say Ish was losing her mind? Maybe he saw that and wanted to escape?"

Ish. . . something about Lila's questions tickled memories I couldn't quite grasp. Maks interrupted my musing.

"Maybe he didn't want to be broken any more. That can drive people to do things they would otherwise avoid."

There was something in his voice, more than the words themselves, that pulled my eyes to him. "What did you do, Maks?"

He shook his head and wouldn't meet my eyes. "Doesn't matter, Zam. Doesn't matter."

After that, our discussions were nothing more than the necessary.

We covered good ground that day and the next. There was a constant sensation as though we were being watched and I didn't like it, but I didn't know how we would avoid it either. Different from when we'd been stalked by the Ice Witch's shadow. This had a heavy menace bleeding through the sensation as though the watcher was enjoying our discomfort. Taking pleasure in the shiver it gave us as we rode.

And on the plains as we were, there was no cover, no way to hide.

If something decided to come after us, we would have no choice but to run for all we were worth.

Again.

That irritated me. How long would I have to run this time? Till Balder dropped and I was on foot? There were so many times in the past when it would've been nice to have stood my ground, to be the lion I was meant to be.

"Your face is an open book, you know that, right?" Maks's words once more drew my eyes to him.

"What?"

"Your face. Your emotions are not hidden at all. I can see you're pissed off about something and then you get this twist in your lips that tells me you're determined. Why don't you hide all that like the other supes?"

He was looking at my lips. I had to clamp them together to keep from smiling. "I don't know. I never bothered. I don't like games. They irritate me."

He nodded. "That's. . . the Jinn are like that. They like games."

"I know they do," I said.

Wow. As if I didn't think it could get more awkward, I opened my mouth and spoke yet again, really putting my foot in it.

"I don't regret any of it, Maks. I should, but I don't."

I looked at him and he was looking away, so I couldn't see his face, couldn't read his eyes. His one hand lifted, and for a split second I thought I saw a glimmer of gold around his neck before he answered.

"I do."

Chapter 13

Merlin flinched at those two little words Maks spoke. "Oh, that was not the thing to say to her, man." He touched the orb, and it spun around so he could see Zamira's face. The horror and shock written across her skin was as plain as day. Maks was right about that little fact; she was not good at hiding her emotions. Or she just didn't care to as she'd pointed out.

It was one of the traits he liked about her. No guessing as to just what she was feeling, or even what she was going to say sometimes.

He blew out a breath, flapping his lips lightly, thinking. He was sure that Maks was important now, sure that he was the other desert born the Oracle had meant when she spoke of the wall coming down and the Emperor being stopped. The only thing that still had him concerned was Maks's loyalty. Would it be to the

Jinn and his father, or would his blood run truer than that?

Because while he wasn't sure, he had a fairly good idea of what Maks was. Jinn, yes, but something else too. Something good and pure that offset the madness that came with a Jinn's power, and that goodness was what kept Maks with Zam. She called to him like a siren to a sailor drowning in rough seas.

Whether she meant to or not, she'd captured him firmly and had become a rock of strength he needed, he was sure of it.

Merlin glanced at the sleeping form of Flora. It was the first time she'd essentially left him alone in months. Not that he minded, but he had things to do that would be easier done without her knowing. He twisted his lips, thinking fast. There would not be time for him to get to Zamira, Maks, and little Lila. They were on their own for now.

Never mind the gorcs still hunting for her. He was far less worried about Zamira on this journey of hers. She'd proven herself more than capable through the Witch's Reign, stronger and smarter than anyone—even himself —could have guessed. He would let her go and see what he could do to help the bigger picture move along.

It looked like it was time he had a chat with Ishtar. That discussion had been a long time coming, and he needed her help if the Emperor woke. But first, he would have to convince her to do the right thing which was far easier said than done. The more stones she gathered to herself, the stronger she became. More like the woman she'd been when the Emperor had reigned supreme.

"No time like the present," he muttered to himself.

Decision made, he paused on the doorstep and looked back at Flora. She was going to be pissed as a wet hen when she woke and found him gone. He grinned and blew her a kiss.

Her anger would be something to behold.

He couldn't wait.

Chapter 14

The clouds above us hid the sun at its zenith when it should have been flooding the plains with bright light. I wished for the sun, for the warmth to chase away the cold that clung to me. But instead I was left in the cold, nothing but the naked earth around us.

Maks regretted what had happened between us, the kiss, the friendship, everything. That could be the only thing he meant when he'd said, "I do." Wasn't like he was fucking well saying he'd marry me. Not that I would have wanted that.

"Well, sucks to be you then," I snapped and urged Balder into a faster trot. We weren't too far from Dragon's Ground. . . maybe I could just. . . I didn't even know what I would do. The hurt and cold in my body was replaced by a burning red-hot anger that was much easier to hang onto. There would be no tears over Maks then. None.

He could fucking well bite me for all I cared.

Lila swept out in front of us doing barrel rolls through the air. While it wasn't exactly warm, at least we weren't dealing with the cutting rain that had pounded on us for days.

I let my mind be occupied with the weather, with dissecting Lila's moves and seeing how beneficial they could be in a fight if she were bigger, with thinking about anything but the man behind me.

"Zam, I didn't mean it like that," Maks called after me. I kept my back ramrod straight.

"You said it. You don't say things you don't mean, right?" I booted Balder harder than I should have and he gave a buck and pinned his ears. "Sorry," I whispered. I didn't need to take my anger out on him. Not for an instant. I relaxed my hands and seat, doing my best to not be tense for Balder's benefit at least.

"Zam, don't be like this," Maks called after me and I tightened my hands on the reins.

I took my feet out of the stirrups and pushed up onto the saddle. Just wait till he got a load of what I was about to throw at him. I shifted into my cat form, ran across Balder's back and leapt off his rump straight at Maks. His eyes widened but, of course, he thought he would be catching a tiny kitten in his big strong arms.

Not so much.

I shifted again at the last second, so my entire body weight slammed into him at full speed. I knocked us both off Batman's back; the horse scrambled out and away from us and I landed on top of Maks as he hit the ground. The air whooshed out of him and he closed his eyes while I stared down at him.

"Don't be like what, Maks? Don't think that was a fucking shitty thing to say? Don't think that after everything we've been through, after I've saved your ass multiple times, you'd think of something better to say than you regret meeting me?"

"Better than a lie, don't you think? I don't want games either. I want honesty." He breathed out as he opened those eyes of his. Eyes that I'd always thought were pretty. They were as blue as ever and filled with a blankness I didn't like.

His words were sharper than any knife and I hated the pain they caused. Because the only way they could cut me like this was if I really cared about him. About a Jinn that I'd thought was a good man. More the fucking fool was I.

Lila swept down around us. "What did I miss? Did you kiss him again?"

I pushed upward and strode back to Balder. "Go away, Maks. You owe me nothing."

"You need my help, Zam," he snapped. "There is no way you're going to get your brother out without my help. And I owe you my life."

His words tore through all the defenses I was so rapidly building. Defenses made of lies.

I didn't like Maks.

His kisses were awful, sloppy and cold.

I thought he was a self-serving asshole.

A Jinn just using me.

Except none of it was true, and I didn't do well with lies whether they were for me or others.

"I don't need you," I said. "So, go, escape the wall and your family and be free of all of this. I release you from any bonds you might feel you have for me saving your life." I finally turned to him. "That's what you want, isn't it? To be free?"

"Yes," he said.

"And I am just one more chain holding you here because you *owe* me." I arched an eyebrow while my heart pounded out of control. Balder danced around me, picking up on all the energy I was throwing off.

Maks nodded once but didn't speak. His hand lifted to his neck and then dropped.

So that was how it was going to be. "I absolve you of anything you think you might owe me. Lila, witness this," I said.

She sucked in a breath. To have a witness was to say that nothing would ever be given my way in recompense for saving Maks's life.

"I. . . I witness your words, Zamira Reckless Wilson," she said. "But are you sure?"

"You are free, Maks of the Jinn," I said. "Assuming that is even your real name."

I turned my back on him and mounted up. "Lila, how close are we to the Dragon's Ground?"

She cleared her throat. "Seven miles. You should be able to see the marker soon."

I nodded and spoke over my shoulder. "Do not follow me, Maks."

"Or what?" he called back.

I shook my head. "I won't do anything, but the dragons might have a different thought on just how crunchy you are."

Lila flew at my shoulder, darting looks at me. "Seriously, what did I miss?"

"He regrets everything, Lila. All of it. And he said it right after I told him I didn't regret it."

She winced. "Well, that was stupid of him."

"Rather." I bit the word out, thinking how I'd like to shove it down his throat. "Tell me he's not following."

She twisted around and then shook her head. "He's just sitting there on Batman watching us leave, his one hand on his chest."

That was what I wanted, but it still hurt. Damn it. "Good."

"Wait," she said. "He's coming our way now. Like, really fast."

I twisted around to see Maks and Batman galloping toward us. He leaned over the horse's neck, driving him hard, pushing Batman through the limp he had. This was no simple catching up to us, and that sense of foreboding finally came home to roost. "Lila, what's behind him?"

She flew straight up, let out a tiny roar, then flew right back down. "Gorcs. A lot of them."

"In the hood!" I yelled at her, and she shot to my shoulder and climbed into my hood. I gave Balder his head and he took off, running flat out. Batman barely managed to catch up to us even going at full speed. I didn't care, and I didn't bother to look at Maks.

The gorcs were fast enough that we could be in trouble, and there was no water anywhere nearby.

"Head for the forest. That's our only hope to lose them there. They will set off all sorts of traps and then the dragons will deal with them," Lila said.

There was a pulse of cold around my neck, the chain holding the lion's head ring cooling so rapidly, it burned, but that faded and then words flowed through me.

Don't you wish to stand your ground? To prove your worth?

"Yes," I whispered to the unknown voice. I was so done with running, with being the smallest one around, with just all of it. And while Bryce was out there waiting for me in one sense, I also knew he didn't want my help. He didn't care if I lived or died, not really. He was my brother, but the brother I'd grown up with had died in the Oasis, and what was left was a shallow shell of the man I'd so admired.

Darcy had abandoned me for Steve. Steve had abandoned me for Kiara. Bryce had left me to fight for myself.

Maks didn't want me.

I slowed Balder, letting Batman pull ahead. "Lila, go to Maks."

She didn't argue, but of course, she didn't know what I planned to do. I could save them both if I stood my ground.

With the gorcs gone, Maks and Lila could find their way to the wall. He could take her with him, they could escape together. That was what the words said to me and I believed them. The silver chain cooled further until it was nothing but a chunk of ice against my skin.

Use the flail, Zamira. Use it and embrace its power. It will not fail you.

I turned Balder around in a slow canter as I reached for the flail. It would kill me. I knew this.

But to save the ones I loved, that was worth it. That was worth death.

"I'm sorry, Balder. You'll go down with me," I said and felt the pangs around my heart. He'd been a good friend to me, better than the two-legged ones I had.

He tossed his head into the air and reared up, striking out with his front hooves. He plunged forward and threw himself into a gallop. I swept my deep red cloak off, let it flutter out behind us, leaving me in nothing but a T-shirt and my cargo pants and the one weapon that could wipe these assholes out.

My confidence grew with each stride. Belief in my own abilities jumping in leaps and bounds.

I could see them clearly now. They'd lost numbers in the river and were down to an even fifty. Still there were far too many, but hope lit through me. I wasn't sure if it was pride, or stupidity, to think I could stop them.

I spoke to the flail. "You can have your pound of flesh when I say so. Not a second before."

The handle warmed against my skin once more, growing tacky. Even if I tried to let go, it wouldn't let me. Not now. I'd just made a deal with the devil's weapon, and I would never be able to go back.

Behind me someone shouted. I ignored the sound.

I held the flail out to my right side and began to spin

it, letting the twin spiked balls pick up speed until they were nothing but a blur beside me. The gorcs saw me coming and roared a greeting, laughing, taunting me.

It was not the first time I'd been laughed at.

Kill them all, Zamira. You can do this. Find your power.

I snarled and leaned into Balder, and he gave me everything he had. We blasted toward the gorcs and the first one reached for Balder's head to pull him down. Balder dodged to the left, and I swung the flail in a perfect arc, driving both balls into the gorc's chest, cracking his sternum.

Time slowed, and I saw the spiked balls move as if on their own as they pushed their way into the creature's flesh, pulling the skin and bone apart, blood floating out on the air like liquid flower petals.

I yanked the handle hard, disengaging the weapon from the gorc. "We've got more, you greedy pig."

Time sped up and the scream from the gorc hammered at my ears as his body was flung twenty feet into the air, end over end before he fell, landing on two of his buddies.

I pulled a kukri with my free hand and threw it at the gorc closest to me, nailing him between the eyes. He was still running then fell forward, putting a furrow into the ground like a rhino coming to a sudden halt. I turned Balder with my legs and he kicked out, catching a gorc in the jaw, snapping it in half. I swung the flail and hit a gorc, and then another, and another. The rage in me built and multiplied. I don't know how many we took down. I only knew that as long as there were any standing, I would kill them.

Creatures of the Jinn, they needed to die.

You can do this, Zamira. Dig deep, girl. Dig deep.

I moved as though this were a dance, a dance I knew inside and out.

A snarl erupted out of me and there was an answering roar from the remaining gorcs. Bodies lay around me and I pushed Balder deeper into their ranks.

He stumbled over a limp body, throwing us both off balance, and then there were hands yanking me from the saddle and the gorcs tore the weapon from me.

Literally.

I screamed as my skin went with it, peeling off my palm like a peach. I kicked and hissed but the gorcs' hold on me didn't lessen. I couldn't shift while they pinned my muscles and bones down so hard. They might as well have trapped me with iron bands, I was held so tightly.

"Looky here, she got Marsum's flail!" the gorc who'd taken it from me yelled, holding it up. I stared at it. A thought slamming through me that was very much my own.

"Now, take your pound of flesh," I yelled, and the flail shone bright white like a flash bomb going off. The gorc holding it screamed and tried to get the weapon to let go, but it was taking what it was owed.

A life.

Right in front of my eyes, the gorc shriveled. Its companions watched with eyes as wide as my own felt. The creature's body was sucked dry as the flail pulsed and glowed. The hands that held me let go and I scrambled forward. The smart part of me that wanted to survive said I should shift and run.

But I was done running. I was done hiding.

These fuckers were going to pay even if it cost me my life.

It won't. You are not alone, Zamira. Let them help you.

The scream that built in my chest exploded from my mouth as I leapt toward the still-dying gorc. I kicked the arm that clung to the handle of the flail, and the bone, brittle as if it had been in the desert for a thousand years, snapped, dangling at the break.

The shriveled gorc lurched toward me, his teeth sticking out past his lips that had pulled back with the loss of his vitality.

I shoved him with both hands, sending him back into one of his buddies. "Not with that, you aren't." I snagged the tip of the flail and the weapon released its hold on his hand and clung to me once more.

Before the remaining gorcs could pull their shit together, I swept into them, going for their legs. Three went down with broken knees before the others snapped out of it.

They circled me, and I moved with them, flowing like the desert wind, hitting, maiming, and then retreating. Strike, wound, retreat, repeat.

"Get that flail from her!" roared the biggest of the gorcs, most likely the leader. If I could kill him, the others might scatter.

I turned my back on him before I could stop myself. What the ever-living fuck was happening to me? The heat of my necklace was suddenly a blaze against my skin and I screamed as it burned into me.

Run! Save yourself! A new voice, one that I almost knew, broke the belief in myself.

And for a moment, I thought it was the sapphire.

I fumbled for it with one hand while I sidestepped the gorcs in what was becoming an intricate and soon to be deadly dance.

"Zam, out of my way!" Lila screamed from above and I knew what was coming.

Fuck, she was going to spew.

I dove to the left, hoping I was right, aiming straight between the legs of the gorc closest to me. He swept down and caught my right leg by the ankle and yanked me up so we were face to face.

"Gotcha!"

"Not yet." I rammed the metal tip of the handle as hard as I could into his chest. It wasn't perfect, but it did the trick, driving its way through his flesh.

He roared and then there were other cries behind me, but I couldn't see. I could only feel the way he twisted his massive hand around the bone in my ankle, could only feel the snap as he yanked it hard to one side, could only hear the tear of my flesh as the bone shot through.

The scream that escaped me went octaves above the last. Fucking hell, if I didn't keep my shit together, I'd pass out, and then I'd be done.

Good. Come home to me, little cat.

That was not my inner voice. Who the fuck was messing with me? I dropped the flail, shocked that it let me go, and fumbled once more for the sapphire. Except it wasn't the sapphire that was heating my skin up. No, the metal that burned me had been given to me by Ish, a ring embedded with her spells to keep the worst of the two curses off my skin.

I yanked the thing from me with a hard jerk and let it drop to the ground.

If I thought things were bad before, I was about to make them a lot worse. But that was the only chance I had of surviving. If I let the curse Marsum had laid on me run free, it would do all it could to turn my life upside down. And I could use that to help me survive by making it think.

"I want to die," I whispered. "Just let me die."

The gorcs turned on one another, scrabbling to kill those closest to them, but they left me alone. For the moment.

Batman slammed through them, Maks riding hard. He leaned so far out of the saddle his hand brushed the ground in a stomach-dropping move. He scooped up the flail, spun and slammed the weapon into two gorcs at a time. Tears streamed down my face.

"I want to die," I said again. My curse would give me the opposite of what I wanted, except this time I wasn't sure I was lying. I felt it through to my bones, this deep loss of hope. Bryce was probably dead.

Maks hated me for what I was. Using me, maybe. The hands on me tightened, grabbing at my other leg, and I knew the gorcs were stretching me out to use me as a shield against Maks and the rage he rained down on the gorcs with the flail.

They were talking to him, telling him they would follow him.

It might be our only hope, for him to take control of the gorcs. They belonged to the Jinn after all.

I opened my mouth to tell him to do it, to claim them. His eyes met mine, and he shook his head, the meaning as clear to me as if he'd spoken out loud.

He was done running too. I knew it in my belly. I felt his anger at his past. I felt the connection between us. He wouldn't have come back if he hated me. Whatever lies I was being fed, from wherever they'd been coming, were just that.

Lies.

The hands on me began to pull. I faced the sky and the sapphire still lay against the skin on my chest. A jewel that was full of power, but I was no mage.

Maks was a Jinn, though, a mage in his own right.

"The sapphire! Lila, get the sapphire!" I screamed up at her, the words turning into a howl as the gorcs around me laughed, my joints stretching.

She dropped from the sky and landed on my belly, sparkling acid still dripping from her mouth. I closed my eyes. "I trust you."

Lila clawed at my shirt and exposed the sapphire, a single drop of acid dropping on my skin, burning me like nothing I'd ever felt. I hissed out the words, "Take it to Maks."

"I can use it," she said and then she was gone, into the sky.

"You're going to die, stupid cat!" the gorc nearest to my head, the one I'd stabbed, said.

I rolled my eyes so I was looking up at him. "We are all dying. Just a matter of speed."

He grinned, flashing his teeth at me while the gorcs died at the end of the flail. I could hear them, could hear their bones snapping and their bodies falling to the ground, but there were so many of them. Too many.

"Zam, hang on!" Maks yelled over the noise. "I'm coming, just hang on."

Hang on? "What the fuck do you think I'm going to do stretched out like a goddess-damned sheet on laundry day?"

The gorcs around me laughed, and they loosened their holds on me some. I didn't understand why my curse wasn't working. Before, when it had been in full effect, I'd been able to manipulate it. But not now.

I didn't understand how it could be broken. The wind around us suddenly changed directions and I saw Lila sweeping through the sky toward us. Her eyes, normally violet, had shifted to a burning brilliant blue, and she screamed a high-pitched wail that made my skin crawl. She rolled through the air, the tips of her wings touching the gorcs as she flew between them.

Each gorc she touched stopped moving, not in a slow-motion kind of way, but as in she'd frozen them in a split second, their bodies covered in a thick sheen of ice that captured them. Between Lila and Maks, the gorc numbers dwindled in seconds to only those who held me between their hands.

I stared up at them. "You were saying about dying?"

They dropped me all at once, but not before Maks drove Balder toward them. My brain wondered when he'd switched horses, but that was all I could come up with.

The flail came down hard on the head of one gorc, released and swung to the next. Lila shot in and touched the last two, freezing them in mid stride so they fell over, their frozen bodies shattering as they hit the hard-packed ground next to me.

I was breathing hard, unable to think straight through what had happened. The urge to die caught me off guard. I only had one weapon left to me, my last kukri blade. I went for it, scrambling to pull it out of its sheath on my leg, but my fingers were numb and slow from the brutal hold the gorcs had on me only seconds before.

Maks leapt from Balder's back and dropped to his knees. "Zam, what are you doing?"

My words were my own, at least. "I don't know! Something. . . wants me to die and I don't understand!" There was more than a little fear in my voice, and I could hear it. Something that knew me well, that had known I'd be angry and wanting to strike back at the gorcs and the Jinn for taking Kiara, something that knew me well enough to know how to hurt me the most.

Three, there were three voices battling inside my head. One believed in me. One did not. The last wanted to kill me.

I shook so hard my teeth rattled. And it wasn't the cold that Lila had produced that sent the shakes through me. What the hell had happened here? Where had my control gone?

Lila dropped to the ground beside us and pushed the

sapphire toward me. I held my hands up, palms out stopping her.

"No, keep it from me. Something is wrong."

Maks touched my shoulder, and I flinched as if he'd struck me too. "You're right, someone is trying to keep us all apart. I. . . I didn't mean those things I said, Zam. I couldn't figure out why I even said them."

"Because you hate me. I'm a lion shifter, despite what I look like."

"No, that's not true. I don't hate you. If anything, I'm trying to keep you safe. You're important to me and part of the small hope I have of destroying Marsum. But I'm not doing a very good job of it, am I?"

His words were soothing the anxiety that had taken hold of me and allowed me to see just how fucking idiotic it had been to charge the gorcs. Something I would have done in my younger years, maybe, but I'd learned a lot between then and now. I was not a child. And yet someone who still thought I was had used my past against me. I closed my eyes, feeling her touch even at this distance, and the thought that she'd tried to kill me cut me to the core. Just as she knew it would. At least one of the voices was known to me. I just couldn't decide which she was.

I looked up at him, my emotions rolling.

"Ish did this."

Chapter 15

The hard ground of the plains was not what I would call a comfortable bed to convalesce on, or in. But I had no choice at the moment. That and the words that had slipped from me seemed to have frozen time, the same way Lila had frozen the gorcs with the power of the sapphire.

Maks and I sat there looking at each other when *really* we should have been dealing with the massive injury on my leg. The thing was, the realization that Ish had somehow set my heart and my mind against me was beyond horrifying. It went against everything she'd ever taught me to believe.

She'd been the mother of my heart, the only one I'd known, and had never shown me a cruel hand. I stared at the glittering necklace I normally wore on the ground beside me. Could she have been manipulating me through it? She'd laid the spell on it herself.

I turned my attention to my leg and grimaced.

The break in my bone was far from clean, but it was still cleaner than the break between Ish and me. The blood wasn't pouring out of me, which meant it had been pinched off somehow. All I could think were bad things like nerve damage and maybe enough loss of blood that I could lose my foot. Never mind the other tears in the tendons and ligaments of my limbs where the gorcs had decided to play tug of war.

Lila danced around us. "Did you see what I did?"

I gave her the best smile I could. "You were damn amazing, Lila. You should keep that sapphire. Not like I was doing anything with it."

"You sure you want to do that?" Maks said softly. "Not that we don't trust you, Lila." He held up his hands as her once-again violet eyes narrowed. "But how do you hide it? The stone is no small thing."

He had a point. Lila frowned. "You think someone would try to take it from me?"

"Yes. I think if the gorcs knew it had any power they would have taken it from Zam first." He sighed and shook his head.

I made myself sit up though the movement sent a shock wave of pain up my leg to steal my breath. "Oh, that's going to hurt tomorrow. Probably get a bruise from it."

Sure, it was a piss-poor joke, but I had nothing left to me but my sense of humor. And even that was stretched thin.

Maks looked around. "I know you aren't going to want to hear this, but we have to move. The gorcs. . . they will have Jinn attached to them, and the Jinn will know that they were killed with a powerful weapon. They will come looking to see who did it."

I groaned. "Of course. And now that my curse is in full effect, they'll show up in three, two, one."

The three of us went very still, listening. But we had some small luck; there was no noise, except for the rumble of Lila's belly.

Maks's hands were gentle as he probed a little at my ankle. "I can set it, but then I think you should shift. I can hold you easier and the jostling will be less."

I stared at him. "You want to set that mess of bone?" I pointed at the shattered end of my lower leg bone. I wasn't feeling it unless I moved, which was quickly freaking me out. Shifters healed fast, but with an injury like this it would take a week or more. That was with the assumption it healed at all. If I was really lucky, it would heal crooked, and that would be it, I would have a bum foot. Or I'd lose it completely.

Bryce's hatred of his body slid home to me harder than ever before. He'd had further to fall too, being the strong lion he had been. "Bryce, fuck, I'm sorry I didn't understand better," I whispered.

"Lila, find her a stick to hold in her mouth."

Oh, Goddess of the Desert, we were really doing this. Maks made his way to my shoulders and helped me lie flat on the ground. His blue eyes were too close. "What did she use to make you want to kill yourself like this? Ish had to have used something that would naturally motivate you, something you wouldn't suspect until it was too late."

I could have lied to him, but I fucking well hated

games of any sort. "I was protecting Lila. And you. Batman couldn't outrun them. He has a limp that will only worsen if we push him too hard. I didn't want either of you to die."

I made myself keep my eyes on his, so I didn't miss the flicker of confusion.

"Why would you want to save me?" he whispered. "I'm one of them, Zam. I've done things I am not proud of. I am your enemy."

Goddess, truth was the hardest thing to speak some days. "Not to me, you aren't."

We just stared at each other, that is, until Lila cleared her throat. "Stick." She threw it at me and it bounced off the side of my head. I turned to her, my eyebrows pinched.

"You want to add to my injuries?"

"Don't make me tickle your catastrophe." She winked, but I saw the strain in her face. She was worried.

I took the stick and pointed it at her. "Henry the Fourth; not his best work, but he had worse." I opened my mouth and put the stick in, clamping down until my sharp canines buried deeply into the hardwood. I didn't know if I should close my eyes or stare up at the clouds above. I settled for staring. Maybe I could focus on the shapes, on the distinct grays that swirled and wove between each other with the push and pull of the wind.

I breathed in, smelling the gorcs, their leather armor, the oil on their bodies, the blood soaking into the ground, the puddles of rain that lay here and there. The smell that was uniquely Maks. The leathery scales on

Lila's body that smelled a little like honey. The breath of the two horses, the stamp of their hooves, the creak of their gear as they shifted weight, the world narrowed to my senses and all I could take in to distract me.

The touch of Maks's hand on my lower leg, the strength in his fingers and the care he took to move slowly, the tremor in the split second before he would set the bone. He was afraid to hurt me.

His hands moved fast and with more strength than even I realized he had. He had always been holding back with me even when he'd tackled me what seemed so long ago. He'd never shown me just how strong he was, and I let my brain go there and only there as the pain rocketed through me, the liquid fire that was agony making my gorge rise at a speed I couldn't stop. I turned my head and puked, stars and black spots dancing across my vision as the world went in and out of focus.

"Shift, Zam. Quickly," Maks said, and I did as he wanted because I couldn't think past the radiating waves of pain.

But I'd not thought this through. The shift shattered what was left of my control on my voice and I screamed as my bones realigned to become the small house cat that was my other form. Every bone in me shook and rattled as I shifted with so much pain that I wasn't sure I'd make it across to the other side of that doorway in my mind. What would happen if I got stuck? What would happen if my body got caught between forms?

I'd be a fucking monster for real then. There would be no fixing *that* catastrophe. I forced my body to keep going, ramming it through the waves of pain until finally there was nothing left but a puddle of fatigue and me as a tiny black house cat shivering on the ground.

I lay on my side panting hard, my eyes closed. "How's it look?" I managed.

"You aren't going to believe this," Maks said softly. "It's healed."

I made myself push up with my front legs though they shook something fierce. Then carefully I pushed to three legs, holding the previously broken one high.

"Seriously, it looks fine." Lila drew close, sniffing. "There's no cut in the skin anymore."

I swallowed hard and put my foot down, testing its strength.

There was a shimmer of something, like a deep bruise, but there was no sharp pain that would indicate a major injury. I took a step, then another and another. "Holy shit, how is this possible? Wounds like that are not supposed to heal so well. Certainly not in a shift."

Maks shook his head. "I don't know, but I think you should just let yourself stay in that form for a while. Don't push it if we don't have to." He stood and turned away, gathered the horses and the flail and then mounted. He paused over something, bent and picked it up. I knew it was the necklace from Ish, the one that held my father's ring. Something about it had brought me to the edge of being suicidal.

"Lila," I said softly while Maks got things together. "I'm so sorry. I didn't mean to put either of you in danger. I think. . . I think Ish did something to make me fight, to face the gorcs on my own."

She shrugged. "Shit happens. I won't turn from you,

Zam. I did that once and I felt the hurt all the way to the tips of my wings. For good or ill, we're in this, I think, together for a reason."

I butted my head against hers and she dropped a wing over my back, sheltering me from the rain that had once more begun to fall. "Thank you, Lila."

Funny, I would have said in the past that Darcy was my best friend. In fact, I always had. Even after she slept with Steve. Because she was a lion, and a part of my pride, and that meant we stood by each other. But this friendship with Lila felt more real than any relationship with any of my pride.

It should have bothered me, but the thought of Lila as part of a new pride that only she and I shared made me smile. I trotted over to where Maks stood beside Balder. I didn't ask, just jumped, and he caught me. His thick coat was layered with wool and a waterproof over-coat. I had no shame left to me.

I crawled up over his neck and then went straight down inside the front of his coat, turning until my head poked out the top. The heat from his body seeped into my own and my eyes slammed shut, fatigue hitting me like a blow from one of the gorcs. Around his neck, he wore a gold chain, the thick links warm from his body. I settled it under my front legs and it kept me from sliding farther into his coat.

"Don't shift while you're in my coat, you'll rip it," Maks said as he swung onto Balder's back. I smiled and turned my head down under the top of his coat, darkness covering me. Breath after breath, my heart rate slowed and the smell of Maks that was uniquely his filled my lungs. Desert, he smelled like the desert, and maybe I'd always picked up on that, the desert and flowing fresh water, a river, a place of safety from the heat of the land I loved.

Home. He smelled like home and I wanted to stay there.

The motion of Balder's steps, the warmth from Maks, and I fell asleep feeling safer than I had in a very long time.

What I hadn't counted on was the dreams. Or that Ish would be waiting for me within them.

I stared, the scene before me fading in and out for a moment before I realized I stood in Ish's private study. The flames of her fireplace were nothing but coals and she sat in her favorite chair, her head in her hands.

"What have I done? Zamira, Zamira, forgive me. I tried to save you, my daughter." She whispered the words while rocking in place.

I said nothing, feeling the truth of the dream for what it was. A vision that I needed to see in order to understand what was going on.

I held my tongue as a knock came on the door. "My lady, there are two satyrs here who beg to speak to you. They come at the behest of Zamira."

Ish's head snapped up and the tracks the tears had left on her skin were clearly visible. What did I believe? A sobbing woman who grieved what she believed was my death, or what had happened to me where I'd felt her power push me toward a suicidal act?

There were two other voices who'd commanded me,

using me. *Who* they were was the question I couldn't answer. But perhaps seeing this would help.

I held still as Marcel and Stella were ushered in. Marcel didn't wait. He launched into the story of the Jinn attacking them and taking Kiara, and how I'd asked them to deliver the message in the hopes that she might do something.

"She wished to save Kiara?" Ish frowned and shook her head. "She went after her brother, did she not?"

Marcel shrugged. "I think so. But she said you were the only one who could do anything to stop the Jinn who had the girl. That you were the only one strong enough."

I was impressed that he hadn't offered to flounce Ish once during the whole conversation. Then again, Stella looked to have a death grip on the back of his arm.

Ish slumped. "If I leave the Stockyards now, all will be lost. Kiara must survive on her own if she is to survive at all. Thank you for your message. You may stay and refresh yourselves for the night, but no longer. I cannot guarantee your safety here."

Stella took a step forward. "My mother told me of you. Ishtar, Goddess of the Lions, Destroyer of the Land. What are you doing? Is it your fault that our world is dying? Your fault the emperor sleeps when he could be making our land great again?"

Ishtar? Was that her full name? It tweaked something in my memory, a story my father had told me, but I couldn't quite grasp it.

Ish's eyes narrowed as did my own at the not so thinly veiled insults. "You know not of what you speak.

The Emperor is a truffle-headed fool with more power than any creature should have."

Marcel stared at Stella like she'd sprouted a second head. "Yeah, so you can go your way. I don't want to go with you. I'm not an *emperorist*."

Stella shook him. "You got Rev killed. You're going to give me a child."

I wanted to save him, but I needn't have worried. Ish snapped her fingers and then pointed one at Stella, her power reverberating through to me even though I stood there in spirit. The curl of power that wrapped Stella made the satyr female squeak and piss trickled down her legs, dripping on the floor. Ish's voice rumbled deeply, making my chest shake. "Go and leave him."

Stella dropped her hand from Marcel, spun on her goaty little hooves, kicked out once and then scurried from the room.

"Thank you, Holy Goddess, if that's who you are, thank you." Marcel dropped to his knees in front of her. "Thank you."

The room wavered and swayed as I was being pulled from it. But why had I seen it at all? I was no dream walker, which meant someone wanted me to see this scene.

Ishtar, was that really who she was? Why would she lie all this time then? I would not have thought any differently of her. Would I?

The dream faded, and I tried to hang onto it if only to make sure Marcel would be safe. Damn it, I liked him too much.

I strained against the bonds pulling me back, Maks's

voice the largest part of it. I stared into the darkness as the door to Ish's inner sanctum opened and in swept a man I knew.

Merlin. I might have breathed his name. He turned, touched his fingers to his head acknowledging me, and then the bastard had the nerve to wink. He *fucking well* winked at me as I slid away from the scene. But I heard his words loud and clear.

"Ishtar, my old friend, we have things we must discuss."

"Merlin, you bastard." Ish lifted a hand to him and the scene was gone, flashed away in the touch of Maks's hand on top of my head, calling me back to the land of the living. I fought the call of his touch, and the way it pulled me from the deep healing sleep. I wanted to stay where I was pressed against his body, safe and warm, breathing him in and knowing that for the moment nothing could touch me. That the dreams were just that —only dreams.

"Zam," his voice had an edge to it that made me shiver despite the warmth between us, "I need you to wake up. We have a rather large problem."

Why was I not surprised?

Chapter 16

Merlin smiled at Ish despite the harsh words she threw at him in her chamber at the Stockyards. Around her, he could see the dancing colors, the different stones she'd collected over the years bringing her back a measure of her previous power. But she was not there yet.

"Well, I should have stayed after that last visit, I agree. It's not nice to flounce and run, don't you think, Marcel?" He turned his eyes to the satyr still on his knees. The young supe stared up at him.

"You flounced her and. . . left her?"

Merlin shrugged. "I was young and stupid."

"It looks like you're old and stupid now," Marcel muttered.

Merlin laughed. Satyrs were always good for a laugh if nothing else. "Fair enough. But. . ." he turned to Ishtar, "I came with a far more important thing to discuss than any previous relationship we might have had."

"It was hardly that." Ish's tone was dry, and she'd pulled herself back together after the initial shock of seeing him, he could tell. She was a hard one to crack and flouncing her had been a bad idea all those years ago. And a large part of the reason why he didn't want Flora with him now.

"Fair enough. A single night of passion then between young hearts." He tipped his head to her and just caught the roll of her eyes.

"What are you doing here, Merlin? I doubt it's to reminisce about the days of old." She moved to her chair and sat, lowering herself with the grace of a queen bred and born to her position.

"We need to discuss the Emperor. He is waking."

Marcel gave a strangled tiny goat cry before he slapped his hands over his mouth. Merlin didn't spare him a glance but instead kept his eyes locked on Ish. "I cannot stop him, Ishtar, Queen of the Desert."

She closed her eyes. "Merlin, you stripped me of my power, stole my jewels and gave them to others, and now you wish me to stop your father?"

Marcel let out a big breath and then there was a thump indicating he'd fallen over. But again, Merlin didn't dare glance to the side.

"You can't stop him any more than I can," he said.

Her eyes flew to his. "You think me weak?"

"I think you know as well as I do that there is only one way to end his life, and there is no way that you or I can do it. We have not the skills, nor the heart."

She covered her face with her hands. "Do not ask me to sacrifice her, Merlin. The jewels are already fighting me. They have been held too long by maniacs, by those who are cruel."

He snorted. "And they got that from you, Ishtar. You were the maniac. That is why we, as a group, decided to take the jewels from you. That and we needed them to put him to sleep." He slapped his hand on a table. "When we stripped you of your power, your humility saved you. Now you would throw it away for power again?"

He knew that she'd started by gathering the last of the lions to her, drawing strength from them. They were her spirit animal, always had been, and when the Jinn had nearly wiped them out, she'd gone hunting for what was left of the prides.

She drew a breath. "I am not sending Zamira against the Emperor."

"She has already broken the hold on one part of the wall, Ish." He crouched in front of her. "She will break the middling part too, I am sure of it. She *is* the Wall Breaker."

"Against the dragons? You are insane. She's small and weak and no match for their strength! I tried to bring her back to me, but someone told her she could do it. Someone told her that she could kill all the gorcs if she found her power!" Her eyes were wild with emotion, mostly fear. She loved Zamira. He could see it in her.

Flora, it had to be Flora who'd encouraged Zam to fight. That was her way, just like her granddaughter. Leap into the deep end and fight your way out.

"Is she alive?"

"She is," Ish said softly. "Though I do not know for how long."

"Marsum just tried to kill her, if I am reading the signs correctly," he said.

She let out a soft cry. "He has found her then. He knows she lives." Ishtar shook her head and covered her face with her hands. "I. . . the jewel from the giants, it has done something to me. Their hatred of her is filling me like nothing else. I don't understand. It is not safe for her to come home to me."

Merlin sighed and held his hand out. "Give it to me then. If you cannot hold it without trying to kill her, give it to me."

"Better that she be dead than facing the Emperor," she snarled.

Merlin took a step back, feeling the power rushing up through Ishtar's body. He could see the different gemstones she held glowing lightly, and it was then he realized that she'd taken them into herself. She'd swallowed them whole.

"Ishtar," he whispered her name, "do not do this. We still need you."

The power rolled around her, and he knew there would be no getting through to her now. There was too much fear, too much shame, and too much strength given to her from the jewels that had held her original power for so many years. Twisted by the creatures that had handled them, they'd absorbed the darkness within the world.

And now that darkness was echoing every ugly

thought she had, and she did not have the heart to fight it.

He took a step back and grabbed the satyr by the arm. "I leave you then, Ishtar, to your plans, whatever they might be."

She drew a breath, and he yanked the satyr up and bolted from the room as Ishtar began to chant behind them.

He could have blocked her, but he was still hoping to avoid using his power. The taste and flavor of his magic would be like a gong to the Emperor. A gong that would break through the last of his deeply spelled sleep.

As he and the satyr raced through the Stockyards, he yelled at those they encountered. "Go! Ish has lost her mind and will kill you all."

The bleating of animals, the cries of the people, it was the Reckoning all over again. Merlin felt it under his skin and it drove him to run faster even as he could feel his own power welling up, preparing to protect him.

This had been his worst idea yet, and that was saying something. He'd had a lot of bad ideas in his lifetime.

He scrambled up onto his horse and booted it into a gallop. The satyr stayed glued to his side, running flat out.

Behind them the ground rumbled and an explosion rent the air.

There was nothing left of the kindhearted woman who welcomed the destitute into the Stockyards. She was gone.

There was only Ishtar, Queen of the Desert, first consort to the Emperor.

He bowed his head. "There will be no hiding now."

"Then I'm going to find Zam," Marcel said. "She's got a knack for staying alive."

Merlin glanced at the young supe, nodding. "Yes, I think we should both find Zam."

Chapter 17

Maks's fingertips ran along the top of my head between my ears and I couldn't help but push my furry self into his touch. Damn feline response to touch. I fluttered my eyelashes without meaning to at him. "Sorry, can't help it."

His face was a careful neutral, but his eyes were soft. "You'd better come take a look at this."

I pulled myself up out of the top of his coat, shivering as the wind hit me, ruffling my fur. I twisted around so I looked in the direction we were headed.

Ahead of us was indeed a large problem, but I had to believe it wasn't as bad as Maks thought. I hoped.

We were near the edge of Dragon's Ground to start, the large blackened marker reaching high into the sky denoting the start of the dragons' territory. At the base of it were two horses and two people I knew all too well.

"How is it bad that we've caught up to Steve and Darcy?" I wiggled back down into his coat. "That was the goal. That means they probably haven't found Bryce. Score one for us."

Lila peered at me from Maks's shoulder, down into my warm spot. "They are being held there for interrogation by one of the younger dragons. A chameleon."

I grimaced and Maks gave a grunt that said it all. A chameleon dragon would be hard to fight if it came to that. They could match their scales so fast to their surrounding area that they in essence disappeared.

"Well, if they are talking, that should be good, shouldn't it?" My brain was still foggy with sleep, and with what I'd seen in the vision that had taken me back to the Stockyards.

Maks grunted again. "From what we can see, the discussion is getting heated."

"How can you see that from here?" We were still a solid mile and a half out. Maks held up a battered pair of binoculars.

Right.

I made a move to climb out, and he put his hand against me through the coat. "No, you need to rest longer if you can."

"Yeah, but if there's going to be a fight, I need to be able to move," I pointed out.

"No fighting," Maks said. "Lila is going to try to discuss passing through."

Before I could tell them that was a bad fucking idea, Lila had shot off his shoulder and was winging toward the group ahead of us.

"The dragons hate her, Maks. That dragon would as soon kill her as look at her."

"She seems to think otherwise." He looked to the sky, following her progress. "And she's got the sapphire. She's safe, and fast. She'll be okay."

Right, there was that. Maks adjusted his seat. "I have your necklace, the one with your father's ring. It's in my pocket."

"I don't want it back," I whispered. No way I wanted those voices in my head again, forcing me to do things that were not my choice, not my decisions. I'd had enough of that shit in my life to want any more of it.

"I cleared it of Ish's spell. She won't be able to track you through it any longer."

I looked up at him. "You said you thought she affected you too. How?"

He put his hand in his pocket and pulled out a dagger in a sheath. "She gave this to me before I left. She knew I would go with you. She was counting on it for some reason. She asked me to help protect you."

I frowned, my cat lips dipping downward. "None of her actions make any sense. They are all contradictory."

"Agreed. Which makes her extremely dangerous and impossible to predict." He slid my father's ring on the chain over my neck and it curled around me, becoming part of the chain on my neck that was woven of my clothing and weapons. "I spelled it to block the curse as best I could. It's not perfect, the way Ish's spell was, but it should help keep the worst at bay, I think."

I could have kissed him, but I knew it wouldn't have been welcome, not really. I turned and watched as Lila swept in over Steve's and Darcy's heads. "Why did she think she could talk to this dragon? You do remember last time, don't you?"

"I do, but she seems to think this one will be better. She said something about knowing him."

A sense of urgency hit me and I tensed, uncertain where it was coming from but listening to it, anyway. "Hurry, something bad is going to happen."

Maks didn't question me, just urged Balder forward. We took off at a gallop, Batman following more slowly. I bit my lower lip, feeling the bad thing coming like a storm rolling in fast and hard. I'd never had this sensation before and the chain around my neck seemed to hum in response. This had something to do with the curse that Marsum had put on me and the damper that Maks had tried to give it.

I was sure of it.

We were within a hundred strides when the bad thing happened.

Lila was between Steve and the chameleon dragon. She had her back to Steve as he raised his gun. Not to point it at the chameleon, but at Lila. We were so close now that Maks was forced to slow the horses. Slowing would get Lila killed.

"No!" I shoved myself out of Maks's shirt and bounded along Balder's neck, leaping off the top of his head and racing across the ground as fast as I could. My leg didn't hurt, but my body was fatigued, as if I'd been sick for a week. I struggled to breathe around the exhaustion.

Steve brought the gun up, every motion seemingly in slow motion, his finger on the trigger of the handgun. I had to be close enough to do this, to make my plan work. I couldn't wait a second longer. I pushed off, leaping straight for his arm.

My claws sunk into his forearm a split second before my mouth clamped onto the flesh. My weight jerked his arm down enough that as the gun boomed, the bullet went low.

After that, pandemonium ensued. Darcy yelled at Steve, Steve screamed at me, and I let go, backing up to where Lila was. I put myself between her and the two lion shifters and squared my shoulders.

I knew where I stood, and it was not on the side of the shifters I'd been raised with, as much as that truth hurt.

My heart thumped hard as the reality I embraced settled on my shoulders. A nose pushed into my back, far bigger than Lila, rippled with hard scales and nodules. Hot breath washed over me as the chameleon dragon spoke softly for such a big creature.

"Why did you save her? She's not one of yours to protect."

I wasn't sure I could safely turn my back on Steve, but Maks had slipped off Balder's back and he gave me a nod.

I turned slowly to face the much larger dragon. I mean, if I'd been able to see him fully. All I could pick up on was this bare outline of a dragon. I lifted my chin. "Lila is part of my pride. And I protect my own."

The words should have sounded stupid coming from the mouth of a six-pound house cat. But the chameleon dragon shimmered until he came fully into view, and he wasn't laughing. He was a little bigger than the horses, and he didn't have wings. His body was long, lean, and snake-like with six legs under him. His eyes were stunning, sparkling like a rainbow, the colors dancing this way and that.

"My name is Pret. I grew up with Lila." He slowly shook his head. "What are you here for?"

I wasn't sure where he was going with this, but I was not going to lose the opportunity. "My brother came to Dragon's Ground to find a fabled healer. I'm looking for him."

Pret sat back and raised himself like a dog. If a dog had six legs and a snake body. "I have seen no one come through here. That does not mean he didn't slip by during the whelping." He tipped his head to one side. "You really mean what you say about Lila? That you will protect her?"

"With my life," I said without hesitation. Lila dropped to the ground beside me.

"And I will do the same," she said.

Oh, all the warm fuzzies that built up in my chest scattered with the words from the idiot behind us.

"Oh, fuck off the both of you. Neither of you could protect a fucking damn mouse," Steve snarled. "And she," he pointed to me as I turned my head to glare at him, "is not the leader of our pride."

Pret lifted an eyebrow. "You are not the leader of the pride?"

He said it so simply, like he really was surprised. Like he thought I could be. "You are looking at me, the house cat, and asking how I am not the leader of a lion pride?

Seriously?" Sweet baby goddess of the desert, it was like a weird comedy. How many times could we say I was not the leader of the lion pride in a single minute?

He shrugged. "Lila was supposed to take over for her father. I would have followed her."

Lila ducked her head. "It was never meant to be, Pret. You know that."

He grinned then and lowered his head to her. "You don't know that, Lila. There were some here that would have stood for you."

She snapped her tail through the air. "Not now, Pret."

Now this was interesting. I wanted to ask her just what he meant because it sounded to me like she was indeed someone important. The daughter of the head dragon, maybe?

Steve took a swing at me with his boot and I dodged him easily.

"No matter the form, I would always be faster than you, asswipe."

"Shift, damn you. I challenge you to a fight for the pride right now. You win, I'll walk away. I win, you'll be dead."

Well, fuck, that was not what I'd wanted. Or was it? The last few years Steve and I had parried back and forth for the ruling of the pride. For the right to be alpha. Yes, I had the right attitude for the most part, but we both knew he was the powerhouse. The one who should have been ruling was Bryce as he blended my temper and Steve's strength.

But that was impossible with his body the way it was.

"Don't do it, Zam," Maks said softly. "He won't play fair."

That hurt more than I wanted to admit that Maks thought I couldn't win. "I accept, you bastard."

"I'll even give you the edge," Steve said. "Two legs, not four."

I nodded, then forced my body into a shift, and oh, fuck, it hurt. I had to bite down on the scream that rose along my throat as my body came back to two legs painstakingly slowly for me. I was on my hands and knees, panting hard. I would not be shifting back to my smaller form any time soon.

Darcy dropped beside me. "Zam, are you okay?"

I lifted my head to look her in the eye, the final splintering of our friendship happening right in front of me. "You sure you can handle me being your alpha?"

She pulled back a little, her eyes narrowing. "Don't do this, Zam. You can't beat him. You aren't strong enough." She believed it, but for the first time in my life, I didn't.

I pushed away from Darcy and locked my knees so they wouldn't shake. "Get back, Darcy."

Lila swept up beside me as the others pulled back. Her jeweled eyes locked on mine. "They are wrong, Zam. You can do this. You're going to kick his ass so hard, he's going to feel the imprint of your foot for the rest of his life."

I laughed, though it was soft and weak, and I knew exactly why Steve challenged me right then. He could smell it on me—I was in a low spot, my body hurting and fatigued from healing.

It would just be that much sweeter when I did exactly what Lila said I would. Everyone pulled back, Pret included. I noticed that Lila flew close to his head, whispering something to him. What was she up to?

I turned to face Steve as Maks called out a warning. Steve wasn't waiting. He'd rushed me while my back was turned like the cheating fucker he'd always been.

I dropped to the ground and rolled out of his way, only just missing the swing of his hand. There was a sharp whistle through the air and I realized he was using knives. So be it. I jumped up and reached for my kukri blades. One had been left in a gorc, and where the other one went, I wasn't sure.

They weren't there.

"You can't ask for a weapon now, Zam," Steve snarled as he crouched, and stalked toward me. "You know the rules."

And there was reason number two he was pushing for the fight now. Without my blades that would cut deeply into him, I was at a serious disadvantage and he knew it. I should have been flattered that he thought so highly of my fighting skills. As it was, pissed off was about all I felt in that moment.

"Come on then." I beckoned him closer with more confidence than I should have. Despite Lila's words of belief, the doubts weighed heavily on me.

Steve swung in fast and hard with his left hand holding the knife. I ducked under it and he caught me with a fist from the right. He hit me in the side of the head, ringing my bell with enough force that I went to one knee, swaying as he laughed. He wouldn't go in for the kill, not fast. No, he was going to play with me first.

Typical cat.

Darcy sucked in a sharp breath. She'd just realized the same thing I had. That this whole challenge was a setup to kill me. It had nothing to do with winning, but getting me out of the way once and for all.

Steve tackled me to the ground in a mockery of the love we'd once shared. His body was on top, pinning me against the hard earth as he put his face in mine, his *very* obvious hard-on shoved against me. "One last kiss, eh, love?"

He slammed his mouth over top of mine, forcing his tongue into my mouth, trying to make me want him again. I knew his style. I softened, letting him kiss me and I kissed him back. Not because I wanted him. Not for a fucking second. But he was dumb enough to think I would.

He let his guard down as he made a contented noise in the back of his throat. He pulled back a little. "I knew you still wanted me."

I drove my knee up into his balls as hard as I could, and his eyes rolled back into his head. "Not so much, pig."

He didn't get off me, though, and I shoved at him, driving my elbow into the crook of his neck to encourage him to move, but he just lay there, shaking. "Kill him now, Zam!" Darcy screamed. "Do it!"

Kill him.

Shit, I wanted to. He would kill Bryce if he ever got

close to him out here, away from the protection of Ish and the Stockyards.

My thoughts took too long. I should have acted instead of hesitating. Steve reared up and slammed his head into mine and bounced it off the rock below me. If I'd thought my head was spinning before, it couldn't compare to the pain that rocketed through it now.

A knife pressed to my throat and there were gasps around us. I held a hand up. "Do not interfere."

"You think your friends could stop me?"

I smiled up at him. "Yes. I do."

He pressed harder. "Then why aren't you letting them save you?"

"Because I don't want you dead, Steve. Not today. If you'd not been such a fucker, I would have told you what happened to Kiara." Maybe it was dirty pool to use her against him in this fight, but I didn't want to die. And he would kill me.

He frowned. "Kiara is in the Stockyards."

"No, she came with me to escape Ish's threat that if you didn't come back with the jewel, she would take the cub."

Darcy started to cry. "Oh goddess, no. That is our first cub in twenty years."

Steve stared hard into my eyes, looking for the lies. "Where is she?"

Maks stepped up. "The Jinn took her. They hit us with a horde of gorcs, covering our path back to Kiara." Not quite the truth, but close enough.

Steve pressed the knife harder. "You bitch, you did this to kill her!"

"I did not!" I roared. "She's like my little sister, you piece of shit, and you ruined her! You fucking well told her you loved her when you were fucking around on her and me both! I would have saved her from you if I could have! I would have cut your balls off if she so much as whispered the word rape to me! But you bent her to your will. You took her innocence, you sheep fucker!"

There it was, the truth finally. I cared more for Kiara than I'd ever cared for Steve. He pulled his head back but didn't move the knife from my throat.

"Goddess, you're telling me the truth." He stared down at me, horror flickering on his face.

"You could still catch them," Maks said. "They won't have made it to the desert sands yet."

"How do you know that, human?" Steve turned on him, the knife easing off my neck. I shoved his hand and rolled out from under him and I knew he'd let me go. He could have held me there, but the realization that his mate and cub were in danger had changed something in him.

Maybe this was what Steve needed to become a better man. Maybe he really did love Kiara.

But if we told him the truth about Maks, Steve would try to kill him, and I wasn't sure who would end up surviving that fight.

"Because he was a slave to the Jinn, idiot. That's how he knows," I said.

Steve jerked as if I'd slapped him. "That's why you ran out of the desert. Why you said you didn't remember."

Maks nodded.

Steve got to his feet and just stood there as if. . . as if he didn't know what to do. He turned slowly to face me. "Swear to me on your brother's life that you are telling me the truth."

I locked eyes with him. "On my brother's life, and the honor of my pride, I swear to you that Kiara was taken by the Jinn."

He tipped his head back and roared, the guttural noise pulling at something deep in me. I wasn't sure he ever would have been so upset had I been in Kiara's shoes, kidnapped and held against my will, when we were together. And it didn't bother me. There was no bitter regret that he hadn't loved me better or well enough to want to rescue me.

I didn't need him, and he knew it.

We were never the right fit, and that was even clearer to me now that I'd found the one I wanted in my life. Even if nothing ever happened between Maks and me, he'd shown me what kind of partner I wanted.

Steve strode to his horse and mounted up. "I'm going after her."

"I know," I said. "Darcy, you should go with him. He's going to need help."

Her golden eyes were full of sadness. "Zam, what about you?"

I looked at Lila and then Maks. "I've got all the help I need here. I've got my best friends with me."

Her eyes closed. "I'm sorry—"

"Don't." I tipped my chin up a little, holding the emotions back. I was losing my best friend. Or maybe

I'd lost her a long time ago and just hadn't realized it. "Just go, save Kiara and I'll save Bryce."

They didn't wait for any other directions.

The two shifters tore off, back the way they'd come, heading south before I could warn them about the gorcs, or the possibility of more Jinn coming as Maks had said they would.

Pret gave a funny chuffing sound. "Clever. I see why you are an alpha."

I glanced up at him. "I was telling the truth."

"Yes, but not until you had to. Clever." He bobbed his head. "I'm a shitty guard, Alpha." He spoke the title to me and I felt it settle over my shoulders. "Which means I regularly let other creatures slip past our boundaries." He winked one of those big jeweled eyes at me. "That and I'm hoping one day Lila will come back to us."

Lila swept upward and planted a kiss on his snout. "That will never happen, Pret. But thank you. You're a good friend."

He rumbled, and I had the impression it was the dragon equivalent of purring. "Lila, I will never forget you looking out for me after my parents were killed by the White Raven."

She ducked her head and flew back to me, landing on my shoulder. "You should go now, Pret. I don't want you to get caught being nice to interlopers."

He bobbed his head, turned, and made his way north along the boundary line. "Good luck finding that which you seek."

I watched him go, his body blending into the forest,

and only because I knew where he'd been could I pick out the shifting in the scene.

"Lila, what did you tell him?"

Her claws tightened on my shoulder. "That we were going to take the jewel from my father. That we were going to take dragons back to the noble and honorable creatures we once were."

"Lila, we're here for Bryce," I whispered. "With Steve gone, we don't need to get the stone."

"And we're here to make the world better, aren't we?" She swiveled around. "Otherwise, what's the point of saving anyone if we can't make it better?"

The weight of all those lives, of all those who depended on us, was heavier than I wanted to acknowledge.

"Okay. We find Bryce. Then we find the stone."

Why did I get the feeling those words were going to come back to haunt me?

Chapter 18

The first hundred feet or so of walking into the forest of Dragon's Ground was damn near peaceful, which should have been warning enough. I walked next to Balder, one hand on his saddle to help keep myself upright.

"Why are you not letting him carry you?" Lila asked.

"Because my legs need to get their shit together," I said. "I'm no good if I'm falling down."

Maks snorted. "Then let yourself rest."

I knew where he was coming from, but I also knew my body. The more I got the blood flowing, the better. Much as I would have liked to ride along inside his coat again.

I smiled to myself and Lila caught the edge of it. "What are you grinning about?"

"I'm alive, and my leg is still attached. That is enough to be happy about, isn't it?"

Maks slid off Batman and moved to walk beside me. "Maybe. But you seem—"

"Do you regret it now that Ish isn't hanging onto you, manipulating you?" I asked before I could stop myself. I had to know how he felt because the longer he was near me, the more I wanted him to stay at my side.

If I had to let him go, then I had to do it now before my heart got any more tangled up in this mess with him.

Lila squeaked and clapped her wings together. "Yes, I want to know the answer to that question too."

Maks cleared his throat. "This is going to be complicated, Zam. You can't possibly think that it's as simple an answer as yes I regret, or no I don't."

I pursed my lips and nodded. "Actually yes, I do think it's that simple."

He grabbed both my arms and dragged me close, catching me off guard. "I am a *Jinn*, Zam. This, whatever it is between us, can never be, no matter what either of us wants. Do I regret? No. But I wish nothing had ever happened because what is between us is growing with each passing minute, and I know there will come a point when we'll have to choose."

I stared up at him, feeling the truth of his words and hating every syllable. "You don't know that."

"I do. You would be used against me, Zam. They will kill you just because. . . because I care about you," he said, and the sadness in those pretty blue eyes tugged me closer.

Electricity seemed to dance between us and I welcomed the feeling on my skin, the draw to Maks stronger than ever before. "They would kill me, anyway."

"Not like they would if they knew how I feel." His hands tightened in a most pleasant way on my arms, reminding me that he could easily throw me down and have his way with me. Not that I would have fought him.

"I don't want to walk away from this, Maks."

"Then I will. For both of us." He pushed me away, but his hands lingered, as if they had a mind of their own. He took a step back, then reached over to his saddle and pulled the flail down. "Here, you might need this."

I took it. And then he bent and pulled a kukri blade —my blades—from each boot. "And these."

I nodded, my throat too tight to speak.

"No, this can't be how it ends." Lila shot between us. "This is not a Romeo and Juliet story. Your two families might hate each other but they don't give two figs about either of you. So, do what you want. Make cute little cubs I can play with."

"Lila, don't." I closed my eyes as if that would stop what I was seeing inside my head. Because the image was all too strong. A life with Maks? I could see it, easier than I wanted to admit. In the time I'd known him, he'd shown himself to be true to a fault, strong, even though the blood coursing through his veins would make him a monster to me.

He blew out a breath. "We need to find your brother."

"Yeah." I nodded. "We do." I turned away from him, hurt more than I thought possible, because I knew he was right. But I needed to find Bryce now. That was what I had to focus on.

I lifted my head and drew in a deep breath, searching for a scent that would pull us forward. I caught the smells of a typical forest in winter, things decaying, small mouse nests, the sharp bite of the wind up my nose.

"Lila, I don't suppose Pret had any indication of where Bryce might have come through?" I asked.

She snorted and flicked her tail at me and then Maks. I could see she didn't want us changing the subject quite so easily, but I was done with that discussion.

"What a pair of idiots," she said.

A half-grin turned up my lips. "Agreed. Now, where should we start looking for Bryce?"

Lila flew up to the tree branches ahead of us. "That's up to you. My job is to let you know about the booby traps before they hit us."

Again, she was right. I suddenly had an urge for a bottle of țuică, wishing I could drown myself in the rich plum liquor.

If I dared shift back to my smaller form, I'd heighten my sense of smell. That could be a huge help, but I wasn't sure I could even shift if my life depended on it.

My father had always known where every lion in his pride was, at any moment in time, and if they were well, sick, hurt, or hale and hearty. It had been a gift of his, a sixth sense if you will. And occasionally, we'd been able to reciprocate with him, connecting our energies with his. He'd made it a game when I'd been a little cub, like a form of hide and seek. But it had been years since I'd thought of it, and years longer since I'd done anything like it. If there was any time I needed the lessons of my father to stick, it was now. "Let me try something." I stopped where I was and closed my eyes.

"What are you doing?" whispered Maks so close, my heart skipped a beat.

"Searching for Bryce," I whispered back.

Maks's presence was too distracting. I turned and handed him Balder's reins. "Stay here. I need to be alone to do this."

Lila snickered from ahead. "Idiots. Both of you."

I clenched my mouth shut to keep from telling her off, because she was right in some ways, wrong in others.

I walked about thirty feet from Maks and the horses to a large evergreen tree. The base had to have been fifty feet around and in between the roots were several depressions that would make perfect seats.

I settled myself into one of the groves and put my hands on my thighs. The trick, as Dad had always said, was to allow the flow of the world to guide you, to find the ripples that showed another's passing.

I felt as though I sunk deeper into the earth though I knew it was just my mind opening to the flow of the world. The lines of passage began to flicker, teasing two of my senses. I could "see" them with both my eyes and my nose. A rabbit, a fox, a dragon the night before, birds and small rodents. The lines lit up in front of my closed eyelids all different colors against the blackness. Carefully I opened my eyes.

The streaks of the other creatures' passages were still

there, though they wavered a moment. I stood slowly, and started forward, letting my eyes light where they would. On a tree, on the ground, ahead, to the side.

There was no sign of Bryce or his big horse, Ali. "Stick close," I said. "Lila, on my shoulder."

She flew to me and settled on my right shoulder.

Besides her weight, I felt Maks's eyes on my back, trying to figure out what I was doing.

The passage of creatures was sparse here though it was a forest and should have been teeming with life.

We walked north, slowly, and I could feel Maks's frustration mounting. I ignored it and him as best I could.

Ahead of me came a flicker between the trees, half-buried on the ground. Gold, as gold as my brother's eyes. I picked up my pace, ignoring Lila as she begged me to slow down.

I stepped around a tree and there it was. Bryce's passage.

"Fuck yeah!" I shouted, unable to contain my joy. There was no other word for it. I was overjoyed at having found his trail. Because it meant that at least for the moment, he was still alive. I stared down at the golden thread, again ignoring Lila whispering in my ear.

Something about being quiet.

I bent down and touched the strand. It wrapped around my wrist, warming me to the core. In it I felt his heart beat and how much he loved me.

Tears bloomed and trickled down my cheeks. Maks was at my side in an instant. "Zam, what's wrong?"

"My brother loves me," I whispered.

He startled. "You doubted it?"

I made myself look at him. "I pulled the spear out of his back. I made it worse, Maks. *I* crippled him."

His eyes softened. "No, you didn't. Those spears are designed to maim, Zam. I remember it all too clearly. It was not your fault."

He. . . remembered it? I stared up at him, my heart beating hard for a different reason. "You were there? At the massacre?"

Maks's jaw tightened. "I was."

Maks was there with the Jinn when my family had been slaughtered. "And you killed lions from my pride?"

He looked away. "Zam, I didn't have a choice whether or not I could be there."

I shoved him hard. "There is always a choice, Jinn!"

That last bit came out apparently too loud. A low grumbling snarl echoed through the woods.

Lila groaned. "Now you've done it."

I snatched Balder's reins from Maks's hand and leapt up onto my horse. "Try to keep up."

There was nothing else to do but put distance between us and whatever dragon we'd woken. Check that, that *I'd* woken.

Anger cut through me, but the connection I'd found to Bryce was solid and I followed it unerringly. Right through three more dragons' territories if the bellows meant anything.

Lila clung to the front of my saddle, shaking her head. "You know, I can't talk them *all* out of killing us."

"We'll think of something," I said because I'd stepped in it good this time. Like the idiot she'd been claiming I was. I was an idiot for thinking Maks, a Jinn, wasn't like the others. Hell, he'd even tried to tell me that it wasn't a good idea. That he was a Jinn just like the others, no good to be around, not trustworthy. And I, foolishly, had thought he was different.

But my stupid heart didn't care. And that was what twisted me up so much. I should have hated him so damn hard, and I just couldn't.

We wove between the trees, and that was probably about all that saved us from the direct fire of the dragons. Three followed us, pissed off as they crashed through the trees, unable to get a good bead on us. One shot off a current of electricity that danced to my right, exploding against the ground, tearing up roots. Balder grunted and dove to the left, crashing us into Batman and Maks.

"What's the plan?" Maks asked.

"Get to Bryce," I said.

"That's it?" he barked. "Seriously, how are we getting away from the dragons?"

I shook my head and shrugged. "No idea. I'm actually hoping it will come to me in a flash of inspiration."

His jaw drooped. I raised an eyebrow. "You'll catch bugs that way, Jinn."

His jaw snapped shut. Yeah, it wasn't nice to use that word for him, not when it was obvious he wasn't happy with the fact he was a Jinn.

But I wasn't sure I could forgive the fact that he'd been part of the attack that had wiped out my family. He'd been there at the Oasis itself. He'd seen Bryce get taken down. What if he'd been the one to do it?

Goddess of the desert and gods of the sky, I wasn't sure what I would do if Maks had been that one. Bad enough that he'd been there, bad enough that he'd killed members of my pride, but there would be no coming back if he'd wielded the spear that had taken Bryce down. I could never forgive him that.

We galloped around the trees, the horses working hard to make the sharp turns, to dodge the incoming fire and electricity from the dragons behind us.

I looked back once and that was when I realized Lila was no longer on my shoulder. We burst out into a clearing that was huge, big enough for several dragons with room to spare.

And there, as if he'd been waiting for us, sat Bryce.

Chapter 19

My brother's eyes lifted and took us in, heading toward him at a full gallop in the clearing, the dragons whose territories we trampled through not yet visible.

"What did you do, Zamira?" he growled.

I lifted both hands, palms up, suddenly feeling ten years old again. "Nothing! I mean, not really."

Behind us the three dragons cleared the trees with a tiny fourth dragon darting between them. She still wore the sapphire.

I wasn't sure freezing and killing the dragons was the best idea. "Lila, don't hurt them!" I yelled up at her.

The three dragons, so different in color, dropped from the sky, laughter rolling through them. That was not the effect I was going for, but I'd take it.

One was pale gray, his whole body looking like he'd been made of smoke and clouds, and his eyes danced with the electricity that had been chasing us. The second was a deep green, a sap sucker if my guess was right, only he had wings, so maybe he was a hybrid of some sort. His scales shimmered, almost glowing. The third was bright red with smoke curling out of his nose. The fire breather.

Awesome. Electricity, acid, and fire. Just the combination we needed to deal with.

"Lila hurt us?" The green sap sucker wheezed the words out. "Lila the Gnat? Please. That's a crock of shit if I ever heard it."

Lila let out a snarl, but it sounded like a squeaky toy compared to the deeper rumble of the big dragons. It only made them laugh harder and my heart hurt for her. This was why she and I got each other. Our own kind treated us as though we were worth nothing, as if we were losers.

We were the same even though we had totally different bodies; the hurt in our lives was the same. They didn't take her seriously, and a part of me wanted to tell her to let them have it. But that wouldn't help us in the long run and I restrained myself.

I held up both hands, turning to the dragons. "We just came to get my brother, then we will be leaving right away. We didn't mean to trespass, but there was no one to ask for permission to come on in."

I felt more than saw Bryce stiffen. I knew he wanted to deny my words, but if he did, we'd for sure be dead.

"How did you get past the border guards, shifter? There was a report of a pair of riders that outpaced Prince a few weeks ago. Said it was a gray horse and a woman in a red cloak." The red dragon stepped forward, his feet sending a rumble through the earth that made the horses dance with nerves. I kept my hands where they were, away from any weapons. I did not want to set them off. Thank the desert gods I'd lost my red cloak with the gorcs. Currently I wore a dark green one that blended into the forest better, pulled from my stash of gear.

I shot a look at Bryce. "I don't know anything about that. Red is a common cloak color. As you can see, I'm wearing green. And I don't know how my brother made it by, but we were able to slip past while the border guard was dealing with two other riders." Fuck, that countered my previous statement of not getting permission. I was a terrible liar, always stepping in it. But for the moment the red dragon didn't seem to notice.

The red dragon squinted at me. "More of your party coming then."

I looked back the way we'd come, and then to the dragon again. "No, the border dragon drove the others off and we slipped by. We weren't with them." Kind of a truth. Close enough that I hoped the red dragon wouldn't sniff out the piss-poorly laced lies.

The red dragon turned his head to Bryce. "And you?"

He shrugged. "I'm a cripple in search of your healer. I've heard she is the greatest of all healers and I have need of a great healer."

The red dragon snorted. "Even if you reached her, which you won't, what are you going to pay her with? She only takes the highest quality treasures, you know that."

"Actually, Fink," Lila shot in front of them, still wearing the sapphire. She touched it with a claw tip. "We do. And you'd best let us pass to reach Amalia."

The red dragon, Fink apparently, turned to her. "You have no say here, Gnat."

She barrel rolled and came to a stop in midair right in front of his face. "I do have a say. I may have been cast out, but that does not change who I am."

"It does," Fink said, and there was a heavy sadness in his voice. "Much as it pains me to say it, you'd have done better to lead our people. If you'd been a boy."

"Hey, she'd have made a fucking fine leader regardless of her gender," I snapped. "She's got more heart than anyone else I know. Do you know she rushed a band of gorcs to save me?"

The dragons all turned to look at me in unison and I felt my blood quiver in my veins. There was no way I could survive a dragon attack. I had to keep my hand clenched into the edge of my cloak so it wouldn't go for the handle to the flail that seemed to call to me.

"She saved you?" Fink raised a scaled brow. "I find that hard to believe."

Lila flew down to me, landing on my shoulder. "We saved each other."

Fink made a motion with his head and the gray dragon leapt up into the air and flew back the way we'd come.

"We shall see. If you truly killed the gorcs, then perhaps we will let you pass. Such bravery is worth rewarding." He flopped down on the ground and Balder danced backward, tossing his head. I soothed him with one hand.

The green dragon, the acid spitter, snorted and a fine mist sprayed everywhere. I backed Balder up fast, the mist falling where we'd stood only a moment before. "Hey, man," I said, "watch that shit, would you?"

Lila laughed. "That's Draken. He forgets what he's got in his guts."

My curiosity got the better of me. "Are you two related?"

She shook her head. "Not really, not any more than any other dragons are related to me."

Fink snorted and lifted a back leg to scratch at his head like a giant dog. "She's related to everyone. That's the blood line of royalty for you."

I kept my eyes on him while I fought to keep my thoughts off my face. Royalty. So, Merlin was right about that.

Maks moved Batman a little closer, and I moved Balder away. I couldn't deal with him, not right then. Not when I was staring up at a rather large dragon that could literally wipe us all out with a single puff of flame. We were close enough that there would be no escape.

Fink squinted his eyes as though he was thinking hard. Or constipated, that was another possibility. "Lila is an anomaly, not only in size, but in her abilities. She looks like her mother's side, which is not surprising being a female." He winked at Lila and she stiffened on my shoulder.

"Piss off, Fink," she snapped.

I had to say, I was impressed. She was giving as good

as she ever did even though she was clearly outsized, outweighed, and out-dragoned.

He laughed, the chuckle a deep baritone. "Yeah, yeah. You know not everyone agrees with what your father and brother did. But there weren't enough of us."

I frowned. "And which one of you stood up for her then?"

His head tipped to the side. "You don't understand dragon politics."

"I understand loyalty," I said. Behind me Maks and Bryce groaned in unison. "I understand what it means to stand with someone in their darkest hour."

The acid spitter, Draken, snorted again. "You're a shifter. Shifters aren't loyal."

Every instinct in me reared up and yet I knew I could say nothing. Because I wasn't strong enough. The shaking in me had Balder dancing sideways.

"You're a fool" was about all I could muster.

Above the trees, the gray dragon swept back into view and landed in the clearing next to Fink. "Gorcs, dead, fifty of them or so, some killed flat, others frozen, though some were thawing."

Lila lashed her tail. "Damn it."

The pale gray dragon shrugged. "I took care of it. Easy when they aren't running around." He grinned at Lila. "Good job, Princess."

Her tail lashing slowed. "You see that we were telling the truth. Will you let us go to Amalia then?"

Fink shrugged. "You know the dangers between here and there?"

Lila nodded. "Yes."

"You know you all won't make it without help?" He shifted his body so he stood on four legs, stretching and arching his back like nothing more than a giant red, scaled cat. His tail lashed the air and then slammed into the ground. "We will take you as close to the wall as we can. You'll be on your own from there, and I won't help you back through the forest."

Was this really happening? We were getting the help we needed without asking. My hand went to the necklace I wore, and I wondered just what Maks had done to it.

Lila let out a big breath. "Thank you, Fink."

He jumped into the air. "I still believe you have it in you, Gnat. For what it's worth."

She ducked her head into my hair and let out a tiny sob. There were no words I had to comfort her because I knew that pain. I lifted a hand to her side, giving her a small amount of comfort.

"How is this going to work?" Maks asked. I turned to him.

"I don't know."

The three large dragons lifted into the air and hovered, their wings sending our hair and cloaks swirling around us. The horses whinnied and then everything kind of happened too fast to stop it even if we wanted to.

The three dragons swooped down and scooped us and our horses into their big talons. Fink took Bryce and his big girl Ali, Draken took Maks and Batman, and the gray dragon took Balder and me.

I sucked in a breath as the scaled talons closed

around us, just hard enough to keep Balder and me from slipping. My legs were pinned to his side as we rose into the air with a few jerking beats of the gray's wings.

Lila shot out of the scaled cage we were in. I stared down at the tops of the trees as we swept over them. "You got a name?" I shouted up at him.

"My mother wanted to name me Blaz for a legendary hero of our kind, but she settled on Trick." He bent his head around to grin at me. "And you are?"

This was the weirdest introduction I'd had to date. "Zam."

"Nice to meet you."

Balder gave a whinny and struggled against his bonds. "Easy, easy, my friend." I soothed him, rubbing a hand along his neck. It would have been better to blind-fold him but there had been no option.

"How far?" I shouted over the rushing of the wind and the snap of leather wings through the air.

"Not too far. Maybe an hour," Trick said. "Amalia is not a kind dragon, you all know that, right? She's. . . difficult on a good day. And she hasn't had a good day since before Lila was born."

Lila zipped around Trick, and I realized she was showing off.

It hit me in a flash. Lila had a crush on the big gray dragon. I grinned. Oh, this was going to be too much fun. "Lila, weren't you telling me about a handsome gray dragon you knew growing up? Is this him?"

She let out a strangled squawk and shot to where she could give me a look that said it all. I'd hit the nail right on the head. I grinned back at her. "Fair's fair, don't you think?"

Trick laughed. "Lila, you crushing on me, little Princess?"

"No." She blurted out the word. "I am not. You. . . you were kind to me."

His laugh was not mean in the least. "Oh please. We grew up together. I call bullshit."

She groaned. "I am not crushing on you. I'm happy that you are helping, yes. I appreciate it. Nothing else."

I didn't have to say anything else really, but she'd teased me enough about Maks that it was indeed only fair.

"But what about all the barrel rolls?" I couldn't see her. "I mean, showing off is a sure sign of—"

"Oh, my gods, you are killing me!" Lila started to laugh. "Fine, I won't tease you about Maks anymore. I get it. Okay?"

"Who's Maks?" Trick asked.

"The guy she's hot for, but they can't be together," Lila said loud enough that I was sure Bryce and Fink who were to my left had to have heard. I groaned.

"Damn it."

Trick tipped his wings, and we dodged sideways to avoid a particularly tall tree. "Cross-species love, it is a temptation. But no *bueno*."

I snorted at his use of Spanish. "You have no idea."

"Oh, I do. I fell for a wood sprite once." He laughed. "I was only five, but damn she was a saucy little spice pot, all legs and this gauzy pair of wings that were too lovely for words."

I laughed and realized that he was a pretty cool guy, uh, dragon. "I like him, Lila. You should work on this relationship."

Trick rumbled. "I don't come from good stock, Zam. A dragon born from a pair of criminals so there would have been no chance even if Lila was not booted out of the grounds."

Lila swept by me, shaking her head. "That wasn't your fault, Trick."

"Not anymore than you being born as you are is your fault, Lila," he pointed out.

Yeah, I liked him.

Ahead of us was a change in the topography. The trees thinned until there was nothing but a bare strip of ground that ran north and south. Excitement snapped through me. I'd never actually seen the wall. It ran from the Witch's Reign down through to the deserts of the Jinn's dominion. But it had been strictly off limits when I was younger, and I'd never gotten close in all my journeys since then.

I stared hard at what I thought might be the wall. A line of rocks, yes, but they probably weren't even three feet high. This was no mile-high fence that we'd been led to believe. Shit, I could have galloped Balder at it and leapt over in a single bound. "Is that. . . it? Is that the wall?" I couldn't keep the disappointment out of my voice. Because my whole life I'd believed I'd been trapped, and what I was seeing was that I'd not been trapped but tricked.

And that fucking pissed me off.

Chapter 20

"**P**iddly, isn't it?" Trick tipped his wings so we had a better look at the so-called wall. Three feet high, I was sure, and crumbling in places, making it even smaller. Here and there I even saw gaps. Fucking holes that I could have walked through with ease.

"*That's* keeping us all in?" I yelled.

Lila swept around in front. "Have you never seen it?"

I shook my head slowly. "We lived a hundred miles inland when we were in the desert. It was considered bad luck to see it." Now I was wondering just why it was bad luck. I mean. . . all the time we were trapped between the wall and the Jinn was a pile of horseshit. We could have escaped.

Why had my father kept us bound to a desert, a place that had stolen his life, a place where our world was destroyed when we could have gotten away?

I was caught in the snare of emotions that I couldn't slow down. Anger, frustration, and confusion trampled through my heart, leaving it aching with this new twist to a story that I had thought I understood.

"It's not just the wall," Lila said, and then she dropped away. Trick followed her at a distance.

"I do like her, Zam. Her size isn't an issue, but her father is." His eyes caught hold of mine, the lightning in them dancing. "He's dangerous. He'll kill her if he finds her here."

"I'll keep her safe," I said over the wind as it rushed around us in a headlong drop. I held my breath, and then just like that, we were on the ground, Trick releasing us.

Balder stumbled a few steps and then righted himself. The other two dragons dropped off their packages. The horses all seemed to struggle with standing on solid ground, but it didn't take them long to get their legs under them.

I raised my hand. "Thank you."

"Be safe." Trick flapped his wings, shooting into the clouds that had begun to form over us. They deepened in color and lightning crackled through them.

Lila came to my shoulder and sat, her feet clenching at me. "He's going to give us some cover, but we aren't going to like it."

Even as she spoke, the rain started, and the temperature dropped. The wet droplets hit us and within seconds froze. "Freezing rain, that's fucking awesome."

"The other dragons will hide. They hate freezing rain." Lila crawled into my hood. I didn't blame her and wished I could do the same. I glanced at Maks and found him looking at me, his eyes full of a heat that could've been anger, or maybe he was thinking the same thing as me. How nice it would be closer to him.

No, bad, bad Zam. Maks is a Jinn. A Jinn who was at the Oasis.

I cleared my throat before speaking. "Bryce."

"You shouldn't be here," he snapped. "I don't need your damn help."

I directed Balder closer to Bryce and his big mare. "Look, you wouldn't have left me to go it alone, would you?"

"Yeah, I would. Because it's a choice, Zam. That's what you don't get. We all have choices and I made mine. I didn't want help. Go home." He snapped his reins against his horse's neck and she started off at a stately plod.

I stared after him, unable to move. Lila clung to my neck with her forelegs, hugging me. "He's right, it is a choice. But you have a choice too. You don't have to do what he says."

She was right, but that wasn't what was holding me there. No, the lies between Bryce and me were too much, and I knew it was time to tell him the truth of his injury.

I swallowed hard. "Bryce. It's my fault you're a cripple. I pulled the spear out. I thought I was helping. I thought you'd be able to heal. I. . . didn't know it would do this to you."

He slowed his horse and turned her around. His face

was a mask, hiding his thoughts from me. "And becoming a thief for Ish?"

"She said she'd heal you if I helped her," I whispered, knowing he'd hear me over the rain.

He stared at me and I wished to every god and goddess I'd ever called upon that he'd give me something, anything but that stone face I knew all too well. "You blame me for you being a thief then?"

"Goddess, no!" I urged Balder forward, but Bryce held up a hand.

"No. You are not coming with me," he snapped.

"Are you not hearing me? It's my fault, Bryce! It's my fault!" The words were too loud, I knew it by the way the horses flinched and the animals in the bush on our one side fluttered away. "You should have been the alpha of our pride. You should have had a better life than this."

"Then you should have let me die on the sand with Father." His words cut into me sharper than any knife. "If this healer can't do what she claims, you *will* finish what you started, Zamira. You will put your kukri to my throat and you will end my life."

He turned his horse and gave me his back. "And for that reason, I will allow you to come with me."

I was shaking so hard I had to put my hands on the pommel of the saddle to keep from falling out. A hand reached for me, balancing me, and Maks's voice solid, a rock to hang onto in this storm of the past and present.

"Zam, none of this is your fault."

"Well, one of us has to take responsibility for this

shit," I snarled and jerked my arm away from him. "Because you sure as hell aren't."

I gave Balder the cue to move out and he trotted after Bryce and Ali. Behind us, Batman limped his way along. Damn it, I needed to tend to him, whatever was ailing him. I wasn't even sure if it was a cut, or a pull of the tendons or what. I made myself breathe slowly to ease the racing of my heart. But even that didn't quell the swelling anxiety and fear that coursed through me.

The truth was out there, and it had not set me free. It had bound me in ways I could not have imagined. There was no way I could do as Bryce asked. No way that I could kill him, the last of my family, the brother who'd been my hero my whole life.

But if he commanded me as my alpha. . . I wasn't sure I wouldn't do it. The cat in me would want to buckle to his demands. Just as Kiara had bent to my will, so would it be the same between Bryce and me?

And I wasn't sure which scared me worse.

I MADE everyone stop after only a short time and silently tended to Batman. His right front knee was swollen and there wasn't much I could do for it. Soft tissue damage was the worst. Best I could do was make Maks walk.

After that, we walked for hours with the wall to our left and the thick covering of the forest to our right. The swath that had been cleared between wall and forest was about two hundred feet wide. Wide enough that any number of creatures could have tromped along its path.

The freezing rain coated our gear and our clothes, and every ten minutes, we were forced to shake it all off. The upside, I suppose, was we weren't really getting wet, not like we could have been.

"Lila, this Amalia, is she very old?"

"Oldest dragon alive," Lila said. "She was around when the wall was built, or at least that was what I was always told. She remembers our history and is our greatest healer. My parents took me to her when I was a child. You know, to see if she could fix what was wrong with me."

"There is nothing wrong with you," I said softly.

"Then you think there is nothing wrong with you?" she offered, and I shrugged.

"That's different. You're amazing."

She butted her head against me. "So are you."

Yeah, we were a messed-up pair, but I knew in my gut we'd been brought together for a reason. Maybe the world was trying to tell us something.

That a pair of useless supes were better than we thought? Maybe. . . maybe.

I glanced at the wall to our left. "I can't believe we've all been so fucking stupid as to stay in here."

Maks grunted and shook his head like I was a fool. "The wall is spelled, Zam. The closer you get to it, the more pain rockets through you until you pass out. Then the guardians can come and pick you up easily." He made a sweeping motion at the swath we walked on. "That's why this is so wide. The dragons can pick up those stupid enough to think the wall is easily crossed."

It was the most he'd spoken to me since the battle

with the gorcs. It was also an insult, seeing as I had been stupid enough to think it could have been easily crossed.

Bryce twisted around in his saddle to look at us. "If you're trying to impress her, insulting her intelligence won't work. I mean, it worked for Steve, but she was a lot younger and dumber then." Apparently, he'd heard what Lila had said to Trick as we'd flown. Just awesome.

"Hey, it did *not* work for Steve!" I yelled at his back.

"It did. He called you smart for a pretty girl, which is basically 'you aren't quite as dumb as you should have been,'" Bryce fired back.

The flush in my skin was instant and I urged Balder to catch up to Bryce. When I was right beside him I reached over and punched him in the arm. "Then why didn't you say something? I was sixteen! I didn't know any better."

He didn't look at me. "I was in no place to protect you, Zam. You might think you failed me by pulling that spear, but I *know* I failed you. I should have driven Steve away, kept you safe from his cheating ass."

His words were not what I expected.

We were quiet a moment before I pulled up the courage to speak again. "I would have listened to you. If you'd told me Steve was bad for me. I would have listened."

"Would you've?" He shot a look at me and I didn't hesitate.

I nodded. "Yes, you were always my hero, Bryce. Even after the Oasis."

Lila stuck her head up and let out a soft snort. "Hang on, you two, we're close."

222

Our conversation stumbled to a stop as the horses slowed without being asked. The air around us seemed to tense; the freezing rain had let up and animals should have been coming out of the woods to forage.

Except there was no movement, no animals, and no noise.

It was as if we'd been stuffed into a vault that muffled everything around us. Even my sense of smell seemed to be affected. I drew a breath in through my nose, holding the air in the back of my throat, but I couldn't identify any dragon.

"Lila, are you sure?" I found myself whispering without meaning to. The sense of trepidation was so heavy, I wasn't sure I wanted to break it.

Ahead of us, the ground rumbled and shook. I watched in fascination as a depression sunk into the soil, showing the impression of a dragon's foot, then another and another. Amalia was a chameleon dragon, which in and of itself wasn't something all that out of the ordinary.

It was the size of her feet that had my eyes glued to each print in the ground as she moved toward us.

Each foot was easily ten feet across.

We were fucked.

Chapter 21

Maks had caught up to us as I watched with fascination and horror as the healer dragon Amalia drew closer. Not far from the fabled wall, her steps were so close now that I could feel the reverberation of her size up through my seat in the saddle, but there was still no smell of her, no sound from her steps or from the breath curling out of her mouth.

Lila flew up so she was between us and the much, much larger dragon. "Healer Amalia, we come seeking your help."

"Little Lila." The voice was distinctly feminine despite the depth of it, and the words echoed around us as if we were in a box canyon instead of a wide-open strip of land. "I see you, and I see you have brought me something to eat. A lion shifter, a Jinn who is not a Jinn, and a shifter who is not a shifter. . . well, well, you have made some interesting friends."

Bryce stiffened at the word Jinn and I cringed. Assuming we got out of here alive that was not going to go over well. I'd deal with it later, though, again assuming there was a later for any of us.

Lila kept her position. "They are my friends. All of them."

"Then what would you pay me with for my help?" There was no malice in the voice, just genuine curiosity. "You know the way this works, little one."

Lila dipped and rolled, showing off the sparkling blue sapphire. "This. The Ice Witch's sapphire. Is it worth something to you?"

Amalia came into view as suddenly as a bolt of lightning. Her body was white, as white as the driven snow, and her pearlescent scales caught the light of even the weak sunlight and reflected it back in rainbows. But it was her eyes that caught my attention as strange as that would seem. Her eyes were as violet as Lila's, though on a much larger scale.

My brain made the connection fast and my mouth spit it out before my faulty brain-to-mouth filter kicked in.

"You're her grandmother, aren't you?" I asked.

Amalia turned her head to me and gave me a toothy grin. "Clever, cat. Yes, I am."

Bryce urged his horse forward. "Healer, it is I who comes begging your help."

She swiveled her head around, lowering it so she was in front of the horse. Ali snorted and spun, trying to get away from the massive predator. "Get off your horse then, boy."

I leapt off Balder and hurried to his side. "Here, let me help you."

"No!" he snarled as he unbuckled the straps that helped him stay in the saddle. My heart lurched as he undid the last one and pushed himself over to the side. His legs dangled, useless. Slowly he lowered himself so that he stood beside Ali, hanging onto her saddle in order to keep himself upright.

Amalia stretched her wings wide and snapped them hard, the crack of wind off the white leather a startling boom that sent Bryce's horse spinning away. He was thrown to the ground, face-down on the ice-coated grass.

I made a move to help him up, but he pushed himself up and back onto his ass, though it looked uncomfortable.

"Can you help me, healer?" he asked.

She looked at Lila. "You truly have the sapphire? It would give you the power you need to stop your father."

Lila grabbed the leather thong and pulled the stone from around her neck, then flipped it to her grandmother. "I either lead on my own, or I don't lead at all. That's how things are done. I don't know why you are even asking me this."

Amalia grinned as she caught the stone spinning through the air. "That's my girl."

The old dragon twisted the stone around between the tips of two claws, looking at it. "So, they brought this. What did you bring to pay me, broken lion? Or did you think I would heal you out of the goodness of my shriveled and jaded heart?"

Bryce reached under his shirt and pulled out a stone I knew—the first stone I'd ever brought back for Ish. The diamond had belonged to a coven of witches, and I'd slipped in, stealing it while they slept. The story had more to it than that, but that was the gist. Unlike most diamonds of value, this one was not clear. Or not completely clear. Throughout the fist-sized stone were jagged black lines that resembled lightning bolts, making it easy to identify.

That first theft had cemented my place in Ish's life, making me an asset despite my size.

"Oh, another pretty. Lovely. But you give that one to your sister. I want this one." She clutched at the sapphire.

Bryce turned just his head and lifted an eyebrow. "Why would Zam need this stone? She's no mage."

Amalia laughed. "You are correct. She is no mage. She is no lion shifter either. So, what does that make her?"

A shiver of apprehension rolled down my spine, mixing with a healthy dose of curiosity. "You know what my mother was, don't you?"

Amalia nodded. "I do, but that is not for me to tell you."

Damn it.

She turned again to Bryce. "You must know this, lion. If I heal your legs, your life will not be as long than as if you would stay here, in your broken form."

Bryce stared up at her. "If I could only walk for one day before my life was taken, this would be worth it."

My throat tightened, and I couldn't speak past the

lump in it. I'd never understood the depth of his pain until that moment.

He'd rather be dead than broken.

Maybe I didn't understand it because in his eyes I *was* broken, and. . . I didn't let it stop me from living.

And that's when the penny dropped. "That's why you hate me, isn't it?"

He looked up at me, a frown dragging his golden brows together. "What?"

"You see me as broken, but I still live. I still fight to have a life even though I'm considered useless. You gave up. That's why you hate me."

He closed his eyes. "I never hated you, Zam. I envied you. You lived with what you were. You never let it slow you down. I. . . I couldn't get past my own brokenness."

A breath slid out of me. "Don't do this, Bryce. I'd rather you were in my life for as long as possible in a chair, than healed for a short time. Please." I dropped to my knees beside him, taking his hands in my own. "I'll beg if I have to. You're my family, the only family I have left."

He set the diamond in my lap and took one of my hands. "I know. But I can't do this anymore, Zam. I was born to lead, to be an alpha. Not to be a burden on those I love."

"You can lead, even now," I said, not caring that the others were all watching this family drama play out. I knew Lila would understand, and even Maks. Much as I didn't want him to, I think he probably understood.

Bryce looked up at me, sorrow flickering through his

eyes. "Before I do this. . . Zam, in case it goes poorly. . . we had different mothers."

His words could not have slammed the breath from me any harder than if he'd punched me in the solar plexus. I struggled to speak.

"What?"

"My mother died when I was very young, and Dad found a new mate in part to take care of me. I never knew my mother, I only knew our mother. But. . . she was not like the rest of us."

I knew he was telling the truth. "And you waited to tell me because?"

"Because it didn't matter to me that you were different. You were my sister." He lifted a hand and put his fingers under my chin. He opened his mouth as if to speak more, but Amalia interrupted.

"Our time here is limited. And the one stone is not enough to warrant me healing you."

"Then take them both," Bryce said.

"No. You will perform a task for me." She grinned at us. "That I will tell you after you are healed."

"No," I said, but I was too late. She reached out and snatched Bryce up with one paw and then launched into the sky.

I shot to my feet, screaming. "BRYCE!"

Lila flew in my face, blocking me. "No, this is how she will heal him. She'll use the lightning and her magic together."

I was shaking so hard, I didn't notice Maks's hand on my arm right away. And when I did, I didn't pull away.

"I fought the lion shifters, Zam. I didn't kill any of them," he said. "I was young and the sight of all that death changed me."

"You didn't stop the other Jinn either, Maks." I turned into him, resting my head on his shoulder. My rampant emotions and fear for Bryce were just too much. I couldn't deny the comfort Maks was to me, how much he fit into my life. We might have been on opposite sides of the war, but that didn't matter while I stood there, waiting to see what would happen to my brother.

The diamond was cool in my hand and I let it drop to the ground. Maks's arms swept around me, anchoring me. "He'll be okay. He's stronger than any other lion shifter."

I looked up at him and then to the sky above us. Lightning danced across the clouds, silhouetting Amalia here and there within the shadows. "He'll die sooner because of this. I don't want to lose him, Maks."

"It's his life. Let him live it." His eyes hardened a little. "He needs to make his choices like you make yours."

I pulled back from him. "He's not your damn brother. *You* don't get a say in this."

"And he's not your child. Neither do you," he barked. "You can't make his choices for him, Zam. You can't keep trying to protect him!"

"It is my job!" I yelled back. "He's all I've got."

Lila swept between us, back and forth. "That's not true. You have me. And I think even though you're fighting, you've got Maks too."

I turned away from her, shaking my head. "It isn't like. . . he's my *brother*, Lila."

I couldn't find the words I needed to make it clear what I was feeling. Above us there came a roar and a boom of thunder that made me reach for the handle of the flail.

The boom was followed by a scream that made the hairs all over my body stand on end and a low hiss escaped me before I could catch it. "Lila, what is this?"

"I don't know." She came to me, landing on my shoulder. "I don't know what it means. Maybe she couldn't heal him after all?"

That was what I was afraid of. That if Amalia couldn't heal Bryce, he'd tell her to drop him. To just end it.

The scream cut off and the storm clouds peeled back so rapidly, there was no doubt it was Amalia and her magic. She spiraled her way down from where they'd disappeared. Bryce was still caught in her talon on her right side.

I held my ground, Maks's words ringing in my ears. I knew he was right, but that didn't mean I had to like it. Amalia landed and let Bryce go.

He crumpled to the ground, his legs useless under him.

I stared at him lying there, remembering all too well what he'd asked of me. That if he couldn't be healed, he wanted me to use my kukri blade on him.

Could I do it, though? Could I kill my brother to save him from the pain of living?

Chapter 22

My brother lay on the forest floor in front of me, the big pearlescent dragon healer behind him. Surreal was the only word I could come up with for what was happening. Bryce had asked me to finish his life if he could not be healed.

I put my hand to the kukri blade that rested in its sheath against my thigh. To use it on my brother. . . even though he'd asked—no, demanded—I do, I was not sure I was strong enough to follow through.

But. . . that glimpse into his pain, that feeling of being broken, I understood, and I would do what I could to give him the peace he craved. It was the least I could do considering my part in his injury.

No one spoke as I approached my brother. Not Maks, not Lila, and not Amalia. I made myself pull the knife and grip it loosely in my right hand. Lila stayed where she was, her tiny grip tightening and loosening over and over. Supporting me the only way she could.

I went to one knee, pulled the blade and buried the tip of it into the frozen ground. "Bryce? Do you want me to end it still?"

He lifted his head and pushed back to a sitting position, then pushed. . . up. Until he stood above me. Wobbling, but standing.

My jaw dropped. "Holy shit, she did it."

Amalia snorted. "It was not what either of you thought. He was not truly wounded."

I stared up at her. "What the fuck did you just say?"

She flopped down on her belly and stretched out, wrapping her tail and neck around our group, circling us close. "The wound in his back healed long ago. He had on him a gift from Ishtar. That 'gift' kept his legs from working."

Bryce yanked the necklace he wore, snapping the chain. From it hung a ring with the head of a lion etched into it. Just like mine. "She said it would help keep the pain at bay and keep the paralysis from spreading. I never showed you because. . . I thought it was a sign of weakness."

I just stared at it; how could I not? My mind was reeling with the implications. Of what Ish was trying to do, and why.

Bryce slowly turned to look at me. "Why would Ish do this?"

He might not know the answer, but I could feel it burning in my belly. "The jewels, this has all been about the jewels, Bryce. I was her thief. I proved it by getting that first diamond when I was supposed to stay in the Stockyards. As long as you were injured, I was guilty of damning your life to nothing. And I would deny her nothing if it meant she might be able to cure you."

Bryce reached for me and tugged me into a classic one-armed brother hug. "She used your guilt to do her dirty work and she kept me immobile for the same reason. To control us."

I wasn't about to let the moment pass. I wrapped my arms around him, my head fitting under his chin. He sighed and put his other arm around me, and I admit, I might have clung to him, needing to feel his strength buoy my own.

"We can never go back to the Stockyards," I said.

"I know. But I have a task yet to do." He dropped his arms and stepped back, turning to face Amalia. "You are sure about everything then? What you saw and what it means for all of us?"

"I am. The Emperor is waking even now. The magic in our world is growing and coursing over the land. There are very few that will be able to stand against him. You need four jewels, and four souls. You have two jewels." She handed the sapphire to Lila.

Then she tipped her head at the cracked diamond. "That one is for a male, one who is broken beyond repair."

Bryce grinned, still holding me with one arm. "Not it. Must be you, Maks."

I tensed, wondering if Bryce would remember that Amalia had called Maks a Jinn that was not a Jinn.

My brother turned his face to Maks. "I'll forgive you for being a Jinn only because you've kept her alive."

Me. Because Maks had kept me alive. "Hey, I saved his life, too, you know," I said.

Bryce tightened his arm on me. "I don't doubt it, little lion."

My eyes welled up. That was what our father had called me. I was never just a house cat to him, but a miniature black lion.

"Don't cry. There is no crying in the desert." Bryce chucked my chin with a finger.

I pushed him with one hand, not hard enough to really even move him but it felt like we were young again, and safe, which was stupid considering everything. "We're not in the desert, dummy."

He laughed, goddess, he *laughed*, and it was like the sun came out on my soul, warming it to the core. This was my brother, the one so quick to smile, so quick to protect others. I reluctantly let him go.

"What is the task you have to do?" I asked.

Amalia flicked the tip of her tail. "No, it is his task I gave him alone. He will know when the time comes."

I stared into her purple eyes and a shiver ran down my spine followed by a spark of strength that started in my belly and spread through me like liquid lightning. "If he dies for this task, I will come back for you, Amalia."

Maks groaned and even Lila gave a startled chirp.

Amalia's eyes narrowed. "You would threaten me?"

"Get my brother killed, and it will not be a threat," I said.

She let out a low rumble. "You see now, Bryce?"

I looked at my brother who was looking at me as if seeing me for the first time. "Yes. I see it."

What the hell were they talking about?

Amalia pulled back from us. "You must gain the gemstone from the dragons. Ishtar left the three most powerful jewels to the end, and you need them all if you are to have even a hope of stopping the Emperor."

Lila flew up to her grandmother and sat on her muzzle. "Will the dragons be free of the gemstone's curse if we take it?"

"It will take time, but eventually, yes, it will fade. Do not touch that gemstone, Lila. It will devour you." Amalia blew out a ring of smoke that floated up and over the two of them.

Lila tucked her wings to her sides and dropped off her grandmother's muzzle. "Then who should carry it?"

"The Jinn who is not a Jinn. It will fit well with his abilities. Do not use it unless you must," Amalia said.

We all looked at Maks. He frowned. "Why are you doing this, old one? Why, when so many of the other dragons would have torn us apart?"

"Those who live on the outskirts are not as affected by the power of the jewel. Those nearest the horde. . . they will not hesitate." She tipped her head to one side. "Three of you can be small enough to slip in unnoticed."

She grinned at Bryce. He glared up at her. "You're shitting me. I get my legs back and now you're telling me I can't use them?"

"I am telling you the best way to get the four of you out alive. Four from the desert, remember that. And. . . watch out for Merlin." She shook her head. "He thinks he is helping, but I am not sure he won't make things worse."

Awesome, that was just what I wanted to hear. "But he's not actively trying to hurt us?"

Amalia snorted another smoke ring. "He is not. But he is the Emperor's son and the one who put his father to sleep all those years ago. His father will be hunting for him to make him pay. There is nothing else I can tell you right now, except that your time is running short. If you wish to find those who were taken into the desert before they face the full wrath of the Jinn, you must go for the stone now."

How the hell had she known about Kiara? Or that Steve and Darcy had gone after her? A seer indeed then.

Her body faded from sight, turning into a mist that blew away on a gust of wind before anything else could be said.

I stared into the space where she'd been. Hope and fear warred inside my chest, and I decided right then that I would only let one of those emotions rule me, and it would not be fear.

"Mount up. Let's get this show on the road," I said as I swung onto Balder's back.

Bryce laughed. "Dad loved that saying, didn't he?"

I grinned back at him. "I only use it because he liked it. I think it's dumb."

Maks and Bryce did as I said, and it took me a moment to realize that Bryce hadn't argued. He'd let me lead. I glanced at him and he gave me a nod. "Lead on. You're in charge here, aren't you?"

My heart clenched, and my eyes filled up.

He frowned. "No crying, I said!"

"Then stop saying things you know will make me cry!" I shot back. I rubbed a hand across my nose and eyes, pushing the worst of the tears and snot away. "Lila, you lead us."

She flew backwards a few feet and winked at me. "I am on it, Alpha."

I pinched my lips together to keep back the exasperated snort that wanted to slip out of my mouth.

Lila turned east and drew us back into the forest. The ice rain had left sheets of—you guessed it—ice dangling precariously from the tree branches. As soon as we stepped under the cover of the forest, the sound of snapping wood filtered through from every direction. "The ice rain, it's dragging the trees down," I said.

Maks rode up beside me on my right, and Bryce to my left. Bryce looked around, his eyes never resting.

"Lila," he said quietly, "what can we expect to face?"

"Dragons." She snorted.

A laugh bubbled up in my chest, but I said nothing.

"No shit," he rolled his eyes, "but anything else besides the obvious? Spells, traps?"

She snapped her wings hard twice, bobbing in the air in front of us. "Well, yeah. Both really. The thing is, coming in this way toward the mound is good. Because there are no traps and spells directed toward interlopers coming from the wall. It just doesn't happen, so why waste the effort?"

I squinted one eye at her. "But? I hear a but coming."

She flipped over once in the air and then nodded. "Yeah, a great big *but*. Gigantic-ass *but*."

Bryce snorted. "What is it?"

Lila flew in loops around our heads. "We have to cross the whelping grounds to get to the mound."

The blood in my body might as well have all been sucked out right there. "You are. . . you're not serious, are you?"

She shrugged. "Why do you think Amalia said what she said about three of us being the smallest, the ones to break in?"

Three. . . but not three. Amalia had looked at me when she'd said that and it was almost as though I could hear her thoughts. "Not you, Lila. You'll stay with Bryce and watch our escape. Maks and I will slip in."

"Maks is as big as me, if you hadn't noticed," Bryce said.

"Not as a caracal, he's not." I drew a big breath, held it a moment before I blew it out in a rush. "We'll slip in, you two nail down the retreat. Lila, you good with that?"

"How will you know if the spells are onto you?" She frowned.

"Maks, you can see them coming?" I made myself look at him. His blue eyes locked with mine.

"You sure you trust me?"

I didn't look away, but into myself. He'd never done anything to harm me or my friends, far more than I could say for those I'd always thought I could trust. "Yes, I trust you."

He seemed surprised by that statement but covered

it quickly with a nod. "Then it is you and me going in. How far is it, Lila?"

"Couple hours," she said.

The four of us rode through the forest with only the sounds of the breaking trees for noise to cover our passage. I was sure at one point I saw a pair of rainbow eyes watching us, and that one of them winked at me.

I lifted my hand, acknowledging Pret's presence but didn't speak to the others. He would either keep quiet or he wouldn't. There was nothing I could do to change his mind.

The hours slipped by and I found myself walking next to my brother. Twice Bryce got off big Ali to walk beside her, a soft smile on his face.

I walked beside him. "I don't know how long it's been since I've seen you smile like that. Before the Oasis. Long before."

He lifted a hand and I tensed until he dropped it on my shoulder. "Do you remember when Shem tried to kidnap you?"

I put my hand over his. "Okay, yeah. Why are we bringing that up now?"

A sigh slid from him. "There is more to the story than crazy Uncle Shem going on a bender. You were what, four years old?"

I took his hand from my shoulder but didn't let him go. "Five. I was five."

"Do you remember much of it?" He quirked an eyebrow up at me, the question gentle but insistent.

I gave a quick nod. "I remember it all."

"Tell me what you remember. Please."

I wanted to roll my eyes, but again there was an urgency to his question.

I looped my arm through his, liking him at my side. I'd been so small when he'd been hurt we'd never stood side by side. I could get used to this, having him here and in my life again.

"I woke up and Shem was in my room. He called me kitten like he always did, and said he had to show me the stars, that they were in a special alignment just for me." I frowned, feeling Maks and Lila watching us, listening. "He scooped me up and put me on his back and then crawled through the window. There were nothing but clouds in the sky and I knew something was very wrong." I stepped over a log, gathering my memories around me.

"I think I knew that he meant me harm but probably didn't understand how bad it could have been. And then he was running, and he had a hold on me and there was a horse ahead of us. Jaxar, the fastest horse in the desert."

Bryce nodded. "And you fought him."

"The horse?" Lila shot up and into the conversation.

I laughed. "No, I shifted and fought Shem. He couldn't hold me. I was too flexible and fast and he couldn't get his hands on me."

"She shredded his hands," Bryce said, and the pride in his voice warmed me. "She ran back to us. Father and I followed the blood trail for days before we found him at a distant watering hole, his hands a fucking bloody mess."

I sucked in a sharp breath. "I didn't know you'd followed him."

He shrugged. "It was my first hunt for a traitor. He claimed you were special that he'd been called upon by the Emperor to protect you. To train you separate from the pride and show you the way of your abilities."

I didn't like the sounds of that. "Did you kill him?" Shem had never come back to the pride.

"I didn't. Father sent me home and said he'd handle it."

Handle it. We all knew what that meant.

Lila caught a gust of air and twisted sideways. "Wow, and that was your uncle? Your family is messed up."

I realized why the story tugged on her. I lifted my free hand and brushed it along her front leg. "Not in blood, but in the pride, yes. He was like a brother to our father."

"And he tried to kill you," Maks said behind us.

I shook my head. "No, I never felt that kind of malice from him. I was scared because in my heart I felt that he would take me away forever." I'd never really talked about that incident. My father had come back from the hunt and I'd slept between him and Bryce for months until I gained my courage back enough to sleep on my own.

I'd created a three-sided stall outside my bedroom window and my first pony, Gemma, lived there, breathing over me as we both slept.

"Why is this important now?" I asked Bryce. "I

mean it's a shit story and all, makes for a good way to pass the time, but. . ."

"Maybe he was on to something," Bryce said. "Maybe you *are* special, and we kept you from that."

"No. I would never want to be apart from you and Dad. As little time as we had with him, I wouldn't trade it for anything."

Bryce tightened his hold on my arm and tugged me into his side, hugging me. "Me neither. Though I really wish I hadn't been such a fucking pill the last fifteen years."

I snorted. "I assumed you were faking all along."

He pushed me away from him, laughing, and I was laughing and even Lila and Maks were grinning.

Peace settled around us in a place that only held death. The stories flowed between us, of growing up in the desert, of the tricks we'd played on our father, of the trouble we'd gotten into. All of it spilled up and out of the two of us, purging the dark side of our relationship and healing old wounds in ways nothing else could have.

Bryce glowed with happiness, and it was warm and felt like there was nothing we couldn't do now that we were together again. *Really* together, not just living the ghostly existence we had been in the Stockyards.

Those hours. . . I would look back on them as the last time I felt whole, when I had those I loved with me and I knew I was. . . enough. Just enough. I didn't feel like the weak link as I had for so many years and it caused a cascade of emotions that I barely held in check. I didn't feel like I had to prove anything.

That sense of wellbeing ended as the sun reached

243

midafternoon, the clouds shifting enough that a few shafts of light slid through.

Lila hovered in the air ahead of us, no longer moving forward. She turned and swept back, landing on the front of my saddle. "The whelping grounds are a quarter mile ahead, and in the center of them is the mound. It is open, a cave that dives deep. You want to go to the very bottom of it. The jewel will be in that hoard of treasures in a small wooden box. The jewel is in a ring setting."

Maks and I dismounted as did Bryce. I looked to Lila. "Okay, where should we come out? Where will you and Bryce be waiting for us? Here?"

She thought for a minute and then snapped her tail once in the air as if snapping her fingers.

"Run east to the marker. We will work our way to the outskirts of the grounds and wait for you there," she said, but there was a glint in her eye. "We need to hurry."

"You have a plan?" I reached out and touched her back. She bobbed her head.

"Yes, I do. But it means leaving you and Maks to fend for yourselves," she said.

Bryce grunted. "I can't leave her."

Lila growled. "You will get her killed. Night is falling. She and Maks will be able to slip into the mound far easier if it's just the two of them. If you were smaller in your shifted form, I'd say you could go, but you aren't. You're a damn lion."

The timing, though, seemed off. "The marker is hours away from here, less if we go hard. Maybe an hour at top speed. The jewel can't possibly be that deep," I pointed out.

"Three miles straight down," Lila said. "And trust me, you're going to have a hard push to get to it." Well fuck, that was not quite what I expected. "And assuming no one notices you're there," she added.

Maks snorted, almost a laugh. "What's new?"

I had to smile. "Can't be worse than an army of ice goblins."

"Or a giant White Wolf, Bear, and Raven," Lila said.

Bryce shook his head. "This is insane. We should be sticking together. That's how a pride survives."

But I heard it in his voice, he already knew it was the best choice to send me and Maks in alone. He would do what Lila and I were suggesting because no matter that he didn't like it, this plan would be our only shot at getting the jewel and getting all of us out of the Dragon's Ground alive.

I went to him and gave him a quick hug. "If we aren't back in a day, go to the desert. Help Steve and Darcy find Kiara. She's pregnant."

He stared at me. "They don't deserve you as an alpha, Zam."

"I'm not the—"

He put his hand over my mouth. "I say you are. And don't you let anyone tell you differently. You are the alpha of the Bright Pride Lions."

"There has been no official trial." I smiled at him, fighting the way his words sent a zing of energy down my spine.

Lila tapped me. "What's a trial?"

245

"I'm betting Steve didn't," Bryce said, and I shrugged.

"Are you really surprised?"

Lila tapped harder. "What trial?"

Bryce looked at her. "To become an alpha, you must prove yourself willing to give your life to save your pride in an official capacity."

"Well, shit, she's tried to save you and she did save Darcy," Lila pointed out.

He shook his head. "It has to happen after someone names her alpha. Which I just did."

I found myself standing a little straighter. "Then you are my second."

He grinned. "I never doubted that. Who else would you pick? That sheep fucker Steve?"

Lila snickered. "He didn't really fuck a sheep, did he? *Did he?*"

I shrugged. "After we were divorced, we caught him passed out in the sheep field one morning. Wool all over his crotch, his pants around his ankles."

She giggled and covered her mouth with her tiny claws to keep the noise down. "Oh, my goddess of the sky, that's hilarious. What I wouldn't have given to see that."

"At least it was after you kicked his ass out," Bryce said.

I snorted. "Still took me too long."

I knew we were both stalling. It was as if we'd found each other after fifteen years apart. His injuries and the lies of Ish had kept us separated and she'd known it would.

I glanced at Maks. "Ready?"

He nodded. "I am."

I gave Bryce one last hug, pulled Lila to me and squeezed her in my arms, and then I shifted to my cat form. I had my kukri blades and the flail on me, and not much else. Because what else was there?

A nose bumped into my side and I looked over to see Maks as a caracal next to me. His blue eyes were the same, but otherwise, he would have passed for a creature of the desert with his sandy coat and black-tipped ears.

"Let's go." I started out in the direction of the whelping grounds.

Lila called after us, or more accurately, after Maks.

"Maks, do not be a poisonous back-bunched toad. Look after her!"

I snorted and looked over at Maks. "Richard the Third."

He rolled his eyes and looked over his shoulder at Lila. "Thy tongue out venoms all the worms of the Nile, Lila. As always."

She laughed, and I joined in. "Very good, the Cymbeline?"

"Yes, I read it in the Stockyards. It had a number of annotations, I assume yours?" He glanced at me as he spoke.

I smiled. "Yes, those were mine." We trotted along at a good clipped pace, leaving Lila and Bryce behind us. My belly grumbled, irritated that we'd only eaten the dried foods we had on us as we'd traveled through the forest.

Before I could say anything, the forest around us

began to thin, the trees broken and charred in places until we stood at the very edge of the whelping ground.

Night was still an hour off, but the dusky, cloud-filled sky was enough cover that we drew as close as we dared to see what lay ahead of us.

Maks let out a breath as though he were a balloon being popped. "How in the fires of the desert hell are we going to cross this?"

I stared at the scene in front of us. How indeed.

Chapter 23

Merlin made sure that the satyr Marcel was able to keep up as they ran from the Stockyards, but he needn't have been concerned. The goat man easily paced the galloping horse Merlin rode.

"We have to pick up someone before we go to Zam," Merlin said.

"Please tell me it's a beautiful woman," Marcel said.

"It is, but she's not for you," Merlin said with a shake of his head. "She is a priestess of Zeus with a wicked temper and I rather like her."

"Damn, a priestess? They are amazing in the sack, you know. Zeus teaches them all his dirty tricks," Marcel said and then continued to ramble on about a priestess he'd known years before and all the fun they'd had, most of which involved positions Merlin knew to be impossible. But they sounded good.

No, Merlin's mind was racing ahead. If Ish could

not be counted on in the least, their problems were far deeper than he'd thought, worse even than he and Flora possibly realized when they'd started this journey. He frowned. He would have to tell her all the truth now and allow for her to leave if she wanted.

His shoulders slumped. He'd been an asshole most of his life, he knew that. It was in his blood after all.

Now, he was doing his best to change, but it was hard. If he didn't tell Flora the truth, then he knew she would stay. That would give him longer to prove that she wanted him in her life. Longer for him to prove that he was not the man the world had known.

He shook his head. That was not the important thing at the moment. No, he had to find a way to Zam. He had to tell *her* the truth about her lineage.

"Fuck," he growled under his breath. Things were getting out of hand in a damn hurry.

"Yes, that's what I've been talking about, flouncing!" Marcel laughed. "Did you really flounce Ishtar?"

His jaw ticked. "A long time ago, yes. I did it to irritate the Emperor."

"Did it work?"

"He tried to kill me, so I suppose it worked," Merlin muttered, and Marcel let out a braying goat laugh that made the hair on Merlin's neck stand at attention. Sweet baby goddess, that was a horrid noise.

It wasn't long before they came into sight of the hut he'd left Flora sleeping in, and before he even looked inside, he knew she was gone.

"Damn it, Flora." He pinched the bridge of his nose.

"Did you leave her a note?" Marcel circled around the hut, sniffing.

"I did. I told her I wouldn't be long, that there was something I had to do." Which begged the question, just what was she up to? "Maybe she went to Zam?" Merlin frowned, thinking. That was possible. But he wasn't so sure. He circled the hut, still frowning. There at the doorstep was something that made his heart stutter. The burn mark from a bolt of lightning, and a thin line of golden sand that lay over top of it.

He spun his horse and put it into a gallop, heading east. Stupid, this was stupid, and he knew it. But what would his world be like if he didn't have the woman at his side he knew he'd waited for all these years.

"Wait!" Marcel yelled. "That's the wrong way! You said Zam is in the west!"

"She is," he shouted back. "Go to her; tell her what you've seen. I must go to the desert!"

The Jinn had taken Flora.

Chapter 24

The night seemed to fall in increments, an inch at a time in the surrounding forest, but that darkness didn't take away what lay in front of Maks and me.

The whelping ground of the dragons was immense. That was the only word I had for it. The female dragons curled around their nests, their noses touching the tips of their tails regardless of their size, color, or body style. Some had wings, some didn't. Some were huge, others were no bigger than the horses.

It was the sheer number of them I couldn't wrap my brain around. Each one curled on a nest that held dozens of eggs.

Maks put his mouth close to my ear. "There has to be a thousand females here."

That was what I'd estimated the number at. A thousand times dozens of eggs? How the fuck had we not had our world overrun by dragons?

I turned to him, whispering my question. "How is this possible?"

"Egg trade." He frowned. "The Jinn make it happen."

I shivered and pressed closer to him. "They take the eggs?"

"The dragons fight them, but, yes, they take the eggs. Any of the females would be lucky to have a single youngling from a big nest. Most end up with nothing."

Something in my heart cracked at the plight of these mothers. I was not a mother, of course, but I could only imagine a child of my own snatched away while I fought to protect them. A low growl rumbled out of me, and I couldn't stop it.

"We can do nothing about it right now," Maks said. "We have to focus on the jewel."

He was right. I knew he was, but I was fucking pissed. The Jinn, I had no words for the amount of hatred I held for them inside my body.

I lowered myself to my belly. "Time to go, Maks. Stay low, follow me."

He nodded and tucked himself low to the ground. He blended in better to the dead winter grass with his mostly brown coat. Better than me with my jet-black fur.

The first nest we had to pass, I crept close and couldn't resist peeking up over the edge even while Maks swatted at me. The closer we stayed to the nests, the better cover in my estimation as their height helped to hide us. It would be out in the open that we'd get picked off before we could so much as say "duck."

The female dragon's eyes were closed. She was a big

girl, about twice the size of a horse. Her body was covered with deep gray scales with flecks of silver and white flickering through them that caught the light of the stars above us. With each breath she took, her body tightened around her eggs, then relaxed slightly, then tightened again. A mother's love. I couldn't deny that she loved her not-so-little eggs. She was nothing short of breathtaking. Her eyes remained closed and I found myself unable to look away as dual tears trickled from them. Her mouth moved silently, and I could all too easily imagine the whispered prayer to her gods to spare her children. I had to look away, the pain in her face, the pain of loss to come rolled from her and into my own body and it was too much for me.

I bit my lower lip until it bled, hoping the pain would keep me on target. I was doing all I could to dislodge the swell of emotions. Maks patted at my hip with a paw, encouraging me forward. Again, he was right. Another time we would help them. But not today. Today we had others to save, but my heart tugged me toward the mother dragons, toward their plight. I had to fight to keep my own breath even, to keep my emotions in check. But I was losing the battle.

We slid from nest to nest as quickly and stealthily as possible.

"Who is there?" A voice boomed above us at the tenth or eleventh nest we tried to pass. I pinned my body against the edge of it, Maks following suit. The female dragon above us rose up, and up, and up. She was slender, whip-like with four sets of wings and a long lean body that was more serpentine than dragon. Golden brown with markings of black and red, she was quite stunning as she searched the area, her eyes scanning for intruders, aka, us. If not for the fact that I knew she was about to see us I could have watched her all day. All she had to do was look down and she'd see me and Maks tucked against her nest. Her tail slid past us, whacking me on top of the head with a flick before it swept upward. She hovered over her nest, looking out around her, curls of smoke trailing out her nose. Her agitation spilled over to the other dragons.

We were good and royally fucked if we just stayed there.

I bit my lower lip again and stayed still, knowing I was about to throw the dice hard, and hope that I could make them believe me. There was nothing else I could do.

Breathing hard, I crept forward. Maks clawed at my hip, trying to stop me. But I had an idea and it would either work or it wouldn't, but we had no choice. We were about to be discovered even if we stayed still.

I stepped out from the side of the nest, sat on my butt, and let out a pitiful meow. The dragons encircling me shot up as if I'd slapped them each with a claw-tipped paw.

I stood, lifted my tail straight into the air and meowed again, then hopped up onto the golden, red, and black dragon's nest. She let out a roar, and I did the only thing I could.

I rubbed my chin against the egg closest to me, marking it as my own—claiming it. I walked through the nest, marking each, feeling the little heartbeats inside, seeing the thin shells pulse with the life within them. The mother dragon lowered to the ground and her head snaked my way.

"I see you, shifter. What are you doing? You can't possibly think you could fight us?" She hissed after she spoke, menace in every line of her body.

"I'm going to find your babies," I said, and my voice choked on the words because I could feel her sorrow as if it were my own. "I hate the Jinn. They destroyed my family and I didn't know. . . I didn't know they were destroying other families too." I looked up at her, lifted myself onto my back legs and put my paws on her face. I rubbed my cheek against hers. "I feel your pain, dragon. I feel it and it makes me want to destroy the Jinn for all of us."

She stared at me, her jewel-bright eyes dark as the ocean filling with tears. "No one has ever seen our pain, little cat. They only think us monsters that could battle anyone, but. . ."

"I see it, mama. And I will hold it to me. I swear I will find those you've lost," I said softly. "I swear it." Goddess, what was I saying? But the truth was, my words were my bond as surely as if I'd made a blood pact. I knew I could never leave these mother dragons to continue to mourn the loss of their children.

The other females drew closer, and I should have been afraid, I should have been fucking terrified at what I was doing. They could eat me with a single bite, tear me apart and all would be lost. But as I'd felt their pain, I felt the trust they were putting in me to follow through.

Any of them could have destroyed us, but they

didn't. With each of those who came to me I lifted to my back legs and rubbed my furry cheek against their scaled muzzles, marking them.

The minutes ticked by, and though I knew I hadn't met every female, there were many who sat around the red, gold, and black dragon's nest.

"You need something to find the children, don't you?" the first dragon asked softly. "You need the gemstone?"

I nodded. "It will save us all if I take it."

She bobbed her head. "Touch nothing else. Take only the gemstone. It is a vile curse and we would be well rid of it." She rolled back away from me. "I see the truth of your words, little cat. You are growing into your own, though I think the journey will be longer than you realize."

I leapt down from the nest and nudged an unmoving Maks. "Come on."

The female dragons watched with curiosity as Maks crept out. Eyes narrowed all around and I knew why. He was a Jinn. Surely, they would know that. What the fuck had I been thinking? Horror and panic shot through me.

I'd just sentenced him to death.

"Don't hurt him. He's helping me!" I leapt to stand in front of him, but the big female swept her head and pushed me out of the way so that she was right in front of Maks. "You are not what you think you are. Any more than she is. Do not let your belief lead you, young one. Follow your heart."

He stared up at her. "I am sorry for your pain. I feel

257

it as does Zam, and it guts me. I swear I will help her find your children."

Oh, shit, I hadn't meant for him to get caught up in that. But he seemed to mean the words. She tipped her head to him.

"As I am sorry for yours," she whispered. "She has opened our hearts with her fierce spirit. But the men of our flight will not be so happy with your presence. Go, we will cover for you as long as we can."

I didn't wait, but scooted out in front, Maks tight to my ass. We raced by the nests now. What would have taken hours of creeping, we covered in a little under ten minutes. The gamble had paid off in spades.

The mound rose ahead of us, a gargantuan heap of dirt and wood that had been woven together. Three hundred feet across and over thirty feet high at the very peak of the mound, it was big enough for many dragons to go inside, but the pathway was set up for only one dragon. Still plenty big enough for two small cats.

As we drew close, I realized it wasn't wood holding the structure up, but bones.

I didn't let myself slow but raced into the entrance with Maks at my side. We only slowed once we were under the cover of the mound. My eyes worked well in the dark, but I knew at some point there would be no ambient light and we would be screwed. Especially if the hoard was as deep down as Lila had thought. Three miles was far underground. Something I should have thought of.

"Maks, did you bring a lighter?"

"Yes." He grunted but didn't shift. "There are spells

here, Zam. I can feel them on my skin. I need to be in the front."

I slowed and let him overtake me. "What do you think they meant by you aren't what you think you are?"

"I'm not sure." His tail lashed side to side. "I never knew my mother. It could mean anything."

I frowned. "I never knew mine either."

"The mother dragons said the same thing about you," he pointed out as we started down a wide slope.

"I know, and that makes me nervous," I said softly. As strange as it was, now that I was slowly embracing who and what I was, and what I was capable of, I didn't want anything else.

I didn't get much further than that in my musings.

"Stop," Maks whispered, his voice urgent. "This is bad, Zam. Real bad."

I looked past him, my eyes picking up dim shapes. "What is it?"

"You see those two statues on either side of the path?" He tipped his nose to the left and then to the right.

The statues were dark stone dragons cut into the wall, as big as real dragons. Their stone wings spread wide but also curled as if they were cupping the air. They stood on four legs, their necks arched so that their muzzles were pointed down on the path we had to walk.

"The position of the wings is weird." I frowned and shook my head.

"The wings aren't what we have to worry about. The mouths, they are pointed at the path. Could be acid will pour out of them, or fire, or electricity, anything is possible," he said. "The spell around them is massive, Zam. I can't break it."

I didn't look at him. The wings had my eyes locked to them. "That leaves us two options. We race through and hope to all that is holy in the earth and sky that we are faster than the trap, or we go over."

He turned his face to me. "Are you serious? You want to outrun a spell?"

My heart picked up speed. "If I take off my chain, my curse will kick into full onslaught. I can manipulate it. I can get us through."

He closed his eyes, pinching them closed tightly. "Marsum knows you're alive, Zam. He's changed the curse. I don't know what he's done, but he's changed it."

I stared at him. "And you thought to wait until now to tell me this rather minor detail?" What the hell was he thinking?

"I didn't think you'd want to take it off!" he snarled. "You don't want to live with the curse, who would? And while you used it to work for you before, it's not like you made any mention of using it again!"

I shoved my face into his so we were nose to nose even though he was bigger than me as a caracal. "Don't hide shit from me, Maks. I can't make decisions that will actually be good if I don't know the fucking truth!"

"Fine!"

"Fine!" I snapped right back at him. There would be no taking off the chain for right now. "Then we climb over. They won't be thinking about that."

"Right, because they would have thought nothing of shifters trying to steal their jewels." He snorted.

I let the growl slide out of me. "Stop being a shit because you're scared. I'm scared too. So unless you have a better idea, I say we opt for speed. Climb the stone dragons as fast as we can."

He gave a tight nod. "You take the right. I'll go left. Maybe that will confuse whatever spell they have going on here. But wait for me as soon as it is safe. Okay?"

"Got it. Stop as soon as bad things stop happening." I lifted a paw and whacked him on the nose. "In case I die, that's for not telling me the truth."

His eyes narrowed, he leaned over and bit the back of my neck and shook it. "And that's for risking our lives without any thought."

His teeth bit hard enough to send a luscious shiver down my spine to the tip of my tail and my legs turned into jelly. I had to fight to hold back the whimper on my lips, the need to push harder against his mouth. In two-legged form, I could only too easily see him behind me, his hands on my hips, his mouth on the back of my neck. Biting me *hard*, then trailing my skin with hot, wet kisses.

I jerked away from him, unable to meet his gaze. "To the right then." Damn it, my voice was husky and breathy and when he answered, his wasn't much better.

"Right, and I'll see you on the other side."

I trotted away from him. Space. I needed space to get my heart under control.

I stared up at the stone dragon and a shiver of a different kind ran through me. I had a feeling this was not going to go as planned.

I hate it when I'm right.

Chapter 25

I approached the stone dragon embedded in the tunnel's wall slowly at first, trying to see if it did anything, or if I felt anything. Like a warning that we were about to set off an alarm or some shit like that.

"Maks?"

"Yeah?"

"When do we go fast?"

Our words, as quiet as they were, seemed to be the trigger for everything happening at once. The stone dragons breathed in, and their wings stretched wide as the sound of stone cracking filled the air.

"NOW!" Maks yelled.

I bounded forward, not waiting for any other encouragement. I put everything I had into my speed and the stone dragon seemed to sense me coming. Fuck a screaming duck, this was about to get ugly. There was literally no way around it.

The dragon twisted its stone head toward me as its

eyes slowly began to open, a brilliant red flickering ember glowing within them.

"Fire, it's going to be fire!" I yelled.

"Go across its back!" Maks hollered, and I didn't dare tell him what I thought of that.

Of course, Captain Obvious, I was thinking of running right under its fire-breathing fucking mouth. I bared my teeth as I ran, irritation driving me.

The stone dragon pulled away from the wall, its body cracking the stone connection. I reached the leg closest to me and jumped with all I had to get up onto its still-bent knee. The rock it was cut out of was slick, and hard to grasp even with my claws. I flexed my paws and dug in hard, using whatever strength the flail and my kukri blades gave me. I glanced at the head as it swung around, the eyes still opening.

Faster, I needed to go faster.

I leapt again, bounding along the thigh and then hip of the stone dragon, stumbling as it wrenched itself free.

The light in the mound suddenly changed as the left-side dragon let out a blast of flame. I didn't dare look. There was nothing I could do to save Maks, there was nothing I could do but try to get through.

We needed that jewel.

We needed to save the dragon babies.

I scrambled upward and a stone wing slammed into me, sending me flying off the dragon and into the loose sand below. I rolled and bolted. There was a crackle of flames.

Run, Zamira, run! I could have sworn my father yelled to me from the other side of the grave.

I turned on the speed, giving everything I had to my legs, my lungs, my muscles. The flames burst toward me, the air heated and the fur on my body sizzled as the flames wrapped around me. I held my breath and closed my eyes.

Goddess hold me tight, I thought.

And then the heat was gone, and I was barreling ahead with my eyes closed. I opened my eyes and there was nothing but darkness and the stone dragons remaining behind me. I slid to a stop.

"Maks?" I called out.

The stone dragons roared in unison.

Oh, fuck.

Though my fur was singed, and I hated the idea of facing the flames again, I couldn't leave him there.

He wouldn't leave me.

I raced toward the dragon statues and had to dig hard to get purchase in the loose sand. "You dumb fuckers are too slow to catch me!"

That's right, when all else fails, use the always solid "piss off the enemy" trick.

Two stone heads turned toward me, flames already spilling out their pie holes. A streak of brown raced out from behind the second dragon, and though he was limping, it was Maks.

"Run, you fool!" he yelled, and I spun, kicking up sand as though I'd just used a litter box. I couldn't help it. They could kiss my furry black ass.

I leaned into Maks and took some of his weight. The stone dragons behind us went silent and we slowed, the darkness holding us.

When we stopped, our breath came in ragged gulps. Maks had a bit of singeing on one side of his face, and the same front leg seemed to be what was slowing him up.

He blinked over at me. "Thanks."

"Yeah, well, whatever." I shook my head, unable to formulate a better response. "You okay?"

"Bruised, a bit burned. Looks like you got a trim?" He sniffed at me and crinkled up one nostril. "Burnt hair."

I bobbed my head and let out breath. "That probably wasn't the worst of the traps set, was it?"

He shook his head. "Doubtful. And we have to get all the way back by them too once we have the jewel."

"No problem, we got this." I took a step and my foot settled into the ground, and sunk.

I grimaced as I looked over at Maks. "Umm. I think I just set off another trap."

"Fuck. Run!"

That seemed to be our motto for everything, but I didn't disagree.

There was a ping of metal against the stone walls. Spears, arrows and other sharp projectiles erupted from the walls on either side. I dropped to my belly. "Go low!"

Maks did what I said and we crept forward, the weapons mostly missing us. One cut across the flesh of my lower back and I fought to keep my belly down, to not rear up in pain.

"Motherfucker!" I screamed. "Piece of shit, whoever built this place needs to die a painful, long death while someone peels the skin of his balls like a fucking kiwi!"

Maks started laughing. "Stop that! I can't keep my head down when I'm laughing!"

"Son of a goat-herding satyr. I'm going to ram a spear up your ass and scramble your guts!" I yelled as something hot zipped across the back of my neck, opening the flesh. I couldn't go any faster.

Maks let out a cry that told me he'd just been hit. "Faster!"

I scrambled forward, army crawling as best I could. My body was pissed off and it took all I had to keep myself not only low to the ground, but moving at a rapid pace.

Then as suddenly as it had set off, it was over. I rolled to my side, panting.

"How many hits did you take, Maks?"

He lay beside me, his eyes closed breathing hard. "Just the one. You?"

"Two. Across my lower back and my neck. We were damn lucky whoever built this didn't think a cat would sneak in."

He grunted. "The lower ones were set up so they could pass through but not hit the floor. We are indeed lucky we have these shapes and nothing bigger."

And we were lucky that I'd taken the hits I had and not Maks. If we'd had our positions reversed, I would have taken no hits and he would have been killed.

I kept that thought to myself. No need to point out what I thought was the obvious. That was his job.

I groaned and rolled to my belly, tucking my paws under me. "I just need to breathe a minute."

He scooted closer, his bigger frame warm, and I

leaned into him. "It's only going to get worse, more dangerous."

I twisted and put my head on his back. "My dad told me about this hero he knew outside the wall. His name was Indiana Jones, and he faced stuff like this all the time. And he was just a human and he survived. If he can survive boulders chasing him and falling into snake pits, then this should be easy for us."

"A human did all that?" Maks adjusted himself so that he curled around me a little, his tail twining with mine. "That's unbelievable."

"Well, my dad was no liar so it has to be true. If Indy can do all that, we can do this."

Maks sighed. "Maybe we should have hired this Indiana Jones to get the stone for us."

I laughed softly and then cringed. The movement pulled on the two slash marks through my back, sending sharp pains rippling across my spine. "I'll be sure to see if Bryce has a way of contacting him. For next time."

We rested there until I started to get drowsy, telling me it was time to move. "Up, we have to go." I stood and groaned as I stretched carefully. I was far from healed but the rest had allowed the wounds to at least start to stitch back together.

Maks didn't sound much better as he pushed to his feet. "Okay, that's two traps. How many more do you think we've got left?"

I laughed, though the situation was far from funny. "A hundred?"

"Gods, don't say that." He scrunched his eyes shut

and then frowned, as he opened them again, his caracal brows dipping low. "Does it seem brighter to you?"

I stared around, noticing a slight glow ahead of us as though it were far away. "Yeah, it does. We don't have a choice, we have to go toward it, seeing as it's coming from further down the tunnel."

We started off at a walk, testing the ground with each paw we put down. Now that the adrenaline had worn off, we were slow, sluggish, and that was a bad sign. I needed to fix this.

"AH FUCK!" I screamed and jumped straight up into the air, letting loose with a cat screech that would make anyone's hair stand on end.

Maks let out a snarl and spun in a circle, his body puffing up, as he looked for whatever had set me off. I dropped to the ground laughing so hard tears gathered in my eyes.

"What, what is it?" His eyes were wide, and his mouth hung open as he panted a little. I could hear his heart as it pounded wildly.

"Got your heart rate up, didn't I?" I grinned at him and his jaw dropped open.

"You. . . are you shitting me?" He gasped the words as though he truly couldn't believe what I'd done.

Laughing, I trotted out in front of him. "Come on, now that the blood is pumping let's see what that glowing globe of death has waiting for us."

"Holy fucking hell, you did that to get my heart rate up? Are you insane?" He threw the question at me.

I shrugged as he caught up, still smiling to myself. "If we're slow, we're going to die. I could feel the lethargy dragging us down." I tipped my head, thinking. "Almost like it was a spell."

He snapped his jaw shut and his eyes narrowed, but not at me. "Damn it, you're right. It was subtle, a pull on us that would lull us into complacency."

Something else was coming, and coming soon.

Just my bad luck.

Chapter 26

Maks continued to lead the way through the darkness of the dragons' mound, testing for spells that would want to leap out and tear us a new one.

"Still nothing?" I asked, pitching my voice low.

"No. Which makes me nervous. I think you were right about that previous spell, it was meant to subdue our reflexes," he said, his voice also quiet.

I bobbed my head in agreement even though he couldn't see me. It made sense that if we made it past the first two challenges that we would be fast, savvy, and on our toes. Best way to kill us would be to slow down those reflexes. The move was clever, devious, and I had to give props to whoever made this place. If we'd been a stitch less smart, we'd be dead.

In other words, Steve, would have been dead ten times over by now.

The tunnel dipped downward at a steady pitch,

and the glow ahead of us grew with each step of our paws. Steady, pulsing, the light was a deep red that made me think not of fire exactly but something deadlier. I just couldn't put my finger—pardon me, paw —on it.

"Hold," Maks said, and I froze between steps with a front paw in the air.

"What?"

He was quiet long enough that the irritation began to flow upward. "Maks, what is it?"

"The ground, do you feel it? Like it's rumbling." He went very still, his ears the only movement on him as they swiveled around. I focused on the ground beneath my feet.

He was right; there was a tremor. One that was growing faster than I wanted to believe. "Well, shit. If I know anything about this place that can't be a good sign."

"No. Keep moving forward. Don't run unless we have to. I think this one is going to try to drive us toward something very bad." He started off in a jog and I hurried to catch up.

I swallowed hard, thinking about what it could be. Water? Yes, it could be water flooding toward us. My blood ran cold at the thought. Gods, not water, anything but water. I could too easily imagine the tunnel we were in flooded with a raging river that filled the space so there was nowhere to breathe, sweeping us along until we stopped struggling. This was not like the river escaping the gorcs. Water of that magnitude in this place would mean certain death.

The rumbling began to shake the walls and I fought not to hurry.

"Breathe, Zam."

"What if it's water?" I blurted out. "We won't be able to escape it!"

I turned my head as a sound like stone on stone whispered to me. "Maks. I think we should run."

"Yeah. Let's go. But don't use it all up."

We took off, fast, but not top speed. I stretched out beside him, tail up and racing as though there was a prize at the end. I suppose there was a prize, but the jewel was more than that. It was hope.

I drew deep breaths in and tried to keep my heart from hammering out of control. The sudden spikes of fear were not like me, and I knew then I must have triggered a spell again.

"Fuck off with your spells!" I snapped and Maks shot a look at me. There was no time to explain, I could only hope he caught on.

We dropped down suddenly, the path disappearing from under us in a ten-foot plunge. I grunted as I hit the ground, stumbled and the sound behind us increased.

Stone on stone, and then a crunch of bone that was as distinct as a boom of thunder. . . What the hell was coming our way? Surely not one of the stone dragons.

We were running almost straight down, easily at a thirty-degree angle and gravity seemed to tug at our limbs, pulling us faster and faster.

There was a mighty boom behind us as whatever chased us took the ten-foot drop. I dared a glance back and my eyes tried to bug out of my head. Behind us was a rolling ball of death that bounced off the sides of the wall. It was not only stone but bones that had been rounded and compressed, and it fit through the tunnel with very little room to spare—in other words, there would be no dodging it. I saw a few heads, skin, and limbs of creatures the boulder had squashed already protruding here and there. I did not want to add to that.

"Oh, hell no. I am not fucking Indiana Jones!"

Maks looked back and groaned. "Shit, just run!"

"It's driving us, you were right." But driving us to what?

I tried to recall what I knew of Indy's adventures, but it was pitifully little. How had he escaped the rolling boulder of death?

The glow ahead and the boulder behind, there was no good way out of this.

Maks and I kept pace ahead of the boulder, but there was no slowing, not for an instant. And there was no chance to speak or come up with a plan.

It seemed like that was the goal. The glow was no longer just light, but warmth too and I could see it coming in through—

"It's a drop-off!" I screamed.

There was no time for Maks to respond. The boulder was only inches off our tails, and the drop-off was there. The tunnel narrowed, and I knew without seeing, the boulder would hang partway out to push us into the drop, but it wouldn't follow us.

"Go to the side!" I yelled and then there was no more time, only reflexes. We hit the opening and I shot to the right, Maks to the left as the boulder slammed into the space. I scrambled against the wall of the cliff we were suddenly on. My paws trembled as I stood on what was essentially pieces of a ledge that weren't a ledge, just tiny rocks that I could cling to. The boulder, having done its job, was pulled back by some inexplicable force.

Grinding, the sound of more bones breaking, of the wall giving away in chunks and pieces. I waited for it to withdraw before I leapt back to the opening. I glanced once at the boulder, but it seemed uninterested in us now.

"Maks?" I yelled for him and shot to the right side.

He was on the cliff, but a good fifteen feet down and clinging by only his front paw.

I let out a breath and shifted into my two-legged form. I couldn't help him as a house cat, not this time.

I whipped off my cloak and held the hood, wrapping it around my wrist once. "Hang on."

"Nah, I was thinking of letting go, see if I could fly," he said, his voice as dry as a popcorn fart. I rolled my eyes and lowered myself to my belly, dangling my cloak. It swayed about a foot above his head.

"Can you push off and grab it?"

"I have to." He growled and then he leapt upward. There was a moment where I wasn't sure that he'd reach it, where I thought he was going to fall, and then his claws sunk into the middle of the cloak and he hugged it tightly.

He was only about forty pounds in this form and I brought him up hand over hand. He flopped beside me and shifted back to two legs.

"Thanks."

"You're going to owe me a lot after this," I said, breathing hard.

"I can think of a few ways to repay you." He turned his head to me and gave me a slow smile.

I struggled to swallow. "What about all this *we can't be together*?"

"Well, at this rate we're both going to die before anyone is going to give a shit who we are flouncing." He grinned. "So why not at least die happy?"

I leaned toward him, fully intending to kiss him when I saw what lay out before us. I froze in mid-movement and just stared.

"Oh, my gods."

"Well, maybe, but we haven't. . . wait, what do you see?" He twisted around, and I just pointed.

At the bottom of the cliff was an island, and on the island was a hoard of jewels, gold, silver, precious metals, weapons, anything of value I could have ever thought of was there. And it was surrounded by—wait for it—

"Is that a moat filled with lava?" Maks breathed out.

"Yeah." I nodded. "I think it is." I stared at it, wondering just how we were going to cross it without being burned to a pair of crispy kitty cats.

I drew a breath and let it out slowly. "First thing first. We need to get down there." I looked around the edge of the tunnel's drop-off. The cliff wall was steep with very few reasonable handholds, as we'd found out, and it was too high to jump. A hundred-foot drop would break bones, if not outright kill even a pair of supes like us.

I dropped to a crouch and then stretched out on my belly so I could look out over the edge. Directly below me, there were notches in the wall almost like they'd been placed there on purpose and not just natural depressions. "Look at this. Think we can use it?"

Maks dropped beside me and we stared together at the cliff wall. "No. There's no way. Even on four legs, damn it. There's no way down, Zam."

He was wrong, though. I reached up to the necklace I wore. "Then we need to change our luck. You said Marsum shifted something in the curse?"

Maks looked at me, his eyes full of worry. "Far as I can tell."

"And you can't change the curse. You can't remove it?"

"I'm sorry, I can't. I mean I could, but it would kill you," he said.

I gave a sharp tug, snapping the chain. "Then we have nothing else to do but see if it will work in our favor."

Maks surprised me. "Yeah, I think you're right. Time to throw the dice and see what comes up."

I grinned and laid my cheek against the cold stone. "Let's hope it's not a pair of snake eyes."

He snorted and rolled to his back. "So you want to just lie here and wait?"

I closed my eyes, letting my senses roam, falling into the same kind of trance I'd used to find Bryce in the forest. "Wait, and the world will provide."

"That doesn't sound like you."

"My mother said it once, I think," I whispered. I

slowed my breathing until I felt the stone below me, tracing the veins of quartz, the deposits of gold and silver, the heat of the lava, the smell of dragon musk so faint, I'd not breathed it in before.

My skin prickled as I let myself sink further, feeling the earth around me, seeing the traces of those who'd passed. All of them dead, but for the lines that streaked through the air. Those were the dragons that had been here, and they vibrated with vitality. Blue, red, green, black, shimmering and dancing. Beautiful, they were stunning in their life forces.

I tipped my head so my closed eyes faced toward the tunnel. The lines of all those lives lost who'd come to steal the dragons' hoard was far more than I would have thought. Hundreds, some new, many older. . . a flicker of gold caught my eyes. The threads of a lion shifter— one that still lived. But how was that possible?

Behind my eyelids came a flicker of the outline of a body, slowly and indistinct at first. The person came into focus and slowly became a woman who could have been my sister with her long dark hair and brilliant green eyes. The angle of her cheeks, the twist of her lips as she smiled down at me, they were so familiar. Memories tickled across my mind, pulling me into the past. She had more curves than me, but otherwise we were very similar in build. I sat up, with my eyes still closed. "Mom?"

Maks shifted beside me.

"Zam?"

I reached out blindly and put a hand on him to

shush him up while I spoke to her. "Mom, we need to get the jewel."

She smiled, lifted a hand to me, and then she faded as she pointed at the tunnel beyond us, then she was gone again. I clenched my jaw and pushed to my feet. I shouldn't have been surprised. How would she know? But that golden thread of a lion shifter, it drew me forward like a beacon. Whoever it was still lived, and he was close. I let my eyes open and the golden thread remained.

"Zam, what are you doing?"

"There's a lion shifter here," I said softly. "Maybe he can help us."

"You think that's a good idea? If he's here, he's here for the hoard. Not to help anyone but himself." Maks pushed to his feet beside me.

I shrugged. "Could be, but then he's going to think the same of us."

I took a step along the golden strand, seeing it shimmer and dance. "He's hurt, I think."

"Great. Another broken lion," Maks muttered.

Another time I would have whacked the back of his head. That was my brother he was referring to, a brother who was no longer broken.

As it was, the golden thread shimmered, faded and then pulsed stronger. I hurried after it up the tunnel we'd come down. The steep angle made my thigh muscles burn and the fatigue of all the running, leaping, dodging and surviving made itself known to me. I let out a low hiss, using the side wall to pull myself farther up.

"Just where is he?" Maks asked.

"Close, that's all I know," I said, distracted by the golden thread. How long since we'd found a new lion shifter? Years.

The golden strand took a hard left turn, straight into the wall across from me. I stared at it. "That has to be wrong."

"What?"

I pointed to the wall. "The lion shifter, he is in there. But that's not possible. How can he be in the wall?"

"He, are you're sure it's a he?" Maks asked.

I reached out and touched the golden strand, feeling the energy of it as clearly as if it were a physical thing. "Yes. I don't know. . . how. . . it just feels like a man."

Maks stepped up to the wall. "Could be a hidden door?" He slid his fingers over the stone, pressing and making swirls here and there.

A sound further up the tunnel caught my ears, and I turned my head to hear better. "Maks, is that the bellow of a bull dragon?"

"Fuck," he snarled. "Help me. There has to be a way to get this open."

I leaned into the wall, feeling for a latch, a catch, something. The bellow up the tunnel came again, followed by a rather distinct voice.

"Trespassers are destroyed!"

"Oh, that is not going to go well for us," I grunted as I shoved on another piece of stone. Nothing, nothing was going as planned.

I reached for my pocket and felt for the necklace as a radical, stupid, horrifying, idea came to me. A dragon that flew was coming our way.

We needed to get to the island surrounded by a moat of lava and no bridge. But a flying dragon? That could be the ticket we needed. Or at least what I needed.

"Maks, shift," I said. He looked at me, nodded and shifted. He stared up at me from his four legs and I pointed at the stone wall. "Now stay here and see if you can get the shifter out, I'm going to get the gemstone."

"Wait, there is a dragon coming!" he snarled after me. "He'll kill you!"

I gave him a half-grin. "We all die, Maks. But today is not that day for me."

Chapter 27

I ran for the end of the tunnel leading down to the dragons' hoard and the jewel, down the slope as I quickly reviewed the half-assed plan I'd come up with. I refused to think of it not working.

And to be fair, at least I wasn't hesitating.

The sound of the bull dragon behind me intensified. "Come on, you big lazy fucker! You want me? Then you're going to have to work for it!"

He roared in response and I could only hope that Maks would stay low, and that the dragon would swoop on by him.

That was the first part of the plan.

The second part was far more ridiculous. I slowed my steps about twenty feet from the drop-off. I slid the long cloak off my shoulders and it pooled to the ground around my feet.

I needed more range of movement and couldn't risk the flapping material of the cloak being snagged by a tooth or claw at the last second. I wasn't interested in being thrown off that way. I turned and faced up the tunnel.

"You coming or not, you big bitch?" I called out to the dragon.

Another massive bellow echoed through the tunnel before he came into view at the crest of the final slope. Black as night, there was not a single other color on his scales, claws, or even the horns that stuck out the top of his head. His eyes, though, were a brilliant violet and, call it a hunch, I was pretty sure I stood in front of Lila's father.

A father who'd run his daughter off for not being what he wanted. Something in me snapped and I hated to say a portion of my plan went to shit right there. Calm, collected. That had been the plan.

"You piece of shit! You gave up on your daughter because she was too small? Maybe if you hadn't been such a worthless father, you would have seen the amazing dragon she is!" I screamed the words, for her, and maybe a little for me.

His violet eyes popped wide and then narrowed. "I have no daughter."

"Bullshit, you motherfucker!" I pointed a finger at him, turned my hand and crooked it toward me. "If you dare."

He opened his mouth and roared, the sound echoing through my chest. His teeth were easily as long as my forearms, and they glinted with the light of the lava behind me.

His muscles bunched, and I made myself not react.

He couldn't know what I planned to do, which meant I had to wait for the last damn second.

The black dragon shot forward, pushing hard with his claws into the rock of the tunnel. He was coming fast, the shards of stone flaring up around him, his mouth salivating.

If he thought he was going to get pussy tonight, he was sorely mistaken.

I waited, my hands outstretched as he came at me, all muscle and teeth. Fuck, I was going to die.

The heat of his breath blew my hair out behind me before I made my move.

I dodged to the left as hard as I could, running up the curve of the tunnel, using my momentum to curl back over the dragon's head. His eyes followed me, and I walked through the door in my mind, shifting from two legs to four.

I finished my flip onto his back as he slid under me and his momentum took us out of the tunnel and into space.

His wings snapped wide, and I dug my claws deep into his scales. "I'm riding you now, you bitch!"

"I am not a bitch. You only use that for females!"

I could not believe he answered me. "Let me explain. I think you're as useless as you think—wrongly—that your females are, which makes you my bitch!"

I clenched my claws a little more as we swept around the massive cavern. He barrel rolled and my fur all stood on end as we went upside down. All it did though was make me hang on more. Tighter.

Harder.

He spun so fast it was like he'd decided to corkscrew his way through the ground. We dropped while spinning and my gorge rose. "That's all you got?"

"Pussy, I'm going to eat you!"

"In your dreams!" I shot back, then let the vomit roll. It spun past me I turned my head and prayed it wouldn't hit me.

No such luck with the necklace removed. My own puke splashed over me, coating my black fur all along my spine.

"You are weak! You are no more than an irritation to me! You think your claws do me damage?" He roared the words as he slammed his body against the wall and rolled into it, the boom of the hit reverberating through his body and into mine.

Fuck! I let go and raced around his belly as he rubbed himself against the rock as if to dislodge a burr, still flying.

I was on his belly and he was upside down when I dug my claws in deep again. He roared, and I remembered the way my claws had affected the young dragons, how they'd screamed that the wounds burned.

"Your son tell you about the cat that clawed his hide, the one who saved Lila?" I asked as his blood began to drip. "Did he tell you how he passed out, how the wounds burned?"

"No, Lila is dead!" he screamed back at me.

"She lives! And she will take the throne!" Oh, why did I say that?

His roar rattled the cavern, and I made myself look at where we flew. He dipped low, heading for the lava.

"What are you going to do, rub your belly in the moat?"

"You are a fool," he snarled as he dropped lower as if to do just that.

I laughed. "I see Lila got her brains from her mother."

"What?" he roared.

The momentum as he swept low was too much. He missed the moat and skimmed over the hoard.

I let go.

I hit the pile of metal, jewels, and other trinkets, rolling end over end.

Sliding to a stop, I stared up as the black dragon soared up and around prepping for another pass.

I pushed up and ran to the very summit of the treasure trove. A better view, I needed a better view of where the jewel might be. The dragon above me roared again.

I had no doubt he would land on the island with me. Perfect.

But first I had to find the jewel.

I scrambled, diving into the pile. If I were an emerald, where would I be?

Laughter reached my ears. "You think to find our gemstone? Is that why you came?"

I turned to see the black dragon doing exactly what I thought he would. He had landed and crept forward with his wings spread wide and his head snaking left to right.

"Well, now that you mention it, yes." I flicked the tip

of my tail, irritated. "Would you mind pointing it out so I can save our world?"

"Lies, all those who come only have lies with which to blind us with, but I know those lies. There is no danger to this world."

I moved with him, keeping enough distance between us that he couldn't get me in a single lunge. "Not even the Emperor?"

He blew a snort out. "Idiot, the Emperor sleeps."

"Eh, not so much." I shrugged. "But you believe what you want, and I'll do the same. Now where is the emerald?"

He lunged, snapping, but missed me. I slid down the slope of exquisite trinkets, tumbling. The pile loosened and went with me, covering me fully.

I hunched down further as the dragon stepped over me, his belly right above my head, still dripping blood. "You think to hide from me?"

I pushed my way carefully out so that my head was above the pile of coins around me. I made myself look away from his body and to all that lay around me. There was nothing but gold, silver, rubies, sapphires. . . not even a hint of green winked at me.

He continued down the slope, grumbling and talking. He reached under his belly and touched the wounds I gave him and let out a long low hiss.

I pulled myself free of the pile of coins and put my belly low, stalking my way to the highest point of the treasures once more. He was at the bottom now, calling me out with that rumbling bellow of his.

"Pussy cat, you are only making your death worse by prolonging this!"

I rolled my eyes. Big words from a dragon missing a sense of smell and humor.

Once more at the top, I gritted my teeth with the frustration soaring through me. I let my eyes close for just a second and that's when I felt it. A pulse of energy tied to the forest, to the trees and to the dragons.

I slowly turned and slid down the slope on the opposite side, following the pull, and a faint line of green that seemed to beckon me forward. A chest no bigger than a ring box was on the sand of the island, all by itself. I shifted to two legs, stumbled and went to my knees, scooping the box up. I flicked the lid and a fat jewel sat in a ring setting, surrounded by diamonds.

I yanked it out and slid it onto my finger, then shifted back to my house cat form, making the jewel a part of the chain around my neck.

My bones and muscles protested the rapid shift and a groan slid from me.

Too many shifts, too fast.

"Hey, you lazy ass!" I grabbed the ring box in my mouth and waited for him to come over the crest of the treasure hoard before I twisted, flung my head to the side and released the box to throw it into the slowly moving lava. "That's what I think of your stupid emerald."

His eyes. . . goddess, they went so wide that I thought they would fall right out of his head and roll to a stop at my paws.

"NO!" He leapt down toward me, his wings wide as he caught an updraft from the heat of the lava.

I ran toward him, dodged to the right, turned and leapt up, catching hold of his tail. I needed a ride out of here now.

This was about to get tough. And that thought made me want to bust out in maniacal laughter as if the journey so far in hadn't been tough.

I settled for digging my claws in deeply and making him howl.

Chapter 28

Lila's father reared up on his back legs, his neck and head twisting around with his mouth wide open, coming straight at me with all those teeth. I distantly wondered if he wasn't a fire breather, just what was he?

I didn't have long to wait.

Seeing as his mouth shot toward me, I could see to the very back of his throat and the green mist that grew within that space.

Mist. Not acid like Lila.

Oh fuck. He was a death dragon.

"Cheater, cheater," I snarled. "You can't catch me on your own, so you resort to your stink breath?" This was bad, like super bad. Beyond bad, to the deepest of hells of bad, deep within the recesses of the baddest realms. One little breath in, one fucking sniff and I was done.

A death dragon's breath was pure poison, one that

would draw the life out of you and give it to the dragon in question, and there was only one death dragon that had ever lived beyond birth that I knew of. He was the legendary Corvalis. That explained how he'd found his way to become the leader of the dragons. Each combatant who had faced him and lost would have given over their life and their power to him as he fought to take control of the dragons.

I had no idea he was even still alive. Or that he was Lila's father. Suddenly his disdain of his daughter made horrible sense. As the legend he was, there would have been no way he could have accepted a daughter he saw as useless and weak.

His mouth snapped shut and his wings beat twice, hard, taking us higher. I caught a glimmer of movement in the tunnel above and I tried to look without looking.

Two men stood there.

Two where there had been one. Maks lifted his hands and I saw nothing, but Corvalis suddenly jerked hard to the side as if he'd been hit. His head whipped around to face the opening of the tunnel and he swept toward them.

"RUN!" I screamed at them as I myself ran up along Corvalis's ridged back. I pin cushioned him with each step, digging my claws in to keep my traction high in case he decided to flip over. He drew closer and closer to the tunnel opening and Maks just stood there, his blue eyes alight with a fury I'd never seen in him.

His held his hands out, palms toward us and there was a shimmer of light as though the air around him bent, and then Corvalis let out a roar and his head snapped to the right.

The momentum of him being blown to the side brought his body in close to the tunnel opening.

This was it, the only chance I would get. I ran across the dragon's back and leapt for the tunnel.

It was too far. I knew it was the second I pushed off with my back feet into the open air between us. I thought about shifting if only to throw Maks the ring.

My eyes met his and his hands swept toward me, his fingers flicking upward, and it was as though I'd been lifted on a gust of wind.

Just enough to get me to the crumbling threshold of the tunnel.

I caught hold of the rock and scrambled forward.

A hand swept under my belly and caught me up. The smell of lion surrounded me, only not lion, but family—a lion related to me.

"Bryce, what are you doing here?" I yelled and stared at the lion shifter holding me, my cloak over his arm.

Not Bryce.

Shem.

My crazy-ass Uncle Shem. And it was then that it hit me. *Shem* was the lion I'd smelled in the dungeon of the Witch's Reign. What the hell had he been doing there?

Apparently, my father had not handled things after all.

"Hey, kitten. Let's go." He winked a golden eye at me, the wild fervor I remembered from when I was child dulled with pain. But it was still there, meaning he was as unreliable as ever.

He leaned back against the wall where I'd sensed him and the rock slid open. He stepped through and Maks followed.

Utter blackness covered us as the infuriated roars of Corvalis rocketed though the stone. The dark wasn't the only thing I picked up on. The smell of shit, blood, and rank lion rammed its way up my nose and I wrinkled my lips. Fuck, that was bad. Like a bachelor pad on steroids.

"Uncle Shem?" I repeated his name because I couldn't—literally could not—believe what I was seeing.

"The one and only." His hold on me tightened. "Stay in that shape, kitten. It'll keep the jewel hidden longer."

"No shit," I growled. He lifted me so I sat on his shoulder and then a match was struck, lighting up the very, very small space.

"We need to get out of here," Maks said, holding the match. The lines of his face were drawn.

I stared hard at him. "You okay?"

"Using magic like that. . . it's draining. And. . . it will pinpoint me for Marsum."

Shem grunted. "You saved her. Don't regret it, boy. She's more important than all of us."

My uncle took a step forward and then another. "Here, we climb to the top." He put his hands into a stone ladder that had been etched into a tunnel that went straight up. I clung to his shoulder, wishing I was with Maks. It wasn't that I didn't care for my uncle, except that I remembered all too well why he'd been run off from the pride.

He'd tried to kidnap me.

I gritted my teeth, turned and dropped off his back, landing on Maks's shoulder. He reached up and loosened his winter coat. I slid in and shivered.

"Still don't trust me?" Shem called down.

"You tried to steal me from my parents, Shem," I called up. "What do you want, forgiveness?"

He barked a laugh. "Well, now, you are your mother's child, aren't you?"

I tucked my head against Maks's neck and breathed him in. He turned his head and pressed his face against my side as if he were doing the same. "You okay?"

I nodded. "Just tired."

The two men climbed for a long time. Long enough that they had to stop multiple times to catch their breaths. The stone around us rattled and the roars of Corvalis never really stopped, but they did fade, which had to be good for something.

The minutes ticked by.

I focused on Maks, on the sound of his heart. On the smell of his skin and the whoosh of his breath over my fur.

He'd saved me. Caught me when I'd leapt without looking. A smile tipped over my lips.

"What are you grinning about now?" He breathed the words out.

"You caught me," I whispered.

"Of course."

"I leapt without looking, Maks, and you caught me."

He chuckled though there was strain in it. "Seems fitting."

"Yeah, it does. But you still owe me."

He had to stop climbing as he laughed. "Yeah, that too."

From above us, Shem stopped and stared down at us, and it was only then I realized that the light was growing.

We had to be close to the top.

"Stay in your cat form, kitten," Shem said.

"Stop calling me that," I yelled up at him.

"You are a kitten," he said.

"I'm a fucking house cat, you idiot!"

Maks laughed, though silently. I admit. It was kind of funny. Talk about being complicated. I didn't want to be called a house cat, but I'd take that a thousand times over being called a kitten.

"We're at the top," Shem said.

I wanted to ask him why he was here, what he'd been doing all these years, how he'd avoided the Jinn and just how the hell he knew about this tunnel.

There was the sound of stone sliding across stone and brilliant light—or it seemed brilliant after the pitch dark—flooded in.

"Stay low," Shem said.

Maks snorted, and I agreed with his snort. It was a dumb thing to say. Like what were we going to do, jump out and do all we could to get noticed? Idiot. It looked like nothing had changed in all the years.

Shem disappeared through the hole above our heads and Maks followed him into the bright sunlight.

I blinked a few times and tried to get my bearings. And then I blinked again because he did not bring us out in the middle of the nesting females, did he? There was no way that he would have known that I had already spoken to and convinced the females to let us pass.

But more than that were the new additions to the nesting grounds. There were male dragons waiting at the mouth of the mound that had me more than a little concerned. Corvalis had called in the troops. The only upside I could see was that the male dragons had their backs to us as they stared into the mound. Waiting for prey to come out the way they went in.

But for how long? How long before Corvalis roared up and out of the mound, announcing that we had escaped him? Time was not on our side.

I jumped out of Maks's arms and he immediately shifted. My uncle, on the other hand, stood and stretched. "Hello, ladies! Long time, no see!"

I didn't wait to see if the males noticed him. They would. And I wanted to be as far away as possible.

I bolted east through the nests while I angled to the south. Lila and Bryce would be waiting for us and unlike those I'd stolen from before, I had no doubt the dragons wouldn't give up. There would be no border they stopped at.

The female dragons breathed over us as we bolted for the mound.

Find the children.
Bring them home.
Carry our love with you.

I couldn't see. Their emotions blurred my eyes and I leaned into Maks as we ran, letting him lead me.

"We'll find them, Zam," he growled. "If it's the last thing we do, we'll find them."

I struggled to see through the liquid until the wind pulled the tears away, clearing my eyes. The sound of the heavier tread behind us told me Shem was at least moving in our direction. I wasn't sure I wanted him with us at all, but for now, he was at least attempting to keep up.

We hit the tree line and dove under cover.

The thing is it's a hell of a lot harder to cover the tracks and bright golden hide of a big-ass lion over two small cats.

A sudden cacophony rose behind us, the roar of a lot of very pissed off male dragons and one that bellowed above them all, full of anger and death.

I knew his roar now as if his blood had seeped into me and I'd known him for a thousand years.

Corvalis was coming for me.

Chapter 29

The race through the forest was nothing short of blind madness. Shem didn't quite keep up, but he held on better than I expected. I tried not to think about what we were going to do when we reached the horses.

There was no horse for Shem. It would be up to me to double with Maks again. Not that I minded. My bigger concern was getting the horses to go fast enough to get out of range of the oncoming dragons.

What I minded was Shem showing up and. . . shit, he had helped us get out of the mound, but something felt off. Maybe it was just the fact that he'd kidnapped me all those years ago. Who the fuck knew?

I panted hard, my body humming with adrenaline. I felt two spells go off around us as we shot through them. But they were facing the other direction—Lila had been right about that, at least.

A section of the forest went up in flames right

behind us, and I thought it was a delayed spell. The flames were followed with a roar that was close enough, I was sure I could feel the hot breath of the dragon ripple my fur. I shot forward, a new burst of energy running through me as the flames raced to catch us. I didn't dare look back.

The heat of dragon-born fire was no small thing as it crinkled the edges of my fur. That was enough to know we had to move our asses.

Shem, on the other hand. . . "Oh, bonkers, it's blue flames. That is bad."

Blue flames were alive, and they sought out their prey. More than likely, us. If I'd had enough breath to respond to him, I would have told him this was his fault. Yes, he'd gotten us out. But why the hell would he have shouted hello?

Unless he wanted them to chase us? Which made no sense.

My heart thundered along and the adrenaline began to fade, the herd behind us increased its speed and we fought to keep ahead of them, my energy near its end. I closed my eyes for a split second, searching for that overlay of colors that would show me our path.

And in that brief moment of calm, I heard his voice. The man who'd raised me, the man I wanted so desperately still to make proud of me.

Dig deep, you are strong enough. I never doubted it, my girl.

I drew a breath and demanded more of my fatiguing muscles. I shot ahead of Maks and he quickly caught up.

He'd been holding back so he wouldn't lose me.

Goddess. Why did he have to be a Jinn?

I looked at him at my side and felt a funny twinge. It didn't matter. None of it mattered as long as we stood with each other.

I would have liked for that realization to have come in a calmer moment, but whatever. This was my life.

The trees began to thin, and through them I saw the tall black charred tree that marked the southern boundary.

Bryce was there with the horses. Lila hovered above his shoulder.

The horses danced. They knew the predators were coming.

"Bryce. Run!" I screamed the words, hoping he heard them. His eyes shot to me, finding me in the canopy under the trees.

He dismounted his big horse, Ali, dropped the reins of all the horses except Balder. He mounted my horse, his face as calm as a summer's day.

Why wasn't he running?

"RUN!" I screamed again, and the dragons behind us roared in response. Lila buzzed around Bryce, trying to get him to move and when he didn't, she flew to me.

"He says this is his moment. What does that mean? I can't get him to go!" The panic in her voice was clear. She would know better than any of us what was coming our way.

No, Bryce. I saw the golden lines running around him. One connecting him to me, others that were faded and I knew connected to our father and his mother.

Those that were faded began to pulse, calling him.

"NO!" I wanted to scream, but I couldn't. There was no breath left in me. No, not Bryce. He put two fingers to his mouth and saluted me as his alpha. I hadn't earned it, and he saluted me as his leader.

"I defend my pride. I defend my alpha, even unto death. I will always be with you, Zamira." He shouted the words and then his head tipped up and he booted Balder hard. Balder leapt forward, bucking and twisting.

"Hiss at him," I whispered as the tears streaked my face. I'd shifted mid stride and was on my belly, watching as Bryce and Balder raced north, drawing the dragons' ire.

I scrambled to get up to him. Maks and Shem tackled me at the same time.

I screamed, and a hand slammed over my mouth and I bit down, hissing and punching. Someone was yelling at Shem to let me go. Lila shot between us and slammed her tail across his face, sending him back. I twisted around and stumbled forward. Maks had a hand under my arm, tugging me away from Bryce.

Shem carefully handed over my cloak, as if it were dangerous. "Here, she'll get cold fast once the adrenaline is gone."

I let Maks put the cloak on me as he spoke. "Zam, listen to me. He. . . he knows what he's doing. He's a fighter. We have to trust him. And he has Balder. Balder can outrun anything. You know that." Maks turned me to face him. I saw it in his eyes though and I couldn't stop the tears. I slumped forward and he caught me. Again, the shift took me without warning. Maks scooped me up and tucked me inside his shirt.

I let him.

It was not weakness ruling me. It was logic. There would be no catching Bryce and Balder, and to try would put us all in danger.

This was the choice of an alpha. The life of one, for the life of many.

The sobs shook me, and I could feel nothing but grief for a man who had been my hero for so long. The man who had been the reason I'd fought so hard to be strong.

My eyes were closed. The lines of gold that tied me to him vibrated and quivered and I sent my heart along them.

The images that came to me were hazy like a dream.

Balder ran hard. The dragons were above them both, ducking and dodging in close. Fire and lightning danced, and there was a moment where I thought they were both going to get bitten in half by a big green dragon with the wingspan of over a hundred feet.

"He is mine!" roared a voice, and Corvalis swept into view.

Of course, he'd seen Maks tuck me into his shirt and now thought that Bryce was him. That I was there with him, still tucked away.

Bryce leapt from Balder's back, shifting in midair. His clothing shredded, and the lion slid to a stop. Holding his ground.

A roar reverberated through him and I cried out. "No, Bryce, no!"

Maks's arm tightened around me as we galloped

away, but my eyes held only to my brother. He was doing this for me, for us. Because he believed in me.

I hated Amalia in that moment. I wished she hadn't cured him. I hated Ish more, for bringing us to these crossroads.

Corvalis dropped to the ground on all fours, facing Bryce. "Return my emerald and I will make your death quick."

There had to be something I could do. I just had to think. Think, damn it!

My mind raced.

Bryce lifted his thickly maned head and let out a bellow that was part laugh, part challenge. "I am a shifter of the Bright Lions' Pride. We faced the Jinn for hundreds of years, we held our ground. I am a protector of this world, dragon. Can you say the same? Your kind once stood shoulder to shoulder with mine to face the darkness. Will you do so again?"

Curses, this had always been about curses and the Jinn.

I shoved my way out of Maks's shirt and landed on the horses neck with a grunt. I shifted so I sat straddled with two legs, balancing precariously. I lifted one hand and touched the necklace I wore. It held my curse from me, and an idea formed. Reckless, but it was all I had to hang onto.

"Stop!" I screamed as I reached forward and grabbed Batman's one rein and yanked him hard to the left. He spun out and I used the lost momentum to leap from his back.

I hit the ground running. "Lila, with me!"

She was at my side in a flash and I looked her in the eye. "What if your size was a curse, Lila? What if. . . this, my necklace, could take it from you?"

I held the necklace up to her, the one with the lion's head ring. She looked at me and I looked right back into those violet eyes. "Will you help me save him, Lila?"

She ducked her head. "I. . . I am not big enough. It's not a curse."

Tears streamed down my cheeks. "Please. It's the only hope I have."

Maks caught up to us as did Shem.

"Zam." Maks said my name and there was so much pain in it. "Please, you can't save him."

I drew a breath, filling my chest. "If I am to be an alpha, then I choose this as my trial. I will save my brother or die trying." I grabbed the shotgun with the grenade launcher and checked it. One grenade left and two slugs. It would have to be enough.

Maks closed his eyes. "Goddess help me, do not make me watch you do this."

Shem slid off Ali's back, naked as the day he'd been born. "You can do this, kitten. You can. You know it in your belly there is nothing you can't do. You just have to believe."

"You're going to get her killed!" Maks roared and his magic pulsed over his skin. There was a flash to the south, and he spun around. "They've sent two Jinn to find me. I have to head them off."

"I will help you," Shem said. "I've been fighting Jinn my whole life."

I looked to my brother, seeing him through the lines of his life as they connected to me.

The dragons around my brother swayed from side to side and I saw a few whose eyes darted to others. As if they knew. I saw Pret, Trick, and Fink. They nodded. It was Trick who stepped between Corvalis and Bryce, his back to his leader.

"We would stand with you, brother. We have seen the heart your family carries in the strength of your alpha."

He didn't so much as bow to Bryce as he tipped his head. A salute from one warrior to another. Hope, fragile and light, filled my chest.

"Lila," I whispered with my eyes closed. "Trick is standing with Bryce."

She cried out, panic in her words, "Against my father? He'll be killed!"

"Yes." I breathed out the word and the connection between Bryce and me tightened as if he saw me watching.

I turned to her. She lowered her head. "Do it, we have to try."

I slid the necklace over her head and it settled around her neck. The reaction was fast.

A deep rumble cut through the air and the clouds that had been hesitant and light only a moment before erupted like a rolling wave of water, black and mean, only there was no rain. The wind whipped and swirled around us in a tornado and Lila was caught up in it.

"LILA!" I screamed her name, leapt up and caught her by a back foot. "I've got you."

Only the wind had us both, sweeping us beyond the reach of Maks and Shem, high into the maelstrom of the clouds. I held on tightly as we were thrown higher and higher.

I wish I'd been able to say goodbye to Maks.

"Wait, I've got you," Lila said as she twisted and wrapped a talon around my middle. I touched the black curved weapon that was easily six feet along, almost as big as Corvalis's. I stared up at her, that blue and silver scaled body the same, only sized way up.

"Holy mother goddess of the desert! LILA!" I screamed the words because she was bloody fucking magnificent.

I mean, she'd always been, but seeing her as she was *meant* to be was nothing short of breathtaking. She let out a roar that cut through the air, and the clouds rumbled in response, lightning dancing around us. She flicked me up into the air and I landed on her back as if I'd ridden this way for years. I tucked my hands under a scale, the shotgun clenched in my arms and hung on tightly as she shot forward.

The scene of the dragons and my brother filled my eyes again.

"Zam, I cannot bear for you to see this again." Bryce's words were spoken, I think, but I couldn't be sure they didn't reach inside my head. I let out a low moan. "Faster, Lila, faster."

She stretched out, her body streaking through the clouds, the moisture of them soaking me as I crouched over her neck, my clothes whipping in the wind. We were going to make it. We had to.

Bryce winked at me. "I am your protector always. I will be with you, Zam. Look for me when I am gone."

We broke through the clouds above the dragons. Above Bryce as he faced them. I lifted a hand to him though he wasn't looking for me.

"No. I am your protector, now, brother," I said softly.

I could only say that a weird madness took hold of me because it was a fucking stupid thing I did, but then again, the curse Marsum placed on me was in full effect.

I am going to die, was what I thought. I didn't want to die, but I was going to. For Bryce. And that would make my death worthwhile.

I stood on Lila's back, the wind tugging at me as I *jumped* off her back and into space, shotgun in hand still.

I fell with my arms wide. Lila dove next to me, twisting into a spiral as she went straight for her father.

The seconds stretched as only those that herald a coming violence could.

Corvalis looked up; his eyes that were carbon copies of Lila's widened. He launched himself sideways, away from Lila.

Toward me.

The emerald stone sparkled on my hand.

I was no mage, it would not save me.

I lifted that hand and pointed the finger at him, shooting at him as if my hand were a gun. Nothing happened, of course, except Corvalis launched toward me.

I rolled in the air, shifting into my house cat form as his claws reached for me.

He passed by Lila as he sought me out as if she were of no consequence.

BFM. Big fucking mistake, dragon.

I dug my claws into his leg, attaching myself to him, digging in deeply as I climbed his body. From below us came the roar of male dragons, and the bellow of a lion.

Lila slammed into her father's back and he twisted around, his mouth opening, the green mist pooling.

I was at the base of Corvalis's neck when he turned to Lila. Her mouth spewed sparkling green acid all over his back that ate through the scales, through the muscle and bone.

But it wasn't working fast enough. I shifted back to two legs, brought the shotgun up and grabbed the grenade off the bottom of the stock. I threw it up and into Corvalis's open mouth. He gagged, and his mouth snapped shut as the grenade went off, blowing a hole through the side of his neck.

He gurgled and the wound healed. "Are you shitting me?" I yelled as he opened his mouth again, only this time there was no mist. Maybe I'd broken his mist maker? I'd take it.

I clung to him with one hand as I reached for the flail with the other. "You're getting dragon blood today, you bastard, so no killing me."

The handle heated so fast in response to my words, I would have dropped it if it hadn't glued itself to my skin. I yanked it from my back and swung it with all I had into the side of Corvalis's head. The twin spiked balls drove in deep, past the layers of scales and into his jaw bone, snapping it in half.

Lila let out a roar, and I looked to her. She gave me a nod, and I yanked the flail from his head. We were spiraling down to the ground rapidly.

"You got this?" I said.

She grinned as the acid dripped from her mouth. "I've got it."

Holding the flail, I back flipped off Corvalis and fell the final fifty feet to the ground. Fifty feet, part of my brain said I would break my legs, my spine. As a shifter I was not strong enough to take the fall.

No. I am strong enough. I am the alpha of the Bright Lion Pride.

The ground swept up, and I relaxed into the fall, loosening my muscles and joints. I hit the ground hard, dropping into a crouch, the flail still in one hand. The shock of the landing reverberated through my bones, but nothing snapped. Nothing gave.

I slowly stood to find half the dragons on one side of me, and half on the other.

I looked for Pret, Fink, and Trick. Above us, Corvalis and Lila battled. I'd done what I could for her.

The moment I took a step forward, Balder was there, galloping for me. I grabbed his mane and swung into the saddle as I raced between the two lines of dragons.

"You heard my second, his words are truth. The Emperor wakes, and we have a choice. Will you stand with us as you once did? Side by side, brothers and sisters in the battle for our freedom?" I held up the hand still holding the flail. "Or will you hide away and let your children be stolen by the Jinn?"

Snarls and roars met my ears. Above us, Lila screeched and I looked up. Corvalis had her neck in his mouth. I had to help her, and there was nothing I could do. But there were dragons here who could help her.

I pointed at her as she wrestled with her father. "She is your queen. Would you let her be taken by a dragon who will never see you free? He holds a thousand dragons' power. If that is not cheating, I don't know what the fuck is."

Trick shot into the air, lightning coursing around him as he went straight for the battle. Fink and Pret were close behind him.

"That is not how this is done!" a blue dragon screeched from my left. He was bunched to launch into the air—at me and Balder. He shot toward us, his eyes narrowed, mouth open as his power roared up his throat. Blue, ice, water, I could see it coming as he gathered it around him. He slammed into me and Balder, sending us flying to one side. Balder hit the ground, rolled, but I heard no snap of his legs, thank the goddess.

I came up from the hit, rolling back to my feet, my adrenaline raging through me as the dragon's mouth came at me. Too close, he was too close, I could never stop him in time. I held my breath.

I was going to die.

There was a flash of gold along the ground, and then the mouth around me was gone.

I stared up at Bryce as he hung from the blue dragon's neck, his massive claws and teeth tearing huge chunks of scale and flesh. The blue dragon's mouth was open as he struggled to breathe through a shredded throat.

"I got this, Alpha!" he snarled.

There was a moment, just a moment where I saw Bryce as my hero as he'd been all those years ago. He'd saved me. He'd saved my life. My heart swelled with pride. That was my brother. It didn't matter to me that we didn't share the same mother. He was the brother of my heart as Lila was the sister of my heart. I took a step toward him, toward the battle.

A pale pink dragon that was more snake than dragon raced in from the other side, big fangs hanging past his thin lips, dripping black liquid. Poison.

I locked eyes with the pale pink dragon. He grinned. I dug in and ran, spinning the flail. "Come on, you big girly fucker!"

He didn't come for me, though. The pale pink dragon caught Bryce with his mouth, clamped down and shook him like a dog with a rag doll toy as his fangs dug in deeply. The snap of bone echoed through the air and I was back again in the Oasis, I was watching him die in front of me. He roared, pain-filled and guttural, but still triumphant. I knew it through my whole body.

This was the death Amalia had warned him about, and he'd embraced it.

To save me.

"NO!" I screamed as I swung the flail upward, slamming it into the belly of the pale pink dragon. "His heart, go for his heart!"

The flail obeyed me, digging in, and I let go of the handle as it pushed itself past the dragon's scales. A worm, a snake under the skin, a parasite that sought only the heart's blood, the flail was alive with its lust for death and blood. The pink dragon froze, and his tail swept around to pull the flail out, but it was too late.

The weapon had drilled in and was gone. I pulled my kukri blades and stood over my brother as the dragons circled around us. We would die together.

"Bryce. This was not how I planned today would go," I said.

He gave a weak laugh, and I dared a glance at him. He was back to two legs, naked, his body. . . twisted from the shaking, black poison flowing from a half-dozen bite marks. "Me neither. But it's a good day to die. With my alpha at my side. My sister standing with me."

Behind me the pale pink dragon fell to the side, twitched once and I *felt* the flail absorb its life. Payment was made.

"Don't count us out yet," I said.

I held my hand out and for lack of a better way to explain it, I called it to me. My weapon, it no longer belonged to Marsum but to me. The flail blasted out of the dragon's chest and straight to my hand. I took hold of it, the warm blood of the dragons cementing my hold on it, my fingers pulsing with its strength. To my other side the blue dragon fell over, gasping out his last.

There was a thump behind us and I held my ground as the dragons circling us slowly backed away. Hot breath whispered around me and I turned. "Lila."

She lowered her head to me, blood dripping from around her mouth and off a gash over one eye. "Corvalis fled."

The gathered dragons gasped. "Not possible." The whispers came as they backed up and raced from the battleground.

Lila was injured, the wounds were deep and bleeding, and as much as I was worried about her, it was nothing to my fear for Bryce.

I dropped to my knees beside him and slid the emerald stone off my hand and pressed it against his flesh. "Bryce, stay with me."

"Not this time," he whispered. I yanked my cloak off and laid it over him, trying not to notice the way his body was broken. One arm was nearly torn off, both legs were shattered, but it was his hips, turned at an impossible angle. His back broken in truth.

I scooped his head up onto my knees as I fought to hold the tears back.

"No. I won't let you, Bryce. You are my second. That will not change." I ran a hand over his face and the first of the tears dropped. "Please, please don't leave me, brother."

He lifted one hand and caught a tear off the edge of my chin. "You are not a little girl any more, Zam. And there is something I must tell you before I. . ." He groaned, the air whispering from him.

"No, no, stay." I wanted nothing more than to give him my strength. To heal him, but I had nothing like that.

His eyelids fluttered, and he took a slow breath, his chest barely lifting. "Your mother. . . was cursed. Like you."

I sniffed. "Bryce, you can tell me later."

"Now, I have to say it now." His face twisted with pain and I leaned forward, pressing my head against his.

"Bryce."

"You. . . the curse will help you. Don't let them take what you are away from you, Zam. You have everything you would ever need just as you are." His hand dropped from my chin and I caught his fingers.

"Bryce?" I whimpered his name.

"Maks, he's good for you. You have my blessing," he whispered.

The tears flooded my eyes. I could see nothing. I could only feel as he slipped from me in truth.

"I love you," I tried to say those three words, goddess how I tried, but they came out a sobbing mess of syllables.

"I see Dad—" The words breathed out of him with a last whoosh of air.

I gasped as he slumped. I clutched him to me, rocking back and forth as the sobs rippled past my lips and turned into screams I couldn't hold back.

The screams were echoed by a roar behind me, Lila adding her voice to my pain. Only it was more than that.

"Zam!" She screamed my name and I twisted to see her on the ground, her eyes rolling back, foam at her mouth. Trick had a front foot on her, holding her down.

"Something is wrong."

I let Bryce go, tears still staining my face as I ran to Lila. "Talk to me!"

"The necklace burns!" she roared.

I clambered up her side and slid down to her neck

where the necklace was burrowing into her flesh. I caught the edge of it and yanked it up. Only it didn't give but snapped away from me and dug deeper into her flesh. I grabbed a kukri blade and dug it under her scale. "I'm sorry!"

I drove the blade in deep and under the necklace, like digging out a sliver. The blood flowed around my hand as I caught the chain on the tip of the blade. I yanked it up, pulling the ring talisman from her flesh, popping it high into the air.

I caught it with one hand and immediately threw it away, the burn of the metal too much to hang onto. Below me, Lila thrashed as her body slid back to the size she'd always been. I scooped her up and held her in my arms as she shivered and whimpered. "I've got you, Lila."

Trick leaned over my shoulder. "They will come back. You need to go. They won't accept that Lila defeated her father. Even though they saw it."

I nodded and looked at my brother's body. Not him, he wasn't there anymore. "Will you make a pyre for him?"

The words, the words should not have been spoken for years, not until we were old and gray, until Bryce had children and his children's children to mourn his loss. I clutched Lila closer and her tiny claws reached around my neck.

"Siblings aren't always blood," she whispered to me. "Sometimes they find you when your heart needs them the most."

I had no words; the pain was too much. A nose

bumped into my back and I wrapped an arm around Balder, hugging him to me as the sound of flames crackled around us. I made myself look, made myself watch as the cloak caught fire and for just a moment, I thought I saw Bryce's lion form standing with his broken body.

And then it was gone, and it was time for us to leave. I turned away, walking, limping my way south.

Chapter 30

The desert called to me, and I followed it south, knowing that my destiny was drawing me forward now. Whatever Marsum had done to my curse, I would fight it without the use of any block.

I stopped after what could have been hours or days, I'm not sure, and quietly used the hacka paste on Lila's wounds and the bruises Balder had caught from his tumble. Lila did the same for me, patching me up while the tears flowed. It was like a river had started and I didn't know how to stop it, a waterfall with no ending.

We walked until we found Shem and Maks. They were coming back for us at a hard gallop and they slid to a stop when they saw us.

Maks jumped from Batman and ran to me, catching me up in his arms. I didn't have to say anything, he knew—somehow he knew. He held me while I cried, both Lila and me, holding us while we leaned into him.

A bellow of a lion snapped my head up. Shem stood

with his back to me, the roar, one of honoring a fallen family member, the acknowledgment that a hero had been lost.

I lifted a hand to Maks's face. "Are you hurt?"

He put his hand over mine. "Small wounds. The Jinn were not expecting me to fight with an experienced lion shifter at my side. We killed them both."

I nodded but couldn't bring myself to say "good."

Lila shivered and peered up between us.

"What are we going to do now?" she asked as Maks pulled a second cloak from the saddlebags and swept it over my shoulders. Was I cold? I didn't even know.

I drew a slow breath and made myself put my pain aside, just for a moment.

"I am the alpha of the Bright Lion Pride," I said softly. "And three of my pride are in mortal danger." I looked up at Maks. "I name you my second, Maks. Will you take that title?"

He stood a little straighter, and his arms tightened around me. "I will always have your back, Zam, no matter how dark the days that come shadow us."

Lila curled into me and I lifted her. "Lila, will you be my second?"

Her head snapped up. "You can have two?"

"I can do whatever the fuck I want. I am the alpha." I made myself wink at her. "I couldn't do this without the two of you—I won't do it without either of you."

Her smile wobbled. "I've got your back, Zam. Sister of my heart, the one I knew from the second I met that you would change my world."

I leaned in and kissed the top of her head. "Sister. You are part of my pride now."

Maks leaned over and kissed her noggin as well. "I want her as my sister too."

Lila snickered. "I don't think Zam wants to be your sister."

I laughed through the tears, laughter and tears flowed between us. Shem dared to come close.

"You three will change this world, I think."

I looked at him, still uneasy but seeing his strengths for what they were. I needed him too. "Will you be my seer, Uncle Shem? As you were for my father."

He bowed at the waist. "It would be my honor, Alpha."

I looked to the south. "Then we go. To the south."

Maks kissed the side of my head. "To the south."

Lila climbed to my shoulder and stared. "You think it will be warmer?"

I laughed softly. "Yeah, I think it'll be warmer."

"Good, 'cause I'm tired of all this ice and rain shit." She flicked her wings and then stretched them out.

We mounted our horses and pointed them south.

I let them get ahead of me, holding Balder back as I stared at the world, a sensation of eyes following me. Not like a shadow, but eyes that I'd felt when I was a child.

Marsum was watching me.

I tipped my chin up. "If you prick us, do we not bleed? If you poison us, do we not die? And if you wrong us, shall we not avenge? I'm coming for you, asshole. You'd better be ready to die."

Chapter 31

Merlin felt the shift in the world. It was subtle, and if he hadn't been straining so hard to pick up a sign that Flora might have left behind, he would have missed it.

Bryce was dead.

The Emperor's hold on the dragons was broken.

And Zamira was coming into her own. Her power was not what the world would think of for a hero, but she was what they needed.

Heart of a lion. Soul of a dragon. Power of a Jinn.

He lowered his head, knowing what would come for Zamira now that she'd set herself on this path. "Hurry, Wall Breaker, Zamira Reckless Wilson. The world needs your heart more than ever."

Afterword

Thanks for coming along for another story! I hope if you haven't checked out my other books you'll take a minute, go to my website and see what else I might have that will tickle your fancy. There's a LOT of books, in several sub-genres which is why I don't put a list here. 😇

www.shannonmayer.com

Acknowledgments

This many books, you'd think I'd run out of people to thank. The truth is, every book is a new journey for me, often with new friends and helpers along the way. This one would surely not have been as good without my editor, Tina Winograd as she really pushed me out of my comfort zone with this book, which IMHO, made it sing. :) Thank you to her, and to my whole team for helping me put this together.